S.S. RAJAMOULI'S
bāhubali
BEFORE THE BEGINNING — BOOK 2

CHATURANGA

ANAND NEELAKANTAN

First published by Westland Publications Private Limited in 2020

Published by Westland Books, a division of Nasadiya Technologies Private Limited in 2023

No. 269/2B, First Floor, 'Irai Arul', Vimalraj Street, Nethaji Nagar, Alapakkam Main Road, Maduravoyal, Chennai 600095

Westland and the Westland logo are the trademarks of Nasadiya Technologies Private Limited, or its affiliates.

Copyright © Anand Neelakantan, 2020

Anand Neelakantan asserts the moral right to be identified as the author of this work.

ISBN: 9789357766494

10 9 8 7 6 5 4 3 2 1

This is a work of fiction. Names, characters, organisations, places, events and incidents are either products of the author's imagination or used fictitiously.

All rights reserved

Typeset by SŪRYA

Printed at Nutech Print Services-India

No part of this book may be reproduced, or stored in a retrieval system, or transmitted in any form or by any means, electronic, mechanical, photocopying, recording, or otherwise, without express written permission of the publisher.

*To my sister Chandrika and
brother-in-law S.D. Parameswaran,
for making me what I am*

Dramatis personae

Achi Nagamma

The leader of an all-women vigilante army. She is fighting against the corrupt and evil people of Mahishmathi.

Akhila

Thimma's daughter. Sivagami is very fond of her.

Akkundaraya

A powerful bhoomipathi who is involved in the transportation of Gaurikanta. He is in charge of the forest lands.

Ally

Brought up by the rebel queen Achi Nagamma, she is an elite warrior and spy in an all-women army. She is not shy of using her sexuality and powers of seduction to get her work done.

Bhairava

A madman who lives near the river. He used to be Maharaja Somadeva's slave.

Bhutaraya

He was the powerful leader of the Vaithalikas. He died during the failed coup against the Mahishmathi king.

Bijjaladeva

The firstborn of Maharaja Somadeva, he is anxiously awaiting the day he will be declared crown prince. He is contemptuous of his younger brother and resents that their father has bestowed the title of Vikramadeva—a title given to the bravest of kings and princes—on him.

Brihannala

A eunuch who is the head of the royal harem. She has her own secret.

Chitraveni

The deposed princess of Kadarimandalam, imprisoned in a palace by Mahishmathi after being defeated in war.

Devaraya

Sivagami's father, who was executed as a traitor by the government.

Durgappa

A bhoompathi who mans the fort of Gauriparvat.

Gomati

The wife of Kalicharan Bhatta, the son of the rajaguru, Rudra Bhatta. She is principled and brave.

Guha

A bhoomipathi in charge of the pastoral lands and the river people. An old man, cruel and cunning, he is revered by his people. He bows only before Maharaja Somadeva.

Gundu Ramu

Sivagami's young, loyal friend from the orphanage. Son of a slain poet, the boy adores Sivagami.

Hidumba

The dwarf is a khanipathi, a step below a bhoomipathi, and is in charge of the Gauriparvat mines.

Kalicharan Bhatta

The son of the rajaguru Rudra Bhatta, he officiates rituals and pujas in his father's absence. He is as immoral and deceitful as his father.

Kalika

She is the head devadasi of Pushyachakra inn, more notoriously known as Kalika's den. She is a seductress and has half the Mahishmathi nobles under her feet. She is adept in the art of kama and supplies beautiful young women to even the maharaja's harem to entertain state guests.

Kamakshi

She was Sivagami's closest friend in the orphanage. She was the lover of Shivappa before she was raped and killed by Prince Bijjaladeva.

Kattappa

A slave, he is dedicated to his work and takes pride in serving the royal family of Mahishmathi. Kattappa served Bijjaladeva, the elder prince of Mahishmathi, and is the son of Malayappa, the personal slave of Maharaja Somadeva.

Keki

A thirty-year-old eunuch, she is the assistant of the famous devadasi Kalika. She is part of Prince Bijjaladeva's camp.

Mekhala

Bhoomipathi Pattaraya's beloved and beautiful daughter.

Narasimha Varman

The incompetent brother of the deposed princess of Kadarimandalam, he has been placed on the throne, but real control lies in the governor's hands.

Neelappa

The favourite slave of Devaraya, who comes to work with Sivagami after thirteen years.

Jeemotha

A pirate, Jeemotha also trades in slaves and provides children to the Gauriparvat mines. He is handsome and uses his charm and wit to get out of difficult situations.

Mahadeva

A dreamer and an idealist, he treats everyone with compassion and love. He is conscious of the fact that he is not a great warrior. He is in love with Sivagami.

Mahapradhana Parameswara

The prime minister of Mahishmathi, he is trusted by the king, who considers him his guru. He is kind-hearted but a suave politician. He was also Skandadasa's mentor.

Maharani Hemavati

The haughty and proud queen of Mahishmathi.

Malayappa

The personal slave of Maharaja Somadeva, he is Kattappa and Shivappa's father. He is a proud man with a strong sense of duty.

Pattaraya

A rich and ambitious nobleman, he is a bhoomipathi, a title of great importance in the Mahishmathi kingdom. He is known for his cunning and ruthlessness. He is a self-made man who rose from poverty to riches through cunning and hard work. He is dedicated to his family and loves his daughter Mekhala more than his life.

Pratapa

The police chief of Mahishmathi, Pratapa is feared by the common people. He is a friend of Pattaraya.

Raghava

Thimma's son, who grew up with Sivagami. He professed his love for Sivagami, but was rejected by her.

Revamma
The warden of the royal orphanage.

Roopaka
A scribe and the trusted aide of Mahapradhana Parameswara.

Rudra Bhatta
The chief priest of Mahishmathi. He is a close friend of Bhoomipathi Pattaraya.

Shankaradeva
The cruel and ruthless governor of Kadarimandalam, he is the cousin of Maharaja Somadeva. Actual control of Kadarimandalam lies in his hands.

Shivappa
The younger brother of Kattappa, he resents being born a slave. He loves his elder brother but is often at loggerheads with him. He was deeply in love with Kamakshi, a friend of Sivagami's, and is determined to avenge her murder.

Sivagami
A fiery young woman, she is extremely intelligent and a trained warrior. She is the daughter of a nobleman of the Mahishmathi kingdom, Devaraya, who was executed as a traitor by the king. The wounds of her childhood have scarred her.

Skandadasa
The deputy prime minister of Mahishmathi, Skandadasa was a man of principles. He belonged to the untouchable caste and was murdered by Pattaraya.

Somadeva

The king of Mahishmathi. He is respected, admired and feared by his subjects.

Thimma

The foster father of Sivagami, he used to be a close friend of her father, Devaraya.

Thondaka

The son of Revamma, who is often drunk.

Uthanga

A boy in the orphanage, made comatose from an accident for which Sivagami feels responsible.

Vaithalikas

The rebel tribe that wants to take Gauriparvat back from the clutches of Mahishmathi.

The Story So Far

Years of simmering resentment in the abundant empire of Mahishmathi is coming to a boil.

Orphaned at a young age, Sivagami is waiting for the day she can avenge her father's death. She hates the king of Mahishmathi, Somadeva, who accused her father of being a traitor and sentenced him to a cruel death. Sivagami's path crosses with the king's, and his family, when her foster father Thimma seeks permission from him for Sivagami's stay at the royal orphanage till she turns eighteen. Prince Mahadeva, the king's younger son, falls in love with her instantly.

Thimma leaves for a secret mission. His son and Sivagami's childhood friend, Raghava, confesses his love for Sivagami, who is taken aback and rejects him as she sees him as a brother. He leaves as well, promising that he will always help her in her mission.

Sivagami takes with her to the orphanage a manuscript that she has inherited from her father. Written in the indecipherable Paisachi language, she thinks it might solve the mystery of what led to his death. She becomes good friends with two other orphans: Kamakshi and Gundu Ramu.

The Story So Far

Maharaja Somadeva's elder son, Prince Bijjaladeva, is anxiously awaiting the day he will be declared the crowned prince. He has a frail ego and is bothered by his younger brother's popularity with the masses. Bijjaladeva is cruel and a bully, and the family slaves bear the brunt of it.

Kattappa, who has his father Malayappa's subservience ingrained in him, is a dedicated slave to Prince Bijjaladeva. Contrastingly, his younger brother Shivappa resents being born a slave and dreams of freedom. Shivappa is in love with Kamakshi, Sivagami's friend. He wants to build a new world and join the Vaithalikas, the rebel tribe that is fighting against Mahishmathi from the forests.

Besides the familial and personal, there is a political power hustle at play for the precious cave stones at the sacred Gauriparvat in Mahishmathi. This mountain is rich in Gaurikanta stones, which are used to make Gauridhooli, the magical powder that gives the weapons of Mahishmathi their great power.

The empire is ridden with political decadence and a corrupt bureaucracy, of which one of the most unscrupulous members is Bhoomipathi Pattaraya. And of the very few honourable people in the kingdom, by far the most honest is the deputy prime minister of Mahishmathi, Skandadasa. He discovers that Mahishmathi is producing Gauridhooli in an underground workshop under the palace. He starts recording the process of making this secret ingredient. Pattaraya is after this secret.

Kattappa goes into the forests in search of his brother. Shivappa, more faithful to his cause than to his brother, stabs him from behind and leaves him for dead in a river. Kattappa

The Story So Far

is enslaved by Jeemotha, a pirate and slave trader. Jeemotha sells Kattappa to Bhoomipathi Guha as a slave. Jeemotha is hatching plans to make a fortune out of Gaurikanta stones. Ally, a member of a secret gang of women rebels led by Achi Nagamma, a mysterious old warrior, allies herself with Jeemotha to find out more about the Gaurikanta stones.

In Bhoomipathi Guha's land, the Mahishmathi government is getting a huge statue of Kali made. Every year, the Gaurikanta stones are secretly filled in a Kali statue and transported into the city. The statue is taken in ritual procession during the Mahamakam festival and immersed in the river Mahishi. The officials of Mahishmathi then fish out the stones from the riverbed and carry them to the underground workshop where they are converted into Gauridhooli.

With the help of Kattappa, on the eve of Mahamakam, Ally destroys the Kali statue and then frees Kattappa from slavery. Ally is caught by Jeemotha. Kattappa rushes to Mahishmathi where he meets Prince Mahadeva and tells him about the coup that Shivappa is planning during Mahamakam.

Kattappa then goes in search of Shivappa and stumbles on Prince Bijjala attempting to rape Kamakshi. He bears the brunt of Bijjala's wrath when he tries to stop the rape. Kamakshi commits suicide by jumping from the balcony. Kattappa immobilises Shivappa, who rushes to murder Bijjala.

Sivagami's treasured manuscript is confiscated and handed over to Skandadasa. When she sneaks into his office to retrieve it, she witnesses Pattaraya murdering the deputy prime minister. She is chased by Pattaraya's men. Sivagami flings her father's manuscript to her friend Gundu Ramu, who is waiting on the other side of the fort wall. Gundu

Ramu is caught by Hidumba, a dwarf and the chief miner of Gauriparvat, who kidnaps the boy so he can take him to the dreaded Gauriparvat mines.

Sivagami inadvertently ends up in the middle of the coup. In fighting off an attacker in self-defence, it appears as though she has saved the king's life from an assassin. The king awards her with the title of 'bhoomipathi' for her act of courage. He also confers Prince Mahadeva with the title of Vikramadeva, a title given to the bravest of kings and princes.

For unsuspecting Sivagami, the first execution she is to carry out is of her foster father, Thimma. It is believed that Thimma might have been one of the members of the Vaithalikas, and was a part of the coup.

Hardened by the injustices of an unequal world, will Sivagami side with the powers she hates and kill Thimma, or will she choose honour and protect her foster father who was fighting for the wronged?

What will happen to Gundu Ramu?

Will Ally be murdered by Jeemotha?

Will Shivappa survive?

Book 2 resumes here.

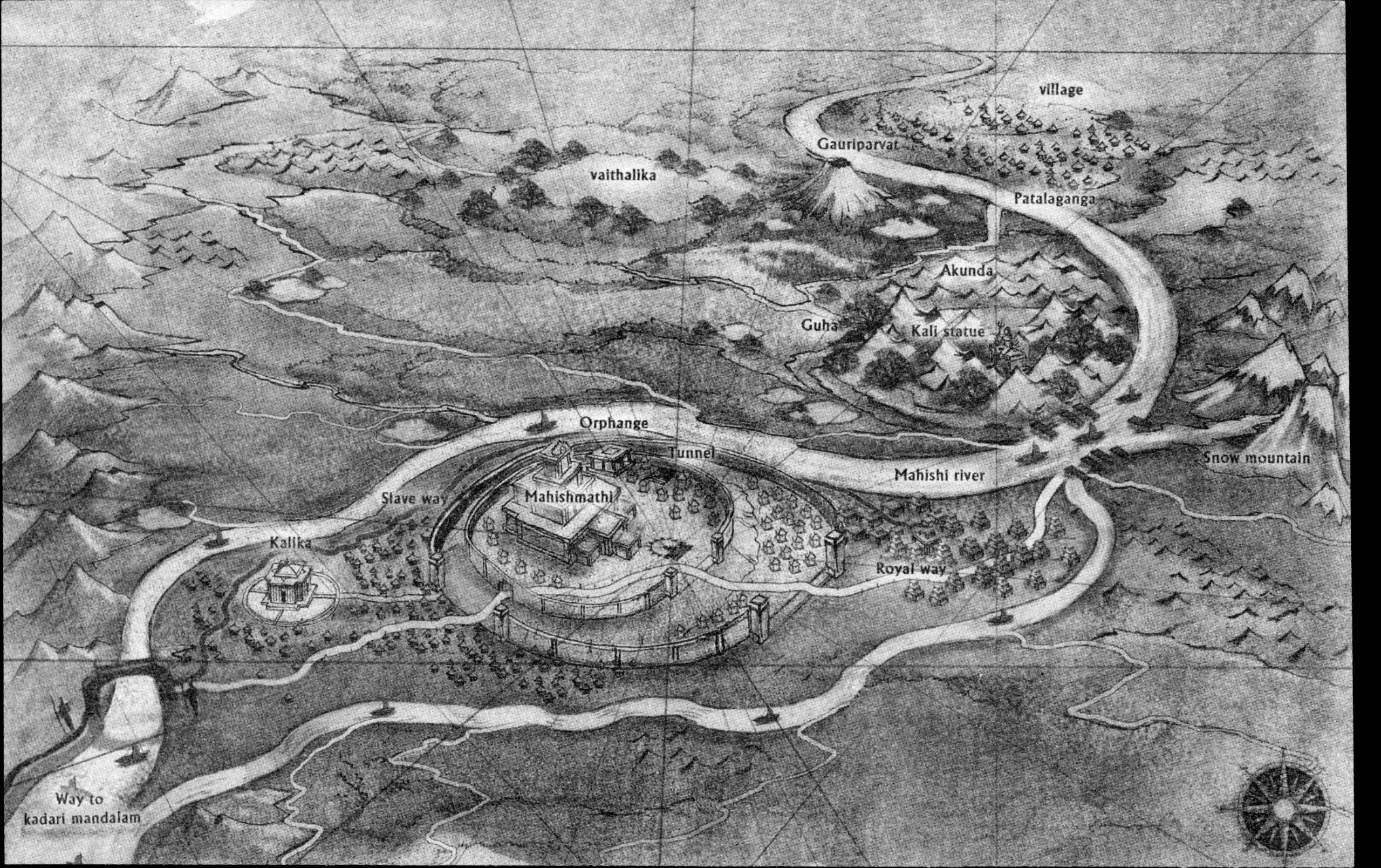
village
Gauriparvat
vaithalika
Patalaganga
Akunda
Guha
Kali statue
Orphange
Tunnel
Snow mountain
Mahishi river
Slave way
Mahishmathi
Kalika
Royal way
Way to
kadari mandalam

Prologue

Sivagami

Thirteen years ago

It was a glorious day. Sivagami could not have felt more happy. She was standing at the gates of the mansion, her eyes scanning the winding mountain path for her father. She was sure he would return today. He had been away for a year, but she would turn five tomorrow, and her father had never missed her birthday. Behind her, she could hear the priests making arrangements for the puja. The kitchen was teeming with cooks preparing the next day's feast and a mouth-watering aroma lingered in the air.

Though it was only late afternoon, mist curled up from the valley. An unusual chill in the air made her teeth chatter. The girl stole a glance at the tall dark slave standing near her. She wished it were his twin, Kannappa, who was with her instead. It was easy to fool Kannappa. Neelappa was sharper. But her father had instructed him to take care of her before he left, and he had been her shadow since then.

'Time to go in, little girl.' Neelappa's gruff tone irritated her.

'You are a bad boy,' she told him.

'I was a boy fifty years ago, little girl,' the slave said with a grin.

'You're always ordering me about: don't do this, don't do that,' she mimicked him, and he laughed.

'Please, Mama, let me stay here. I want to see Nanna coming,' she pleaded, once again wishing it were Kannappa who had the duty of looking after her today.

'You will catch a cold. Besides, it is time for prayers. Your mother is waiting for you.'

She could hear the prayer bell from the puja room in the mansion. The smell of incense and payasam wafted their way, and she was tempted to go in. But her father was coming. She had missed him so much. Payasam could wait. The puja could wait. She continued to stand there stubbornly, cocking her eyebrow, daring Neelappa to force her into the house. 'It is Sivagami's order. Mama, you go and pray. I will wait,' she said.

Neelappa bowed and said, 'Your wish is my order, Maharani.'

She grunted and turned to scan the mountain path. *There he is, there he is,* she wanted to cry out. Suddenly, she felt Neelappa lift her up from behind. She pummelled his arms and screamed for him to let her down as he began walking towards the mansion.

'Nanna is coming, Nanna is coming. Leave me, Mama,' she cried.

'It will take a long time for him to come uphill, and you can finish your prayers by that time,' he said as he carried her to the puja room. Inside, her mother was doing the arati to Amma Gauri. Kannappa was standing in a corner.

'Ayyo, why are you making her cry, Neelappa?' Kannappa said as he rushed to take her from his twin's arms, but Neelappa shoved his twin away. He put her down near her mother and withdrew quietly.

'Nanna is coming, Nanna is coming,' the little girl told her mother excitedly. Her mother smiled without pausing her chanting.

By the time her mother had finished chanting the hundredth stanza of the Devi stotra, Sivagami heard the familiar sound at the mansion gate. She ran to the front door, gleefully crying, 'Nanna, Nanna.'

Outside, it had already grown dark and the servants were lighting the lamps. Silhouetted against the darkness, framed by the entrance, Devaraya stood still. Deadly still. His head and shoulders were stooping, as if he were carrying a huge burden. Sivagami ran towards him, her arms wide open. She stopped near her father, waiting for him to lift her up, for him to swirl her in the air and shower her with kisses. But he continued to stand there like a statue, staring at his feet. Her father's wavy hair, always carefully combed, now lay dishevelled around his haggard face. Strands of grey ran through them. Devaraya had grown a chest-long beard, his clothes were soiled, his toenails black, split and curled. Something was wrong. Terribly wrong. Gone was his smile, and a look of abject resignation had taken its place on Devaraya's once-handsome face.

This image of her father, shattered, would be the one that came to mind whenever Sivagami thought of him.

Behind Devaraya stood his favourite slave, Bhairava, who had accompanied him on his journey to Gauriparvat.

Bhairava was sobbing and rambling incoherently, as if he had gone insane. Neelappa ran up to Bhairava and shook him, seeking an explanation, but nothing Bhairava said made sense. Neelappa slapped Bhairava to bring him to his senses. Bhairava let out a cry of pain and ran out of the mansion, shouting, 'Ruin ... ruin! Lost, gone ... gone.'

Devaraya continued to stand still; his eyes lifeless, like that of a ghost.

'Nanna?' Sivagami's voice cracked. She was on the verge of tears. She heard her mother come up to them, and when she looked up, she saw that her mother was already crying.

'What happened? What happened, Deva?' her mother asked, holding on to Devaraya's shoulders. Devaraya didn't respond and Sivagami started crying. Like a man shaken awake from a deep sleep, Devaraya snapped back to life.

'Kadambari, Kadambari,' he repeated Sivagami's mother's name, as if he had heard it for the first time. Then he swept her into an embrace and started sobbing on her shoulders.

'I am a sinner, Kadambari. There could be no one crueller than me. I have shattered lives, I have destroyed families. I am a sinner, Kadambari.'

'What happened, Deva?' her mother asked again. Sivagami felt afraid. It was the first time she had seen him cry. And what did her father mean? How could he be evil, this man who was kind to everyone, who had taught her to treat everyone equally and with compassion. How could he be cruel or a sinner?

She heard a commotion at the mansion gate. Her father turned to look, and his face became white as a sheet. 'Neelappa!' he cried.

The slave, who had been staring at his employer, snapped to attention. He plucked the lance that was fixed on the wall, turned and screamed a command. Sivagami saw slaves and servants rushing out. They were carrying axes, kitchen knives, garden tools, whatever they could lay hands on. The mansion gate swung open and horse-mounted royal Mahishmathi soldiers galloped inside. The slaves, under the leadership of Neelappa, stood like a wall on the flight of steps leading to the mansion, protecting their master. When the soldiers reached the mansion, Sivagami saw that Uncle Thimma, her father's dearest friend, was with them, along with a few officially dressed men. Uncle Thimma was the commander-in-chief of the Mahishmathi army.

'Nanna, Uncle Thimma has come,' Sivagami said, turning to where her father had been standing. But the room was empty. The lifeless eyes of stuffed stags stared down at her from the walls. Their curved horns threw snake-like shadows around the room. Her grandfather frowned at her from a framed portrait, as if accusing her.

'Nanna, Nanna!' she screamed, as she ran down the cavernous hall in desperation, stumbling over vases, tripping on the carpet and hurriedly getting up. She continued to run, banging on each closed door she passed. She could hear the clanging of swords behind her, at the mansion entrance. She saw Kannappa and Lechmi standing near the puja room. She ran to them, calling for her father. Lechmi picked her up, but she wriggled down. She heard her father's muffled voice from within and her mother crying softly. She wanted to barge in, tell him that Uncle Thimma was there and everything would be all right. There was no need to cry.

She pushed past Kannappa and opened the door. Her father was lying prostrate in front of the Shiva Linga. Her mother was sitting by his side, her palm on Devaraya's back, eyes closed, tears streaming down her cheeks.

'Uncle Thimma has come,' Sivagami said, and saw a shiver pass down Devaraya's spine. He scrambled up, and called out to Sivagami. She rushed into his arms. He lifted her up and showered her with kisses. Sivagami could hear the shouts of men as they approached the puja room. Her father heard too, and tried to pass Sivagami to her mother, but she refused to let go of Devaraya, hugging his neck tight with her skinny arms.

'Let her not see me getting arrested, Kadambari,' Sivagami heard her father whisper. She hugged him tighter as her mother pried her away from her father. Her mother gave her to Lechmi.

'Take her in,' she heard her mother say, and Lechmi grabbed her and ran out. Sivagami fought her, pummelling the maid's back, face, wherever her little hands could reach.

'Don't look, daughter, don't look,' the old maid repeated, wincing in pain as she ran to an inner room. But Sivagami looked, and she saw Uncle Thimma putting handcuffs and a chain on her father. She bit Lechmi's cheek and the old maid howled in pain. Her grip loosened and Sivagami slipped from her arms. She fell, got up and ran, but they had already dragged her father away.

'Uncle Thimma, Uncle Thimma,' she cried as she ran. She couldn't understand why he was being so cruel. Wasn't he her father's dear friend? By the time she had reached the door, they had shoved Devaraya into a closed chariot. She ran down the steps, calling for her father, and stopped in her tracks, shocked to the core. On the courtyard lay Neelappa, motionless. There was a wide gash on his forehead, and he lay in a pool of blood. There were other lifeless bodies—a few of her father's servants and a few Mahishmathi soldiers.

Terrified, Sivagami couldn't move. She was shaken from her stupor by the sound of a whip cracking. She looked up to see the soldiers had formed two columns, one on either side of the chariot in which her father had been bundled. Thimma was at the head of the columns, on his black stallion. He shouted out an order, and the columns began to move. Her father's tenants and servants crowded the road in front of the mansion, wailing. Some shouted slogans against the maharaja of Mahishmathi. Some lay prostrate on the ground. The soldiers rode on, gathering great speed, the chariot clattering on the gravel. The whips stung anyone who stood in the way, and the chariot ran over those who were on the ground.

Sivagami ran behind the chariot, weeping as she stood by the gate, watching the column vanish down the hill. They were taking her father to Mahishmathi.

She ran back to her mother. She wanted answers. She wanted to know why the soldiers had taken her father away. She ran through the mansion, where silence hung like death. She found her in the puja room, sitting like a statue. When she saw her mother, Sivagami's questions died in her throat. She climbed onto her lap and lay her head on Kadambari's heaving chest. A teardrop, her mother's, fell on her forehead.

'Amma,' she whispered.

Her mother gave a start, as if she had only just realised that her daughter was there. She hugged her close and murmured, 'Everything will be all right. Everything will be all right. Everything will be all right.'

Sivagami went to sleep in her mother's lap, trusting that Amma Gauri would protect her. Loud noises woke her up; she saw that she was lying on the floor and there were strangers in their puja room.

'That is the whore,' a man who had sacred ash applied all over his body said in a shrill voice. There was laughter. Though Sivagami was hearing the word for the first time, by the reaction of her mother, she understood it to be an evil word.

'A Brahmin's tongue shouldn't be polluted with such filthy words, Rudra Bhatta,' her mother hissed.

'Ah, Savitri, the virtuous wife of Satyavan.' Rudra Bhatta laughed and waited for his companions to laugh with him. 'Whoring around with a slave while your husband does treason. A whore giving lectures to the rajaguru. I bow to your brazenness.'

Kadamabari moved forward in a flash and slapped Rudra Bhatta hard across his face. Startled, he covered his nose with his hand. Blood gushed through the gap in his fingers and dropped to the floor.

In a nasal voice, he cried, 'Arrest the whore!'

Kadambari stood proud and erect even when the soldiers handcuffed her. Her eyes never left the face of the rajaguru. The soldiers dragged her out, swinging their swords at anyone who dared try halt them. Sivagami ran behind them, crying for her mother. Her mother was saying something to her, but she couldn't hear over the din. She saw her mother being slammed into a cage that was in a cart. Sivagami tried to reach out but her little arms could not even reach the base of the cage. She ran around the cart as her mother cried for her. She saw the soldiers dragging Kannappa and throwing him into the cage, along with her mother. The cart jerked forward and began to move. They were taking her mother away! Sivagami ran behind the cart, crying. She didn't even hear her father's servants calling out, shouting, trying to stop her. She wriggled away from Lechmi's grip and continued to run. They had taken away her father, she could not let them take away her mother too.

She overtook the procession and stood before it. The courtyard was filled with the sounds of horses neighing, the screeching of wheels, and the curses of soldiers. She stood before them, defiant, not allowing them to move. Dust swirled around. A horse peed, filling the air with a pungent smell.

'Run over the pesky fly,' Rudra Bhatta screamed. A soldier in the front moved his horse towards her but she stood her ground. Someone picked her up and threw her into a cage that was hitched to her mother's cart. She tried to break free, but the bars were too strong. She could see her mother stretching her hands, trying to reach her. The carts rumbled down the mountain path towards Mahishmathi. Sivagami stopped crying—she knew she would see her father soon.

When they reached the huge palace grounds, there were thousands of people there, jostling against each other, booing as the carts headed towards the pyramid-shaped platform where the king sat during the Mahamakam festival. Made in the shape of Gauriparvat peak, it was known as Gauristhalam, the stand of Amma Gauri.

'Whore, whore, whore,' the crowds chanted. In the cage ahead, Sivagami saw her mother standing, head up, defiant. Kannappa was banging his head on the bars. The carts sped through the mad crowd, throwing up clouds of dust, crushing the gravel. Despite their speed, people were running behind them, pelting stones at them. A few clanged on the bars of Sivagami's cage, terrifying her.

A pebble found its way in and hit her on her forehead. The pain was blinding, but she had no time to cry. She had seen her father. He was standing at the top of the pyramid structure. If only they would open the cage and let her free.

As the carts approached Gauristhalam, Sivagami could make out Maharaja Somadeva, her father's dearest friend, sitting on his throne. Why was he allowing her father to be chained?

The carts came to a halt a few score feet away from the foot of Gauristhalam. People were screaming and baying for blood—their blood—her father's, her mother's, Kannappa's. The king raised his arm and a tense silence descended. Soldiers opened the cage and led her chained mother and Kannappa to the platform. When they opened her cage, Sivagami jumped out and ran towards her father. Dodging the soldiers, she ran up the steps of Gauristhalam. Her father was only a few feet away when someone grabbed her.

'Uncle Thimma,' she cried at the man who had lifted her. 'Ask them to free my father. Ask them to free my mother.'

In reply, Thimma tried to put her head on his shoulder and pat her back. When she struggled to look back, he hushed her, saying, 'Don't look, daughter. Don't look.'

A guard threw Devaraya at Maharaja Somadeva's feet. The king touched Devaraya gently.

'Show me a way out,' the maharaja said with a smile.

Sivagami, lying against Thimma's shoulder a few feet away, felt relieved. The king would free her father now, she was sure.

The crowd began roaring in anger and she had to strain her ears to hear what her father was saying.

'Stop what you are doing there, or else everything will be destroyed,' her father said.

'Show me an alternative, friend.'

'There is only one alternative.'

'You are a genius, find another method.'

'Not for you. Not again. Amma Gauri, I swear, had I known what you were doing, I would never have remained your friend. You are heartless.'

'You don't know politics, Devaraya. It isn't as easy as reading some stupid books and inventing something.'

'Politics will destroy you and our country.'

'Fool.'

'I *am* a fool, Soma. I should have gone to the public. Warned them about the danger they will face, if not today, then soon.'

'I'm sure you can find another way. You're a genius. Help me, Deva. I will give you one more chance.'

'All right. Allow me to talk to my wife.'

The maharaja nodded. Devaraya dragged himself towards Kadambari. Abruptly, he turned to the people, and a hush filled the arena.

'Citizens of Mahishmathi. I am sorry, for I am responsible for what is happening in Gauriparvat. You should hear about the deceit—'

Sivagami saw her father collapsing to his knees, blood oozing from his ears. Pratapa, a junior officer, had hit Devaraya's mouth with the hilt of his sword. Devaraya tried to get up. His chains rattled. He was trying to say something, but it came out incoherent. The king gestured to a minister.

Parameswara knelt before Devaraya and offered him some water. He whispered something to Devaraya and, the next moment, Devaraya spit out the water mixed with blood on the minister's face. Parameswara stood up, livid, and gestured to a junior minister. Pattaraya came forward and said, 'Citizens of Mahishmathi, you heard Bhoomipathi Devaraya confess about the deceit he is responsible for in Gauriparvat.'

Devaraya was struggling to get free. He rattled his chains and screamed, but his words were still incomprehensible. Pattaraya continued, 'He has deceived our beloved king, His Highness Paramabhattara Gauritanaya Mahishmathi Samrajya Vishwavijayi Suryakulothamma Ranaveera Dheera Bhudeva Gowripadavihara Rajaraja Maharaja Vikramadeva Somadeva. Our maharaja considered him a friend—nay, a brother—and entrusted him with the care of our holy Gauriparvat. But he defiled the holy mountain by allowing the beastly Vaithalika tribe to set foot on her holy abode. He, Bhoomipathi Devaraya, scholar par excellence, the inventor of various war machines and the famed Gaurikhadga, the sword of Gauri, which helped Mahishmathi win all the battles we fought, betrayed our beloved country. You heard him mention deceit. You heard him say how sorry he is—'

Parameswara stopped Pattaraya with a gesture. Maharaja Somadeva turned to Devaraya and said, 'Do you confess, my friend? If you do, I shall spare your life.'

In reply, Devaraya glared at Somadeva.

Rudra Bhatta stepped forward. 'While the traitor was selling state secrets to Kadarimandalam, his characterless wife whored with a slave.'

'A lie, a blatant lie,' Sivagami heard her mother cry.

Sivagami lay her head on Thimma's shoulder, whimpering helplessly.

Pratapa shoved the slave Kannappa forward. 'Slave, confess.'

Kannappa groaned in fear. 'He has confessed,' Pratapa declared. He gestured, and two guards put a noose around the slave's neck. The loose end of the rope was in Pratapa's hands. The next moment, Kannappa was kicked down from the platform. After a brief struggle, his lifeless body lay limp. It swayed slowly, at the end of the rope, turning towards Sivagami.

'Bhoomipathi Devaraya, witness the fate of your wanton wife,' Rudra Bhatta said. Soldiers were building a pile of firewood below the Gauristhalam.

'Devaraya, have you changed your mind?' Sivagami heard the king ask.

'Have you changed yours, friend?' her father replied, in a tired yet firm voice. The king shook his head in disappointment. He snapped his fingers and Rudra Bhatta ordered Kadambari to be brought before him. Sivagami saw her mother standing erect, proud; there was no fear on her face. The soldiers had lit the pyre and its flames reached almost the tip of the Gauristhalam platform where they were standing. Sivagami could feel the heat. Flames spiralled upwards, dancing in the curling smoke.

'Woman, confess your crime. Did you sleep with the slave?' Rudra Bhatta asked.

Kadambari's reply was a look of disdain.

'Then prove your chastity by the trial of fire,' Rudra Bhatta said, and pushed Kadambari into the raging fire. Raising his holy staff, he yelled, 'Like Sita Devi, let the woman prove her chastity. If she didn't sleep with the slave, she will emerge from the flames alive.'

Sivagami was too shocked to react. 'What is happening to my mother?' she asked Thimma.

She saw his eyes were brimming with tears. 'Don't look darling, don't look,' he repeated, as if in a daze.

Her mother's shrieks were drowned in the frenzied chants of the crowd that kept repeating, 'Whore, whore.'

Devaraya lunged at the maharaja with all his strength but was caught by Malayappa, the personal slave of the king who, until then, had been standing like a granite statue by the maharaja's side. Devaraya was no match for the burly slave, who held him by his throat in a vice-like grip.

'Chitravadha,' Sivagami heard the king order softly.

'Chitravadha to the traitor,' Pattaraya cried aloud.

After a shocked silence, a wave of excitement passed through the crowd. Thousands of lips repeated, 'Chitravadha, chitravadha.'

Sivagami looked at Thimma in confusion. She could see his face was drained of blood. He tried to close Sivagami's eyes with the palm of his hand. Sivagami pried open his fingers. Her father was already in a cage which was being lifted high on a pole. A board was hanging from his neck. The cage went up, up, up, blocking the blazing sun. The crowd waited with bated breath. Faces, black, brown and fair, glistened with sweat. Not a leaf stirred. Not a sound broke the deathly silence, except for the creak of the lever as the wooden cage was moved up. Then, a horn was sounded.

The crowd turned as one towards the fort, craning their necks. Something flashed above a tower. And a huge eagle flew over the crowd swiftly. The crowd cheered excitedly, 'Garuda pakshi, Garuda pakshi!' The cage now hung a good two hundred feet above the ground, swaying gently. The giant eagle swept down and perched on the bars of the cage. The crowd screamed in excitement. Sivagami looked on, transfixed, her limbs frozen in shock. The bird was feeding on her father.

Her father's cries of pain were drowned out by those from the frenzied crowds, drunk on patriotism. It was over before it had begun, and the bird left to the tower of death, leaving an empty cage swaying in the air. The crowd grew silent, watching in awe as the bloodied cage cast a dark shadow on the Mahishmathi king.

After a moment, something slipped from the cage and swirled down. It crashed on the ground and bounced. When the dust settled, Sivagami ran to it. With trembling hands, she picked it up. It was the board that had hung from her father's neck. On it was written 'TRAITOR', but the writing was now smudged with blood. Her father's blood.

The crowd had recovered from the shock by now, and in one voice was shouting with patriotic fervour, 'Jai Mahishmathi!'

ONE

Sivagami

'Jai Mahishmathi!' the crowd roared.

The arena was the same, the king was the same, and the chants were the same. 'Kill the traitor!' 'Traitor, traitor, traitor!' 'Jai Mahishmathi!' the crowds screamed. *Thirteen years have made no difference,* thought Sivagami. People were still bloodthirsty. It didn't matter who killed whom. It was just entertainment for them. The rulers knew this well, and used it to control people, to keep them subservient. They regularly arranged these spectacles for the crowds because they helped to instil a sense of pride for their nation. Once that pride was born, it didn't matter whether they starved like dogs or lived like pigs; they still felt their country was the best in the world, that their ruler was their god, and they, the ruler's blind devotees.

Sivagami stood in the arena, gripping her sword tight. They had brought him in chains and freed him before her. He looked tired. When their eyes met, he smiled, and her heart sunk. 'Uncle Thimma, forgive me,' she whispered as she stole a glance at the maharaja of Mahishmathi. He was sitting on his throne, his arms resting on the lion-shaped armrests, and his eagle eyes watching her.

'Redeem yourself, girl,' someone cried. 'Prove you aren't a traitor like your father.'

Sivagami had one chance. She had to be careful. There was a way to save Thimma. A risky way, an insane one, but that was her only chance. When Maharaja Somadeva had told her to kill Thimma, Sivagami had asked for a duel for a reason. She might be dead by evening, but she was determined to avenge her father's murder by taking out the man who was responsible for it before dying. That would be her redemption. She had unknowingly prevented Thimma from doing it by ending the coup. Now, she would do it for her father and Uncle Thimma.

She didn't care who ruled this blasted country after that. But the evil man who was responsible for all of this had to die. She closed her eyes in prayer, trying to push away the fear that was creeping up her spine. 'Amma Gauri, I promise Maharaja Somadeva will not see tomorrow's sunset,' she whispered.

Just then, she saw soldiers bringing Akhila and Bhama to the arena. They were in chains.

Maharaja Somadeva called out, 'Thimma, for old times' sake, I shall grant you this. You lose, you die at the hands of your foster daughter. You win, you still die in the gallows. But, if you win, I shall pardon your wife and daughter.'

Thimma's face was impassive.

Sivagami's heart sank as she looked at Bhama and Akhila. She hoped she would lose to her foster father. How else would she face Akhila? She turned towards Maharaja Somadeva, who was smiling smugly. Somadeva, the God—an omniscient, omnipotent, evil God. Everything was his leela, a play. Like all gods, he rejoiced in the misery of those who depended on him. Inflicting misery was the mark of power. God is power. Power is God. She gritted her teeth and gripped her sword. Somadeva may seem omnipotent, but he was no immortal.

The conch sounded the beginning of the duel and the crowd exploded with joy. It would be a bloody show, where a daughter would fight her foster father and kill or be killed by him.

The sun was a fiery hot ball above her head. Sivagami wiped the sweat on her forehead with the back of her hand. She was deaf to the waves of cheering and shouts that waxed and waned around her. She was focused on her task. Sivagami crouched, her sword crossed across her shield, her left leg bent forward, her right stretched behind, the way Thimma had taught her long ago. She could see the man she had loved as much as her father taking a similar position against her. In minutes, they would be aiming for each other's throats. Her mouth went dry. She would get one chance. If she missed it, that would be the end of her dream, her vengeance. She would die a miserable death, one among many who were crushed under the inhuman system of Mahishmathi. She wasn't even sure she would be able to achieve what she was planning. The king sat so far and so high. She glanced at him. The diamonds in his crown glittered in the sun as he laughed at something his courtiers said.

This is just bloody entertainment for the royals, she thought bitterly. Years ago, her mother's murder and her father's sentence had also been just that for the king and his subjects.

She fought back the sob that threatened to overwhelm her. The heartless king and his cronies were enjoying the spectacle of a daughter fighting her foster father. Bijjala was there, drinking wine from a crystal glass. Her gaze fell on Mahadeva, who turned his face away. The slight hope she had nurtured that he would intervene on her behalf, died. *They're all the same*, she thought bitterly. She cursed herself for thinking about him even at this moment, when she was staring at the possibility of an ignominious death or even worse, a despicable victory that could be had only by killing her beloved foster father.

Sivagami forced her attention back to her plan: she had to find a proper spot and a proper time to execute it. She had no idea how her foster father would react. She didn't want to think about how the crowd would react, in the unlikely event of her plan succeeding. Perhaps there would be riots, perhaps she would be lynched to death. But nothing mattered, if she could lay her hands on him.

Sivagami attacked Thimma with all the speed she could muster. It had to appear natural, it had to seem like an accident. Thimma sidestepped her charge with an ease that drew a thunderous applause from the crowd. She almost fell, but steadied herself at the last moment. Her eyes met those of Maharaja Somadeva. He was looking at her with an amused smile. Thimma could have easily thrust a sword into her back when she was struggling to regain her balance. Instead, he stood watching her, lazily swinging his sword. Sivagami suppressed a sob. He was being kind to her. He was giving her a message to kill him and get on with her life, be a bhoomipathi.

Sivagami braced herself and attacked Thimma again. She swung her sword at him, careful not to hit him. He sensed what she was doing. He charged at her, and soon she was struggling to par his thrusts and swings with her shield. Sparks flew around her. The crowd erupted in enthusiastic cheering. They were getting their money's worth of entertainment. Even this duel between father and daughter would make the coffers of Mahishmathi richer, irrespective of who won or lost.

'Sivagami,' Thimma hissed as they were locked in a deadly combat position. 'Don't even try what you are thinking.'

Sivagami struggled to get out of the entanglement as Thimma pushed her back. She wasn't even surprised that he had figured out what her plan was. Even in his old age, the ex-commander of the Mahishmathi army was a formidable warrior who could easily read what his opponent was thinking.

'Leave me, Uncle Thimma,' she hissed back as she slipped away, disentangling their swords. 'I am going to kill him.'

They pranced around, each not willing to kill the other, yet each trying to get their way. Thimma swirled to entrap her between his shield and his body. He got her, but she blocked his sword with hers. Their swords formed a cross before her eyes, she trying to push away his and he trying to whisper some sense into her.

'You will get yourself killed.'

'He has to die. He killed my father,' she said as she struggled to get away from his grip, 'and if you lose today ... Akhila ... Aunt Bhama ... what will happen to them?'

'You are the last hope, daughter.' She heard Thimma's voice crack. 'For them, for the people. I trust you. Kill me and make them believe you are one of them.'

'Leave me,' she said, half sobbing; she tried to push away his sword with her own as it pressed towards her face.

'Kill me, daughter, and live for tomorrow,' he said, and in the next moment, her sword snapped into two. She heard the upper half clang to the ground behind her. She stared at the ragged part she still held in her hand in surprise. The crowd had gone silent. Thimma still had Sivagami in his grip.

He hissed in her ears, 'Now thrust your broken sword down my throat, daughter.'

She slammed her shield into his face, and he collapsed to his knees as blood spurted from his nose. She knew she had cheated; this was not allowed according to the rules of a duel. But she didn't care. She rushed to the edge of the arena and stood, panting.

The crowd roared, 'Kill him, kill him. Kill the traitor.' Memories of her father's execution rushed to her mind. The king watched her with interest. She contemplated rushing towards him, up the steps of the pyramid. But soldiers were certain to cut her into pieces before she reached the first step. Would she be able to hurl the broken sword at his throat from such a distance? Sivagami noticed that Kattappa's hand was on the hilt of his sword. He was staring ahead, but she was sure he had intuitively read her intention. She had no choice other than to take the chance. She had to get to where the king sat.

Thimma was getting up. She ran towards him, yelling at the top of her voice. She grabbed him, as if tackling her opponent in wrestling, and together they toppled down. Her head slammed hard on the ground and, for a minute, everything went blank. When she opened her eyes, Thimma was standing above her with his sword held high. The sun blazed behind his head, like a halo. The crowd was silent. Her shield lay a few feet away, shining in the sun.

'Don't kill Akka!' Akhila's voice pierced the silence.

Thimma swung his sword and Sivagami tried to block it with her broken sword. He kept swinging his sword at her as she struggled to block him. She was being pushed towards the pyramid. Sivagami knew Thimma was not trying to kill her, but was attempting to knock the broken sword from her hand. At the bottom of the pyramid, with twelve steps separating them from the king, he paused. He stood panting, leaning on his sword a few feet away, waiting for her to stand up. Her back was towards the king, and she rushed at Thimma, planning to turn at the last moment and hurl her broken sword at Somadeva. Her aim had to be perfect. Earlier, she had planned to make it look like an accident; now, she no longer cared. Thimma wasn't going to allow her to do what she wanted. Sivagami was sick of all the political intrigues. All she wanted was for the king to be dead.

She was about to turn and throw her sword, when she saw Thimma hurling his sword.

Time slowed down. She watched Thimma's sword hurtling above her head, towards the king, spinning, catching the sun at its sharp edge and glinting. The crowd was on its feet. Sivagami looked on, expecting the sword to pierce Somadeva's throat. Instead, she heard the clang of the sword hitting a shield. In a flash, Kattappa had moved in front of his king and blocked the sword with his shield. Kattappa moved aside, revealing Somadeva's smiling face. He took the sword in his hand and examined it. He looked at Parameswara, who snapped his fingers, pointing at Thimma. Soldiers began rushing towards them, with their spears and swords held out.

Thimma smiled at Sivagami as if to say, *See, this is what would have happened if you had gone ahead with your plan.* She understood. He had sacrificed himself to teach her one final lesson. An imperceptible nod was his final command. As the soldiers rushed towards Thimma, Sivagami steeled her heart and threw the broken sword she held at Thimma's throat.

The crowd awoke from its stupor and cheered. 'Victory to Bhoomipathi Sivagami devi. Victory to Bhoomipathi Sivagami devi!'

The soldiers stopped near Thimma, who lay still in a pool of blood. The sword that his daughter had hurled at him jutted out of his throat. His lifeless eyes were staring at Bhama and his child. Sivagami wanted to rush to Thimma, hug him and beg for his pardon. She wanted to fall at Bhama's feet and beg forgiveness. She wanted to cuddle Akhila and mourn for the father they had lost. Instead, she climbed up the steps of the pyramid, towards the man who was responsible for the death of her parents, and now, her beloved uncle Thimma.

Sivagami knelt before Maharaja Somadeva; she could hear the cheers of the crowd, and the curses of Bhama. She felt the cold edge of steel on her forehead, on her left shoulder and on her right. She heard the priests chant some mantras, the faint tinkle of bells, the roar of the crowd. She winced when the rice and flowers that the priests threw fell on her.

Somadeva commanded her to rise. Sivagami struggled up, fighting to keep her shoulders from stooping with the weight of guilt, determined to look Maharaja Somadeva straight in his eyes.

A priest stood by the side of the king, holding a golden plate on which lay a sword.

'You behold the Gaurikhadga, the sacred sword blessed by Amma Gauri,' the priest said, as mantras continued to be chanted around them. 'Do you promise to serve the kingdom of Mahishmathi in life and in death?'

'I do,' Sivagami mumbled.

'Do you promise to serve the shadow of Amma Gauri, the supreme sovereign of Bharatavarsha, the commander of the legions of God, the lord of the eight directions, the emperor of seven realms, Gauridasa, Kadarimandalam Kulasekharantaka, Nagavamshakulottama, Gaurivallabha Mahavikrama Bahubali Putra Vikramadeva Paramabhattara Chakravarthi Somadeva Maharaja?'

Sivagami hesitated for a moment. 'I do,' she said.

Maharaja Somadeva smiled.

'In life and in death.'

'In life and in death,' she repeated.

Maharaja Somadeva picked up the holy sword, handed it over to Sivagami, and said, 'Behold the new bhoomipathi, Sivagami devi.'

The crowd erupted in cheers. Sivagami stood like a statue. Behind her, soldiers were taking away the body of her uncle Thimma for cremation. She could hear Bhama continue to curse her.

The king announced that Sivagami would be sworn in as one of the bhoomipathis after the thirteen-day mourning period for her foster father. While standing beside her mortal enemy, after promising to serve him in life and death, she wondered for a second whether it was her quest for power that had made her so heartless. Was her desire for revenge just a veil to hide her ruthless ambition?

She was shaken out of her pointless examination of her conscience by the announcement Parameswara was making.

'Maharaja Somadeva, in his infinite compassion, has decided to spare the traitor's wife and child. The wife will be auctioned as a slave on the day of the anointment of the new bhoomipathi, and the girl will be admitted into the royal orphanage.'

The crowd cheered in appreciation. They had been given one more spectacle to look forward to. What could be more pleasurable than other people's misery?

The king awarded his slave Kattappa a gold necklace for blocking the sword that Thimma had flung at him. After his younger son's role in the failed coup, a grief-stricken Malayappa had withdrawn into a shell and Kattappa had taken his father's place as the king's personal bodyguard. Her mind in turmoil, Sivagami silently looked on as the reward ceremony was conducted.

As she watched, overwhelmed by the feeling of emptiness, she didn't see Bhama fainting. It would be later, while sitting in her new office, her mind still numb, that she would hear about Bhama. Her foster mother had died of a broken heart, leaving Akhila an orphan.

TWO

Kattappa

The grave looked sinister in the moonlight. Something scurried away as Kattappa approached. Mist curled through the tree branches. An owl hooted above him. He frantically searched for Shivappa's grave, but every gravestone looked alike. He began to panic. He stopped by a tree, trying to calm his frayed nerves. A dog howled from afar. Another one answered from a shrub nearby. A couple of bats flurried away from the tree. The waters of river Mahishi were inky black. Was that a shadow behind the banyan tree that stood on the riverbank? He rushed to check. No one. His nerves were making him paranoid. When he finally identified Shivappa's grave, he collapsed on all fours. Kattappa checked for the air hole he had left and sighed in relief.

Malayappa had refused to even touch Shivappa's body, which had worked in favour of Kattappa. Had his father touched it, he would have realised that Shivappa was not dead yet. Kattappa had used marma vidya, the ancient martial arts technique of making a person inert for three days. That was the only way he could save his brother. Had they known he was alive, they would have hanged him in public. Now, he had many witnesses for Shivappa's burial.

But it was the third night now, and time was running out for Shivappa.

'Sorry, Shivappa. Sorry for being late. I shall get you out now,' Kattappa said, his voice cracking. Then, with horror, he realised he hadn't brought a shovel. How was he going to dig his brother out? There was no time to fetch a shovel. He started digging with his bare hands. Someone tapped him on his shoulder. He turned and froze in fear. The last man he wanted to see was standing behind him.

'You're a bigger fool than I thought,' Malayappa said. 'Here is a shovel. Take him out fast. I don't want him to die so soon. I want to ask him a few questions before I hand him over to the authorities.'

By the time Kattappa had managed to open the lid of the coffin, the eastern sky was streaked with grey and he was sweating profusely. He looked around, scared someone would see them. Malayappa was sitting on a rock, watching him dig out his brother. Kattappa kept an eye on his father. He had thought he had fooled the old man, but ...

A bird whizzed past him, screeching loudly. He gathered courage and looked down at his brother. Shivappa's blank eyes stared back. Was there accusation in them? He averted his gaze and blindly reached out for his brother's neck, fumbling for the nerve joint to revive him. He paused, as if he had remembered something. He removed his dhoti and tied his brother's arms together with it. Malayappa walked towards him.

'Don't,' Malayappa said.

'Nanna, he may—'

Malayappa cut him off with a gesture. 'Move,' Malayappa said, shoving Kattappa out of the way. He lifted Shivappa and placed him on the freshly dug ground. Kattappa stood by, uneasy. There was a knot forming in his stomach. He was nervous about how Shivappa would react once he was revived. He looked around again to see whether anyone was coming. He had a strange sense that they were being watched.

Suddenly he heard a racking sound. His brother was coughing uncontrollably. He doubled over, clutched his belly, and writhed in pain. Kattappa's eyes welled up. *My Shiva has come back, cheating death,* he thought. Malayappa, impassive, sat on his haunches. Shivappa continued to cough. A thin stream of blood oozed from the corner of his lips. Kattappa leaned to help, but Malayappa pushed him away.

'He wants water,' Kattappa cried. His father did not say anything; his face was set in stone. Kattappa ran to the river, took some water in the cusp of his palms, and ran to his brother. But by the time he reached Shivappa, the water had drained out.

'He needs water, or else he'll die,' Kattappa said, angry at his father's indifference. He ran back to the river and plucked wild taro leaves that grew in abundance on the shore. He filled water in a big leaf and ran back.

'Drink ... drink, brother.' Kattappa dripped water from the leaf onto Shivappa's parched lips. The first few drops ran down Shivappa's cheeks. Then, with the gusto of a parched man, Shivappa started drinking. The water Kattappa had brought wasn't enough and he ran down to the river again to fetch more water. As he collected water in a leaf, he heard a commotion and looked back. His father and brother were arguing loudly. He dropped the leaf and ran.

Kattappa heard his brother scream, 'I didn't rape anyone! Your duty-bound son helped that bastard Bijjala spoil my Kamakshi…' Kattappa's heart skipped a beat.

'You joined the traitors, you beat up one prince and were about to murder another,' Malayappa shouted.

'Move away, I have no time to argue with a deluded old man who thinks slavery is a blessing. You're the traitor of the Vaithalikas. You've taught us all wrong. Oh God, why am I wasting time on you. Stay away. I am going to kill that bastard Bijjala today.'

'Shivappa …' Kattappa shouted as he reached them. Shivappa looked at him and his face filled with hatred and derision.

Before Kattappa could react, Shivappa dodged Malayappa who was standing in the way, and tried to dart away. Malayappa was quicker. He threw his leg out and tripped Shivappa, who fell flat on his face.

'Tie him up,' Malayappa said to Kattappa. Shivappa was lying still. Kattappa approached him gingerly.

'Drag him to the king. I will not allow any of my sons to act against our oath.'

'They will hang him, Nanna,' Kattappa cried in dismay.

'Let them.'

With a heavy heart, Kattappa removed his turban to tie up Shivappa. He leaned down and held up Shivappa's left hand. He tied one end of turban around his brother's wrist. As he reached out for Shivappa's right hand, he wondered why his brother was lying still, allowing him to tie him up without a struggle. His gaze fell on a gash on Shivappa's forehead. Blood was dripping into the sand. Had their father killed him? Kattappa reached out to turn Shivappa's face and, like a wounded wolf, Shivappa bit Kattappa's fingers. With a howl of pain, Kattappa freed his hand and Shivappa shot up, toppling his brother. He had Kattappa's shovel in his hand.

'Stay away,' he said, brandishing it in front of him. 'Let me die after killing that dog who murdered my Kamakshi. No, don't come near. Stay away.'

'Put that shovel down,' Malayappa said calmly.

'For the last time, please don't try and stop me. Don't come near. No ... no ... stop there, Nanna. Don't come near me. I don't know what I'll do. Stop ... not a step more.'

But Malayappa kept walking towards Shivappa, who was backing away. With a wild scream, Shivappa lunged forward and brought the shovel down on his father's head. Kattappa rushed forward and caught his father, who collapsed in his arms. Everything afterwards was a blur. Kattappa would only remember the heaviness of his father in his arms, the pungent smell of his sweat, his incoherent words, his father's last convulsive movement. He would remember the clang of the shovel that Shivappa would fling before a dying Malayappa. He would remember the pain and surprise in his father's eyes as he lay dying in his lap. The image of Shivappa that would remain with him would be that of a screaming, howling man, crying with guilt and anger as he vanished into the mist.

His father's lips moved and Kattappa tried to catch what he was attempting to say. 'Kill him ...' His father's words hung heavy in the air before they dissolved forever. Kattappa let out a howl of grief when he saw that his father was now lying lifeless on his lap.

Kattappa became alert. He could hear the soft rustle of silk. A breeze carried the fragrance of jasmine. 'Move,' Brihannala said as she sat beside Kattappa and checked Malayappa's pulse.

'Poor man. Such a precious life wasted.'

Kattappa shoved Brihannala's hand away. Anger had replaced grief. He began to lift his father's inert body, but, with a strength that took Kattappa completely by surprise, the eunuch pushed him away, and lifted Malayappa's body.

'Poor man is going stiff,' the eunuch said, and started walking towards the riverside. Kattappa tried to stop her.

'Move away, you fool,' Brihannala said. 'You want to be hanged? You want your action of faking your brother's death to come out? You want your brother to be hunted down and stoned to death like a rabid dog?'

Kattappa stood, blinking his eyes in confusion. Brihannala walked away, and he had no choice other than to follow. They reached the riverside and Brihannala placed Malayappa's body down. Kattappa's lips trembled with emotion as the grief burst forth again. His father looked as if he were asleep. So serene and calm. Then he saw that Brihannala was removing Malayappa's dhoti.

'What are you doing? No, no, I won't allow it,' a shocked Kattappa said.

Brihannala ignored Kattappa. She made a noose at one end of the lungi and put it around Malayappa's neck. She threw the other end over one of the branches of the banyan tree.

'Are you going to continue wailing or are you going to give me a hand to save your neck?'

Kattappa stood frozen, watching the eunuch with burning eyes. Brihannala hoisted herself onto a branch of the tree.

Cursing Kattappa throughout, she yanked the body of Malayappa up and tied the dhoti to the branch. Then she jumped down and studied her handiwork. Malayappa's feet swayed two feet from the ground.

'Passable,' Brihannala said, dusting off her palms.

Kattappa stood, tears streaming down his cheeks.

'If someone asks, say your father has been depressed since your brother's death. You found his body like this, hanging from this tree. Poor Malayappa committed suicide because he couldn't stand the thought of his son being a traitor and a rapist. Sounds so tragic.'

Kattappa turned swiftly and reached out to smack Brihannala across her face. The eunuch was quicker. She gripped Kattappa's wrist mid-air, and said, 'Boy, I have full sympathy and all that. But don't think I am doing all this for you. You deserve to be nothing but a slave. I am doing it for your brother. The revolution needs him. So stick to the story I told you, or get yourself hanged. Either way, I don't care.'

She let go of Kattappa's hand and started walking away. Kattappa ran behind her and tried to block the eunuch's way.

'Where is Shivappa? Where is he?'

Brihannala looked at him for a moment. Then she broke into fits of laughter. 'Go and lick the shoes of your master. You are fit for only that.' She pushed Kattappa from his path and continued on.

Kattappa screamed after the vanishing figure of Brihannala. 'Tell my brother that no power in the world can stop this Kattappa from fulfilling my father's last wish. Tell him I will hunt him down and lynch him to death like the dog that he is.'

THREE

Shivappa

Shivappa ran through the bushes, falling down, getting up and continuing to race forward with no destination in mind. His eyes were blurred with tears. He had killed his father. He could still hear the wails of his brother, and he wanted to get as far away as possible. He knew, though, that he could run anywhere, but the agony of his brother would haunt him forever. He hadn't intended to kill his father, but … Shivappa didn't want to think about it anymore.

Running blindly through the woods, his face was scraped by low-lying branches many times, but he didn't want to stop. Suddenly he collided with a thick branch. He fell and everything went blank for a moment. When he opened his eyes, a craggy old face was staring back at him. Shivappa tried to get up, but the man pushed him back, slamming him to the ground with a strength that belied his lean frame.

'Forgive me, Your Highness,' the old man said in a grumpy voice.

The words 'your highness' pulled Shivappa from his daze. 'Who are you?' he asked, trying to wriggle away. The man looked insane.

'Your slave, master. I am Neelappa.'

Shivappa didn't hear the answer of the slave. He was yet to regain his strength after three days of confinement in a casket. A lump was forming on his forehead, and his head throbbed. He was drifting in and out of consciousness.

'Leave me, slave. I want to kill Bijjala,' he muttered.

The slave's grip became firmer. 'Apologies, master.'

'Leave me. We are brothers. We fight the same war,' Shivappa said, and the next moment, his head exploded with a blinding pain.

'Hail the king, hail the king, hail the king.'

Shivappa struggled to open his eyes. The manic chanting was boring into his head. He could smell incense, hear a rhythmic tinkle of a bell and something being showered over his head.

'Hail the king of Vaithalikas!'

Shivappa slowly opened his eyes. On his lap and on the floor, he found flower petals. When his vision cleared, he saw three men standing in front of him. One had a tray of flowers, another held incense and the third, Neelappa, the slave who had captured him, held a small bell. Neelappa knelt before Shivappa and said, 'We are sorry to be so harsh with you, Your Highness.'

Shivappa tried to get up, but found he was bound to a rickety chair. He was inside a hut with a roof made of rags.

Many faces were peering inside, watching him with curiosity. Shivappa had never seen such grotesque faces. Some lacked noses, some had no ears; the cheeks of some had rotted away. Lepers! Shivappa almost screamed, wondering whether he was trapped in a nightmare.

'We have crowned you as our king, Your Highness,' Neelappa said, and it was then that Shivappa realised that a cloth turban adorned his head. He shook his head and it toppled down. Neelappa picked it up reverently and placed it back on his head.

The three men cried, 'Hail the king of Vaithalikas. Hail King Shivappa.'

The lepers behind them giggled. A woman leper came forward.

'Hail the king of Vaithalikas,' she said.

'Who are you?' Shivappa asked, trying not to look at her face. The disease had eaten away half of it.

'I am the queen of lepers. I am Sundari. Not a leaf moves in my kingdom without my knowledge. You shall lack nothing in this Sundari's kingdom, Your Highness. I have been paid well to keep you here.'

'You've been paid to keep me chained? Who paid you?' Shivappa asked, and Sundari cackled.

A figure made its way through the group of lepers and walked into the tent with a torch in hand. The figure bowed low, and when she raised her head, Shivappa saw who it was.

'Brihannala!' Shivappa yelled. 'What insanity is this?'

Brihannala gestured for the others to leave. When they were alone, Brihannala said, 'How are you liking the kingship, Your Highness?'

Shivappa glared at him. Brihannala smiled and said, 'Haven't you got it yet? The few Vaithalika survivors of the failed coup have elected you their king. Ideally, it should have been your brother, being the eldest surviving son of Malayappa and all that. But Kattappa is incorrigible—he's too loyal to the Mahishmathi throne. They have pinned their hopes on you, Shivappa, you being of Vaithalika royal lineage. I thought I should help the poor souls.'

'Bah,' Shivappa scoffed. 'What if I don't want to be king? I was once sold the dream of a Vaithalika rebellion and freedom by Bhutaraya. All I got was the death of my girl. I want to kill that bastard Bijjala and die. I want to kill that bastard,' Shivappa said, as he rattled the chair and struggled to get free.

'You've just sat on your throne. Don't break it, brother,' Brihannala said, pointing to the rickety chair. She placed a hand on Shivappa's shoulders and peered into his eyes. 'Whether you want to be a king or not is immaterial. Without a figurehead, the rebellion is dead. The Mahishmathi army is scourging the forests as we speak, setting fire to distant Vaithalika villages. People are fleeing. They want a leader, someone under whose banner all the forest tribes can gather, and the mantle has fallen on you. Sorry, brother. We can't let you die. We cannot allow the failure of a great cause so you can avenge your personal loss.'

'Ha, try stopping me.'

Brihannala smiled. 'We *have* stopped you, friend. I am no Vaithalika, but I am their well-wisher. You shall remain here until we deem it safe for you to move around. This is the lepers' village. No soldier will dare to come here.'

Brihannala drew herself up and called out, 'Malla.'

An old leper walked in. With his bulging muscles and broad chest, the leper's body belied his age and infliction. Malla came and stood beside Shivappa, his arms crossed over his chest.

'My dear king of the Vaithalikas. This is Malla. Your bodyguard. I have paid the head of the leper village enough to ensure no one comes in and no one goes out of this ... hmm ... palace. Malla will take care of all your other needs. You will be absolutely safe here, my king. Let your feverish brain calm down, let your foolish thoughts of killing Bijjala fade away. Then we shall send you to your kingdom in the forest. My mother, Achi Nagamma, will be waiting for you with an army.'

'I am going nowhere without butchering Bijjala.'

Brihannala didn't respond, but only bowed her head briefly and then left.

A few weeks passed before Brihannala returned. She walked into the tent with Neelappa and his two Vaithalika friends. Neelappa and the others fussed over Shivappa. He was still in shackles, with lepers standing guard. Even while sleeping, they had kept him chained to a hook in the wall, like he was some beast to be tamed. Yet, they talked to him with utmost respect.

As Neelappa gave Shivappa a haircut and the others helped him into old but good clothes, Brihannala said, 'We have some news that may be of interest to you: Bhoomipathi Pattaraya and his daughter ran away from Mahishmathi immediately after Mahamakam.'

'Why are you telling me this?' Shivappa asked as Neelappa freed him.

'Oh, I thought you wanted to take revenge. The king has ordered Prince Bijjala to catch the fugitive, and the prince has left the city with his personal army to hunt down Pattaraya. So, if you want to avenge the death of your girl, we are at your service.'

Shivappa felt a surge of excitement. He took a few steps but then stopped. He retreated to his chair and sat down again. Brihannala stood with her arms crossed, watching Shivappa with an amused smile.

'Why? Has the fire of revenge died down?'

Shivappa crossed his legs and leaned back on his chair. 'Ha, you think you are the only one with brains. You waited till Bijjala had left the city to free me, and then you come here saying you want to help me chase him in the forest, eh? In the forest, where your people can grab me and take me to…' Shivappa snapped his finger, 'what is the name of that woman? Ah … Achi Nagamma.'

Brihannala laughed. 'What about your plans to kill Bijjala?'

'I'm going nowhere before killing Bijjala. He is the prince of Mahishmathi. He is bound to come back. I shall wait here to have my revenge. You have provided me a kingdom. What if it is of lepers? I shall rule here.'

'What if I order Malla to throw you out of the leper village?' Brihannala snapped, losing her cool. 'The Mahishmathi army will have captured you before you even blink. They will hang you and your stupid brother together.'

Shivappa started laughing. 'What do you take me for, Brihannala? Do I look like a jackass to you? My life is as precious to you as it is to me. Remember the words of praise you showered on me? The king of the Vaithalikas ... the revolution ... the rallying point ... all tribes will come under the banner of the scion of the Vaithalikas and all that. Without me, your revolution is dead. Ensure I am protected and well looked after in this village of lepers. I shall wait for Bijjala to return and have my revenge. I shall have it in my way at a time I choose. I have learnt not to rush into trouble.'

'We shall help you, brother,' Brihannala said. 'It is easy to kill him in the forest. A well-aimed poison arrow—'

'No. Hiding behind a tree and shooting an arrow at Bijjala isn't my idea of revenge. I want the bastard trembling in my hands. I want to crush him under my feet. I want to smash his manhood with a hammer. I want to see the fear in Bijjala's eyes when he sees me. I want to enjoy his pain. So, I shall wait—like an elephant that waits for many years to get back at its tormentor. And until Bijjala comes back, you shall provide for me, eunuch. Unless you fancy the idea of my brother, you and me hanging from the same gallows in the Mahamakam grounds.'

Brihannala stomped out of the hut, and Shivappa sat on the rickety throne with a smile on his lips and yelled, 'Malla, get me a drink.'

FOUR

Bijjala

'I hate that bastard,' Bijjala said.

'I too hate that bastard,' Keki said, filling a crystal goblet with a sparkling liquid. 'Which of the many bastards does my dear prince hate?'

Bijjala glowered at Keki. 'Pattaraya, you fool.'

'Ah, Pattaraya.' Keki smiled. 'He cheated us all.'

'If only I had got him that day,' Bijjala said. Pattaraya had slipped through his net. He should have gone along with those incompetent soldiers to catch him. He had been in the sabha when Maharaja Somadeva was listening to the passionate pleas of that pretty girl, Sivagami, against the death sentence given to her foster father, Thimma. That was also when she had accused Pattaraya of murdering Skandadasa. No one knew when Pattaraya slipped away from the sabha. By the time Mahishmathi soldiers had reached his home to arrest him, he and his daughter had vanished.

'Is it a prince's job to hunt for some fugitive?' Bijjala

grumbled. 'Had my father ordered me to conquer some country, I would have happily done it.'

'This is work fit for a lowly dandakara, Prince. I see your brother's hand in this. You are out in the jungle while Vikramadeva Mahadeva is gaining support from other bhoomipathis. He sits in the palace, surrounded by luxury, and getting trained to be crown prince under that old fool, Parameswara.'

Bijjala nodded, but he was thinking about something else. What bothered him more was the unfinished agenda he had left behind. He lived in fear of Kattappa revealing his secret about the death of Kamakshi. He was unsure how his father would react. Mahadeva was sure to use it to his advantage if he found out about it, and there would be enough courtiers who would side with the new vikramadeva, who was one step closer to the throne than Bijjala. Kattappa should have been eliminated, but the king had made him his official bodyguard and personal slave, and killing Kattappa had become an almost impossible matter.

It was while he had been plotting to eliminate Kattappa, shame his brother and a hundred other wonderful things, that his father had ordered him to find Pattaraya, and told him to not return to Mahishmathi without him. So here he was, in the wilderness, in search of a fugitive. Hunger, fever, long treks through the jungles, fights with wild tribes, harried by wild beasts—all of these were taking a toll on the pampered prince. Bijjala smashed the crystal goblet he was drinking from.

'Oh, that was the last one, my prince. Now you'll have to drink from a coconut shell, like the rest of us,' Keki said.

Bijjala fumed. 'I am fed up, fed up, fed up. I don't know why I don't get information from any of these bastards.

They pee when they see me. They fear me, but always give me wrong information. These savages ...' He pointed at the villagers who were squatting in a semicircle, watching three old men being whipped by soldiers.

Keki said, 'You need to be more diplomatic, prince. You have to make people respect and love you.'

Bijjala stared at Keki. 'Everyone respects me,' he said. Keki shrugged. After a pause, Bijjala said, 'Tell me how.'

Before Keki could respond, Bijjala's attention was drawn to the whipping. 'Why have you stopped?' he screamed at a soldier.

'He ... he has fainted,' the soldier stuttered in fear. Bijjala flung the half-eaten peacock leg he had been gnawing at, and it hit the soldier across his face. Bijjala stood up, swept away everything on the table with the back of his hand, and kicked the table. There was a tense silence.

Keki whispered, 'Control your anger. This is not the time. Go easy on your men. Laugh.' Bijjala continued to stand there, furious. Keki prodded him again, and finally, Bijjala laughed. Keki laughed louder. The soldiers looked at each other, and slowly they began to laugh too, nervously.

Keki whispered something to Bijjala and the prince walked towards the trembling soldier and patted his back. 'I talk straight and act straight. I am frank, tactless and, perhaps, you may find my words harsh. Sometimes my concern for my men gets the better of me, but I want only the best for you. You follow my orders and I shall protect you.'

The soldier stared at Bijjala. Keki gestured for him to bow, and the soldier hurriedly knelt to touch Bijjala's feet.

'Stop him,' Keki murmured to Bijjala.

Bijjala stopped the soldier from falling on his feet and said, 'Anna, please, you are elder to me. Don't do that.'

As they turned and walked away, Keki whispered, 'Good. You're learning fast. Just try this for a few days and they will die for you. It is easy to fool our people.'

'This is fun,' Bijjala said.

'Enjoy it,' Keki said with a grin.

As they reached the villagers who were tied up, Keki said something to Bijjala. The prince nodded, snapped his fingers and said, 'Free the old men.' Keki murmured something to him and Bijjala stopped the soldiers who had come to free the old men, saying, 'Wait, I shall do it myself.'

Soon, Bijjala was carrying the old man who had fainted over his shoulder, while the other two limped behind him, holding the prince's shoulders for support. Bijjala placed the old man on the floor and attended to him. An astonished group of onlookers watched in silence. The man slowly regained consciousness and Keki whispered to Bijjala, 'Now hug him.'

'He stinks,' Bijjala whispered back.

'Hug him twice.'

Bijjala held his breath and hugged the old man. Keki wiped her tears and cried, 'Prince, prince, how kind-hearted you are.'

'Have you gone mad?' Bijjala hissed.

'Wait and watch,' Keki said. She fell at Bijjala's feet. 'You are the embodiment of mercy, my lord,' she cried.

Standing up, Keki said softly, 'From today, start addressing all the old men you meet as mama, the women as mami, and the younger ones as anna or akka.'

'What is this nonsense you want me to do. Am I bloody actor?'

'Politics is a big drama, prince.'

By night, Bijjala was basking in the adoration of the villagers he had whipped and beaten in the morning. Bijjala let Keki do the talking. Keki expressed Bijjala's deep sense of shame in being strict with the people earlier. Bijjala tried to look contrite, and when Keki gave him a small sign, he folded his hands in a gesture of apology. There were loud protests from the crowd. An old woman said she couldn't bear the prince of Mahishmathi apologising to them. Keki nudged Bijjala and the prince went forward and touched her feet. The woman was in tears when she planted a kiss on his forehead. Bijjala tried not to wince from the wetness of the kiss.

Bijjala could see that Keki's guidance was working. He was receiving the same adoration he had seen people give Mahadeva. Bijjala was generous with wine, meat and rice. He rewarded a few folk singers in the village with gold bracelets for composing couplets praising him.

In the morning, tearful villagers bid goodbye to Prince Bijjala. They promised that they would search for Pattaraya, and inform him if they had any news of the fugitive.

After a month more of scouting through villages and staging many such farces, Bijjala longed to be back in Mahishmathi. He hated his father for sending him on this mad chase; a murderous rage gripped him and he wanted nothing more than to finish off his father.

It was another monotonous day. Bijjala studied the undulating valley that stretched ahead as far as the eye could see. Smoke was rising from four places in the distance. They could be villages, but each was separated by miles of forest. It would take several weeks to check each of them. A captain,

Karthikeya, asked him which way they should proceed. Bijjala grunted, irritated that he was forced to take another decision. Then, his sharp ears caught a strange sound. The breeze was carrying it from the valley. He hissed and his men became quiet. They could hear boisterous laughter, followed by someone talking loudly in a strange tongue. Whoever was coming up the jungle path did not know the golden rule of the forest: To survive, keep your mouth shut.

Soon, three men came into view. They didn't even see Bijjala and his men until they were a few paces away. When they noticed them, they gave a friendly smile. They were foreigners, rustic, lean and in nothing more than loin cloths, and with palm leaf hats on their heads.

'Lost your way?' one asked with a thick accent.

'We can help, but it will cost you money,' the other quipped.

'Lots of money.'

'And we can't share our food. Especially with a huge man like you. He looks like he can eat a whole pig,' the youngest of the three said, pointing to Bijjala.

'That will be a sight. A pig eating a pig,' the first responded, and all three laughed.

Soon, they were hanging upside down from a tree, their heads six feet from the ground and begging for their lives in all the languages they knew. Between sobs, screams and profuse apologies, they told their story. They were men from Kedaram, an island far east of Kadarimandalam shores. They had come as pilgrims to the temple of the lion goddess, Simhamukhi, in the forests north of Kadarimandalam, when they heard about a fortune to be made quickly. Some noblemen in the kingdom of Mahishmathi were paying silver coins, matching weight to weight, for river stones. It required good divers, as these stones lay two hundred feet deep in a fast-flowing river. To the men of Kedaram, diving and swimming came more naturally than walking or running. They were men of the seas; men who had made their king rich by fishing for pearls. The priest of the temple gave anyone interested a crude map for a fee. The eldest among the three was carrying this map.

Bijjala stared at the map and, to his surprise, found that it was Bhoomipathi Guha's land. Why was Guha paying silver for stones? Perhaps they were not stones but diamonds, and that bloody Guha was doing something illegal. That made Bijjala grin. He imagined his father's face when he broke the news to him. For him to find out that the supposedly smart and intelligent Mahadeva didn't know anything about this illegal operation. Bijjala wanted to go back to Mahishmathi and break the news immediately. He would hang Guha with his own hands. That would make him front-runner in the race to the throne once again.

But Keki reminded him about the king's order not to return without Pattaraya. Bijjala screamed in frustration and took out his anger on the hapless men of Kedaram. He punched their faces to pulp and their screams turned to whimpers. He asked them about Pattaraya again, and the men, who had initially said they hadn't heard about anyone with that name, soon started pointing in all directions, claiming they had met a middle-aged, obese man.

By midnight, two of the Kedaram men had died and the third was at death's door when Bijjala stuck gold. Keki's mention of the beautiful woman who was accompanying the middle-aged man did the trick. The younger man had seen the pair in a run-down inn in a rarely used jungle path leading to Kadarimandalam. The inn was run by an old man called Muthayya, and it was the haunt of lawless men, slavers and other shady characters.

By morning, Bijjala and his men had left in search of Muthayya's inn, leaving the dead bodies of the three men hanging upside down from the tree branch.

A fortnight later, Pattaraya was on his way back to the inn after another aborted attempt to reach Kadarimandalam. He was shocked to see his beloved daughter tied to a pillar in the veranda of the inn. He ran to her, shouting out in panic. His daughter Mekhala yelled a warning, but it was too late. Pattaraya froze as he was surrounded by the soldiers of Mahishmathi. Bijjala stepped out from behind the pillar. He drew his sword out of its sheath and strode towards Pattaraya. He grabbed the hair of Pattaraya and yanked his head back, exposing his throat. He pressed the tip of his sword, drawing a drop of blood.

It was then that Pattaraya began roaring with laughter.

FIVE

Sivagami

A few officials were huddled by the gate of the sabha, talking in low tones. They stopped as Sivagami approached. She could feel their eyes on her as she walked on with steady steps, trying to seem confident. She wished there was someone to tell her how she to conduct herself in the sabha. She looked around as she entered. Without the king and his paraphernalia, the huge hall looked empty and cavernous. Sivagami had thought she was late, but she was in fact early.

The servants were arranging the chairs, cleaning the carpets and polishing the brass lamps. They stared at her with curiosity and fear. They weren't used to having a woman as bhoomipathi. They didn't know how to address her, how to stand before her respectfully or how to show respect without feeling like they were somehow losing their manliness. The scribe Roopaka walked in, shouting orders at the servants, and paused when he saw Sivagami. An unnatural smile stretched his thick lips as he walked up to her.

Sivagami had heard his name spoken by Pattaraya and she knew he was corrupt to the core. Roopaka bowed to her, partly in jest, partly in respect of the protocol. She responded haughtily, asking him to take her to her seat.

'Of course, gir—devi,' Roopaka said, correcting himself quickly. Sivagami knew the slip was deliberate. He was sending her a message that she was nothing but a chit of a girl. When he took her to the seat, she was taken aback. It was at the rear end, in the fifth row to the left. Only servants and palace maids stood behind her. Even junior officers had seats closer to the throne. In a place where the importance of an official was judged by the distance he was from the seat of power, her position was a powerful message—to her and to the general public.

'Are you sure this is the right seat?' she asked, knowing well what his answer would be.

'Let me check,' Roopaka said with a suppressed smile. He took out a sheaf of palm leaves and made an elaborate drama of going through each of them. He made sure that Mahapradhana Parameswara's seal was visible to her as he shuffled through the palm leaves. She stood there, gritting her teeth, as he took his time checking the seat she had been allocated. Officials were walking in now, and the sabha was slowly filling up. They looked at her with unabashed curiosity and whispered to each other. She heard a middle-aged man whispering to his companion that the evil age of Kali was responsible for such malevolent events. In the age of Kali, Shudras, Chandalas and women would rule over learned Brahmins and Kshatriyas. His companion agreed, adding that at least one Chandala, Skandadasa, had met the end he deserved. And this woman would get married soon; then she would be busy with raising children and household chores. The older man laughed and said, yes, a woman's place was not in the sabha, but in the kitchen. Or in the harem, his companion said, and the men laughed heartily.

Sivagami itched to give them a sharp retort but controlled her anger. Roopaka finally looked up from the palm leaves and said, 'There is no mistake.' He smirked and then lead her to her seat with an elaborate show of respect. He took his uthariya and brushed off imaginary dust from the chair. Sivagami sat at the edge of the seat, then thought about the men's comments. She pushed herself back and sat firmly on the seat, resting her back on the chair. Roopaka watched her with amusement.

'Get me some water and refreshments,' she said, snapping her fingers. The colour drained from Roopaka's face. He recovered quickly and shouted at a servant who was tying up a curtain in a corner.

'Idiot, didn't you hear? Devi Sivagami wants some water and refreshments. Come here you fool. Run. Why are you loitering there? Is this your grandmother's wedding?'

The servant came running, bowed low to Roopaka, and then stood scratching his ear. Sivagami's skin burned at this slight. Even the servant wasn't facing her. Roopaka barked at him. 'What are you waiting for, you fool?'

The man whispered something to Roopaka and the bureaucrat nodded his head and tut-tutted. He turned to Sivagami and said, 'Devi, there is an issue. I don't know how I forgot. No one is served refreshments in the sabha. Not even water. It is considered an insult to the king.'

Sivagami blushed as Roopaka smacked the servant on his head and said, 'Donkey, you should remember such things; you should have instructed her as soon as she came in, right? She is young, she is new. How is a woman supposed to know all these things?'

Roopaka was making sure that the insult was felt. He was putting her in her place. Her ears burned with anger.

'If you are hungry, Devi, I suggest you come to the dining chamber. Hey, idiot—what are you gaping at? Run and tell the cook that Bhoomipathi Sivagami devi is hungry and she will be coming to eat. Run, run ...' He then turned to her with a smile.

'Enough,' Sivagami said. 'I shall go to the dining chamber later. You may go.'

Roopaka smiled. 'Devi, don't feel embarrassed about asking questions. I have been working here for more than two-and-a-half decades. I am always at your service.'

Sivagami dismissed him with a gesture. He gave an elaborate bow and left. She sat, her ears and cheeks burning with embarrassment.

She had never thought being a woman would be such a big handicap. As the hours crawled by, she understood it wasn't just Roopaka; every person in any position of power did not take her seriously. When the sabha broke for lunch, she was the lone woman seated among a sea of turbans in the dining room. Some came to wish her well. Some were all praise for her beauty. Some were patronising, explaining things to her as if she was born dumb as a mule. Some treated her with disdain. The subordinates talked behind her back. If she tried to be haughty and withdrawn, she read in people's faces that they considered her arrogant. Her attempt to be charming made the men feel like she was making advances. It made some men scared of her, and some oozed lechery even in the most innocuous conversation.

By evening, she hadn't participated in one important conversation. Where she was seated, she couldn't even hear the entire debates and deliberations going on in the sabha. She fought back tears of anger and frustration. A sense of inadequacy swept over her. It was clear to her that the path she had chosen—to worm her way into the Mahishmathi administration, finding fault lines and striking it at the right moment—wasn't going to succeed anytime soon. And she didn't have the patience to wait that long.

She observed the maharaja while the debates went on—he was calm and composed. Too calm and composed, she felt. It seemed like he was faking it. He laughed too much and used his charm to humour even minor officials. Through the day, her eyes kept searching for Prince Mahadeva. He was nowhere to be seen. She missed him and felt uneasy about it. Mahadeva was the son of her enemy, yet his smiling face came to her mind unbidden.

When the sabha came to an end and the royal entourage passed by her with the king in the lead, Sivagami noticed that his hair and beard had grown greyer. He had dark circles under his eyes and the look of a man besieged by worry. Something was unravelling in Mahishmathi. If she had to achieve her goal, she thought, she shouldn't be wasting time in the corridors of bureaucracy.

'I hate her, tell her to go away.'

Sivagami stood in front of the closed door. The setting was familiar, the mood was familiar. Nothing had changed. Rather, it had become more depressing, if that was possible. She was in Revamma's orphanage in Dasapattana.

'Akhila, daughter, please ...' Sivagami called out, on the verge of tears. Every day, she would walk down to Dasapattana, hoping against hope that Akhila would change her mind and give her another chance. She couldn't blame Akhila—she had made the poor girl an orphan; she had killed her father and caused her mother's death. All Sivagami wanted was for Akhila to give her a chance to prove she loved her.

Behind her, she could hear Revamma tell Thondaka, 'All are not unhappy living in this poor Revamma's place. Some have become too big. Yet, Amma Gauri is great. She has made some proud ones come to Revamma's home and beg every day. Amma Gauri, Amma Gauri ...'

Sivagami had learnt to ignore these veiled barbs. Revamma was obsequious in front of her, constantly saying that Sivagami was now a bhoomipathi while she, poor Revamma, was a humble servant. Sivagami could taste the venom of jealousy in every word the old woman muttered.

She finally gave up and turned to leave. As she walked out of the orphanage, Revamma bowed deep and said, 'Devi would come tomorrow also, I hope.' Thondaka giggled.

Sivagami ignored them. She walked away, her shoulders stooped with the burden of guilt. She missed her old friends in the royal orphanage. She missed Kamakshi tremendously, but the certainty that death provides acts like a balm. What was impossible to bear was the uncertainty that a missing person invokes. She didn't know what had happened to her dear friend Gundu Ramu. All her attempts to trace the boy had been futile. So many had died in the fire and stampede when the coup had taken place. Had Gundu Ramu been one of them? It broke her heart to think that he had sacrificed himself for something that had nothing to do with him.

Initially, she refused to believe he had died, but as the days passed, she had started losing hope. That the boy had been carrying the precious book of her father made her loss even more devastating. The book was something that had connected her with her father, but to grieve its loss was like betraying the memory of Gundu Ramu. The night of the Mahamakam festival had shattered her life and changed it forever, she thought sadly. The death of Kamakshi, of Skandadasa, and the disappearance of Gundu Ramu followed by the duel with Thimma and Bhama's death—it seemed as though misfortune was following her at every step.

As she walked home, she thought about ending the charade she was playing. She hadn't even got the chance to meet the king after her coronation as bhoomipathi. With bitterness, she understood that the king had beaten her in the game. He was a veteran player in the art of statecraft. He had made a spectacle of her, and then given her a token position. He had played to the gallery and bolstered his image as a just and generous king, a king who had forgiven the daughter of a traitor. She had walked into a trap. *What a fool, what a fool*, she derided herself.

It was almost dark by the time she reached home. She hurried to make some gruel. She had to feed Uthanga. The poor boy would be starving. She had shifted him from

Skandadasa's home to her own house—she felt she owed him that much. It was her fault that the boy had fallen down the steps when they were inmates in Revamma's orphanage, an accident that had caused him to lose the use of his body. Sivagami fed him, bathed him, made him sleep, but she felt she needed him more than he needed her—he was now her only friend. He was the only one who didn't judge her deeds. Even if he did judge her, she had no way to know.

She found herself pouring out her innermost thoughts, her frustrations, her hopes as she fed the boy His expression never changed, yet, after talking to him, she always felt lighter—his gaze seemed to bore through her soul.

That evening, as she wiped his mouth with her shawl, she felt vulnerable, lonely and helpless. She wiped her tears and then changed her mind. There was no one to see her cry anyway. Sivagami let the tears warm her cheeks. Maybe they would thaw the ice that was forming in her heart. She felt sad, but it was all right. Sivagami felt human when she cried.

She was startled when she heard a voice calling out her name. She sat still and listened. Was she hallucinating? There was a soft knock at the door. She opened it and saw an old man standing in the shadows.

'Daughter,' he said. There was a moment of silence—he looked at her as if he were reassuring himself. She saw his shoulders shaking as he broke into inconsolable sobs.

Sivagami's heart skipped a beat. 'Neelappa,' she muttered disbelievingly.

She had thought the slave was dead. Where had he appeared from now? She stepped forward to receive him, and found herself enveloped in that familiar bear hug. He was laughing and crying at the same time. She couldn't hold herself back.

'Where were you, Mama? Where were you for so long?' Sivagami said as she hugged the old slave tight. She sobbed on his shoulder. Finally, she held his hand and made him sit on the veranda. She put her hands on his shoulders and looked at him with tear-filled eyes. She had not smiled so wide for a long time. His curly hair had turned completely white and time had done its mischief on his rugged face.

'Do you want to hear a story?' he asked, as if she was still the five-year-old he had left behind. She nodded with the same enthusiasm and sat down beside him. He started narrating his story. He had survived the attack when the soldiers had come to arrest her father, and decided to leave Mahishmathi after the death of his twin brother Kannappa. He had wandered around the world, working as a galley slave in barbarian lands and later, after winning his freedom, as a sanyasi in the snow mountains of the north for many years. He had taken a wife in the land to the east and sired six children, but had lost everyone in a war that broke out in those distant lands. He had travelled back south and had reached a few days before Sivagami's duel with Thimma.

'Thank you for avenging your father and mother. Thank you for killing that devil who got my brother killed,' he said as he took Sivagami's hands in his and kissed them. Sivagami stiffened and the old man sensed it.

'Did I say something wrong?' Neelappa asked.

'Thimma was more than a father to me,' Sivagami said.

'But ... but he arrested—'

'He brought me up ...' Sivagami said. Her voice choked up. '... and I killed him.'

The old man sat perplexed, not knowing how to respond. Finally, he nodded and turned away. She caught his wrist. 'You were away for a long time. If you promise to live with me, Mama, I shall tell you some stories.'

'You have a long debt to clear, girl.' The old man smiled through his tears. 'You made me tell you countless stories.'

Sivagami laughed. The loneliness she had felt just an hour back seemed to have disappeared. A light had come to her life, and it would never be dark again. That was what she hoped.

Sivagami headed back towards her house after settling Neelappa in a small hut that stood by the gate. She stopped in her tracks. A man was standing in the shadows. She slowed her gait and her hand went to the dagger she kept hidden at her waist.

'Sivagami.'

The tenderness in the voice startled her. Prince Mahadeva stepped out of the shadows and bowed to her with his customary chivalry. She stood stiff, scared he would hear her pounding heartbeat. She was afraid he would see the effect he was having on her. *Don't fall for him, don't ...* she told herself.

'You live here?' he asked, looking about him at her modest home. A wave of shame swept through Sivagami.

'Welcome to the palace of a bhoomipathi,' Sivagami said, looking past him. Her sarcasm was a shield.

'You look tired,' he said awkwardly.

'The job of bhoomipathi is tiring. Too much work.' She wanted to bite her lips. Why was she even having this conversation? She should have bowed to him, given him the formal respect due to a prince. Instead, she was talking like he was her lover and they had had a tiff. She was happy he couldn't see her blush, thankful that it was dark.

'I am sorry the mahapradhana didn't allow you to have your father's mansion. Sometimes the administration is so wrapped up in rules and traditions, that it almost becomes inhumane.'

'Yes. Not giving me an old and crumbling mansion is the only inhumane thing this country did to me.'

'Sivagami ...'

Sivagami closed her eyes. She didn't know how to deal with Mahadeva. Why was she being so cruel? She should have acted as if she were in love with him and killed him when the opportunity arrived. Instead, she was exposing her most vulnerable side—her self-pity. She collected herself.

'I am sorry, Prince. I have had a long day. Forgive me.'

He smiled, and in the moonlight that illuminated a part of his face, she couldn't help noticing that his smile was bewitching. He smiled from his heart. There was no guile in him. His smile hurt.

'I will try my best to get you your inheritance. I will talk to my father.'

She didn't reply. He moved closer to her. Her breathing became shallow.

'Sivagami, I know you have your reasons to hate my family. What my father made you do to your foster father Thimma was deplorable. Sometimes, I can't understand my father. He is a good man, but ...' Mahadeva paused.

Sivagami stood stiffly. *You don't know even half of what he has done to my family, Prince*, she thought. She forced a smile.

The prince is a fool, use him—a voice inside her said. But she couldn't bring herself to. However hard she tried, with him, she became herself.

'Sivagami, I know you don't like me. If I were in your position, I would've behaved the same or worse. But that doesn't change my feelings for you. Call me a fool, if you want. But I believe there is nothing in the world that can't be changed with love. Irrespective of how you feel towards me, I shall continue to love you.'

'Go away,' Sivagami said, struggling to control her tears. *Fool, fool, fool,* a voice whispered deep inside.

'Go away,' she said with sudden fury, this time looking straight at his face. 'I hate your family. I hate everything to do with Mahishmathi.'

'Hate is a choice, Sivagami. So is love. My choice is and will always be, to love you.'

'I want to kill you and your father and your brother and all the rotten men who rule this accursed country.'

'Killing will solve nothing. Violence never works, Sivagami.'

'It has worked for your father. He enjoys having people hanged or arranging duels where fathers kill sons or daughters their father.'

'Things will change for the better, Sivagami. There is always hope as long as we are true to ourselves. I believe in the inner goodness of all humans.'

'Only princes who live in gilded palaces can mouth such inanities. Have you even seen the world outside your palace, Prince? Have you ever been hungry? Have you ever known a fear of the future? Have any of your loved ones been taken away from you by someone so powerful that only thing you can do is to wring your hands and beat your chest in agony?'

'No, I haven't, Sivagami. But that doesn't mean I can't feel the pain of others. That doesn't mean I can't raise my voice against injustice.'

'Ah, I heard that voice. Did the cat get your tongue when I was duelling Uncle Thimma?'

Mahadeva looked down. After a moment's silence, he whispered, 'If you had raised your voice against my father, I would have stood by you. I thought you duelled with Thimma because you wanted to be a bhoomipathi.'

That hit Sivagami like a bolt of lightning. He had touched on something she had been grappling with since that awful day. Had her ruthless desire for power and revenge given strength to her hand? She had no answer. Without a word, she hurried into her home and slammed the door shut. Mahadeva's apology from outside was heartfelt. 'Go away, just go away before I kill you,' she whispered. She had to learn to hate this fool. After sometimes he heard his horse galloping away, and she felt a deep sense of loss.

That night, she tossed in bed, trying to gather up enough hatred towards Mahadeva. *He had no right to say what he did,* she cursed. But the image of his smiling face, the way a strand of hair fell on his broad forehead, the way the tip of his nose reddened when she spoke, the way his eyes sparkled and lips parted made her uneasy. With fear and anxiety, she understood that this was going to be one of those rare nights when she would forget about the raging thoughts of revenge, when her sleep wouldn't be disturbed by memories of the gruesome deaths of Skandadasa or her father or her mother. An impossible future was laying claim to her heart, slowly wiping away the scars of the past. With an iron determination that left her drained, she fought such thoughts. But when the breeze played with the curtains and the crescent moon gave the sky a smiling face, she wished for once that she was a normal woman who could feel the thrill of being sought after by the prince of the kingdom.

She woke up at dawn from a disturbed sleep, and thought she heard the neighing of a horse. She stepped out of bed and saw Mahadeva walking through the gate of her home. Behind him was the most majestic stallion she had ever laid eyes on. Forgetting herself, she ran out and pulled the door wide open.

The morning sun illuminated the tips of his curly hair as he walked holding the reins of the stallion. It was a majestic beast with a shiny black coat and mane that had streaks of gold. She had always loved war horses, but had never owned one in her life. The ones in Uncle Thimma's home were the cart-horse type, of the breed Bahalika.

She ran out and stood a few feet from the stallion. It stood with its head held high, proud and dignified. Puffs of white mist from its nostrils made it look like a celestial beast. She glanced at its chiselled muscles and gently swaying tail. The sun's rays glanced off its mane, making the golden hairs turn transparent.

'Arratta?' she asked, as she put out a hand to caress its shiny coat. She had only heard about the exotic horse breed.

'Khamboja,' Mahadeva said, and it took her breath away. Khamboja was the finest breed of stallions, the ones used by emperors and kings. It was worth a fortune. She pulled back her hand and turned away from the prince.

'I can't afford it,' she said.

'I didn't come to sell it,' he said. After a moment of hurt silence, he added, 'It is a gift.'

'I don't want any gift,' she said and hurried back into her home.

When she was closing the door, she heard him say, 'The prince of Mahishmathi doesn't take back a gift he has bestowed. It is up to you to accept it or let it free.'

She slammed the door shut and stood with her back against the door, trying to catch her breath. She hadn't invited him in. She hadn't said a kind word to him. He had come with a gift for her, and she had treated him cruelly. She was angry with herself, angry with Mahadeva for pushing her into such embarrassing situations. He was the son of the enemy, he had no right to impose himself on her like this, she tried telling herself. But he hadn't been anything but kind to her from the beginning. How was he responsible for what his father did? She could've refused the gift in a more polite way, she thought. She could've thanked him, given him the respect due to the prince of the country, and yet stood firm. Yes, that is what she would do. She would apologise for her impoliteness but would refuse the gift. She opened the door and marched out.

He was nowhere to be seen. The stallion stood grazing on the sparse grass in her courtyard. A sparrow was perched on its back and it flew away, chattering in protest as she ran towards the gate. The street was empty except for a lone milkman walking with pots of milk hanging from a bar across his shoulders. He asked her whether she wanted milk and she ran back into her courtyard without bothering to answer him.

The stallion raised its head as she approached it. She touched its head and it snorted. She ran her fingers through its mane. Soft, silky. She took the reins, put her left leg on the stirrup, and gracefully pulled herself on to the saddle. Sivagami nudged the horse with her right foot and it started off on a gentle trot.

She turned it towards the gate and gentle cantered through the streets. Soon, before she knew it, she was racing down the royal highway. The muscles of the beast throbbed between her thighs, and she could feel the sheer power in its legs as it pounded the granite stone streets. Early-risers enjoying their morning gruel leaned from their balconies to watch her speed past. A few street children ran behind her, hooting and howling, encouraging her, imitating the *cluck cluck* noise of the horse's hooves, but her speeding horse left them far behind. She felt free as the wind and, finally, she allowed herself to smile.

A few days later, Sivagami was tying her horse in the stables of the palace administration complex. She saw Mahadeva standing at the top of the flight of stairs to the sabha, and decided to wait for him to leave. She continued to stand in the stable, caressing the horse's neck.

'You ride so well.'

She turned, startled, and saw him coming through the stable gates. A slanting beam of sunlight falling through a gap in the roof, separated them. The air was thick with the smell of horses and hay. She turned back and continued to caress the horse. He crossed the beam of sunlight and stood by her side. His hand joined in caressing the mane of the horse. He was so close, that she forgot to breathe.

'What do you call him?' he asked. She hadn't thought of a name for her horse yet. She remained silent. He waited for her answer.

'Vajra,' she said finally, saying the first name that came to her mind.

'As in diamond?' he asked.

'As in the weapon of Indra, the king of gods,' she said, smiling for the first time.

He smiled back. They stood caressing the horse without speaking a word. Sometimes, despite their best efforts, their fingers brushed against each other's, and every time it happened, her heart skipped a beat. The spell was broken when a servant came to call the prince. The mahapradhana was waiting for him, the servant said. Mahadeva hurried away after saying a brief goodbye. She stood there for a long time, her heart brimming with an inexplicable happiness. When she finally left the stable, she realised she had forgotten to thank him for his wonderful gift.

That evening, when the sabha was over, Mahadeva came up to her. He asked her whether they could ride out together the next morning. She hesitated, and finally left without giving him a reply, leaving him in agony.

Her mind was in turmoil and, as soon as she reached home, she went to check on Uthanga and poured her heart out to the mute boy, who lay staring at the ceiling. 'My heart says something, my head says something else, Uthanga,' she said. After sitting in silence for some time in the room that smelled of ointments and bitter Ayurvedic herbs, she went to her room with a grim determination to rebuff Mahadeva's overtures.

As she lay tossing in bed, Neelappa knocked her door and came in. He squatted on the floor despite her protests and requests that he sit beside her.

'I can see something is gnawing at you. You need to live, daughter. Don't worry too much about the future. Sometimes it is better to listen to your heart than your head.'

The next dawn was a beautiful one. To her surprise, Mahadeva was waiting for her by the gate. She was too taken aback to hide her pleasure, and she give him a small smile when he brought his horse up to hers. They trotted along, side by side, for a while, picking up speed as they left the city. They raced up the winding mountain path, laughing as they braced against the wind and splashed through streams. Before she knew it, they were in front of the rusted gates of her father's mansion. Sivagami slowed down her horse, feeling breathless under the weight of countless memories pressing down on her. They dismounted and stood at the edge of the cliff overlooking Mahishmathi. Mahadeva took her hand in his.

A rusted giant iron bow that Devaraya had designed lay partially hidden in the overgrowth where Vajra and Mahadeva's mare grazed on fresh blades of grass, occasionally sniffing each other's faces and rubbing noses. Sivagami and Mahadeva walked around the grounds of Devaraya's mansion. For her, it was a trip down the path of nostalgia. For him, it was a journey to her past. Before they knew it, it was evening. A slight breeze played with their hair as they continued to stand in silence, amidst the chatter of birds. No words were spoken, none were required. When the sun bowed down after the day's performance, when the butterflies hurried to have one last taste of nectar, when the champaka tree showered the earth with its withered flowers, Mahadeva drew her to him and kissed her. The past dissolved, the future vanished, and the world around them disappeared. There was she, and he was within her. The ruins of her father's mansion stood like a brooding giant, witnessing the event. The past has a way of seeping in through the cracks of the present and rusting the future. But at that moment, Sivagami didn't want to think about anything.

A few weeks later, Sivagami came home in the evening and was surprised to find Neelappa assembling a chariot.

'A bhoomipathi shouldn't be riding just a horse, daughter. You need to have a chariot,' he said with a grin, wiping sweat off his lined forehead with the back of his hand.

She didn't have the heart to tell him that the king held the prerogative to offer such privileges to officials. Chariots, the colour of flags, the right to put different coloured roof tiles— all these were used to motivate officials. Sivagami would never ask the king for the privilege of a chariot. But neither could she stop the old man in his attempt to do something for her. When the chariot was ready, she was forced to go to the mahapradhana's office for permission to use it. As luck would have it, he had stepped out for some work, and she was compelled to meet Mahadeva.

The prince came out of his office to admire the workmanship of Neelappa. Much to her embarrassment, he gifted him a gold necklace. Neelappa beamed with pride. He pleaded with the prince that he be reinstated as Sivagami's personal slave, and Mahadeva promised him that his wish would be granted. He then turned to Sivagami and invited her for a walk in the palace gardens. She saw Neelappa grinning meaningfully and, ignoring the old slave, gave a small, reluctant nod. Mahadeva's face lit up with her answer, and she felt a pang of guilt. *Am I using him*, she asked herself, as he grabbed her hand and guided her to the gardens.

He showed her the mango trees he had planted when he was a boy; he pointed to the jackfruit tree he and Bijjala would climb and then dangle upside down from the topmost branch. A squirrel darted across their path and, for no reason, it made them laugh. Sivagami was realising that joy could be found even in small things.

They strolled down the granite-paved walkways. He stopped to feed the countless parakeets that were squawking insistently. When they reached the garden of flowering vines, he held her hand and looked at her face. She braced herself for what he was about to say, mind frantically racing for what would be an appropriate answer. But he didn't say anything. Perhaps he had read her mind and was scared of one more rejection. Perhaps he hadn't felt the need to say anything, for he had seen love in her eyes. She wasn't sure herself. They stood under the arch where jasmine vines lay entwined like lovers. A gentle breeze carried the heady scent of saptaparni flowers and bamboo grooves whispered their admiration.

He walked her back to his office and Neelappa, who was sitting on his haunches at the door, stumbled up and bowed. Sivagami blushed when she saw the smile on Neelappa's face. Once again, the prince assured Neelappa that he would take care of his request. He helped her climb into the chariot. His warm palm rested only for a brief moment in hers, but as the chariot rumbled back to the city, she found herself smelling her hand and smiling to herself. Her palm smelled of the exotic red flowers that the prince had called roses—a flower she had never seen before. Mahadeva had told her he bought it from a barbarian merchant who had come from some unknown land in the west, and whose skin was white like a ghost.

'One day, my daughter will be the queen of Mahishmathi,' Neelappa said, startling her. She quickly brought her hand down. His comment had brought her back to reality. What was she doing, she chided herself. There was no place for such thoughts in a mind filled with the fire of revenge. A fire she feared was being covered in ashes now. Far away, she could see the gopuram of the Kali temple. On an impulse, she asked Neelappa to take her there.

As she was praying, she caught a glimpse of Rudra Bhatta peeping from a window of the chief priest's mansion bordering the giant temple complex. Their eyes met briefly before the priest slammed his window shut. Sivagami was struck by a sudden thought. If there was a weak link in the impenetrable Mahishmathi administration, it was Rudra Bhatta. The Brahmin may be petty and sly, but he was also a coward. The royal priest must remember what had happened to her father. He was an insider. The mystery that Mahishmathi was holding so dearly to its heart could open through him. She would pay him a visit, and she would do it when he was least expecting it.

SIX

Ally

Ally eyed her creation critically. She had done her best in the dim moonlight that filtered through the crack in the covering of the well. She reached out to alter the eyebrows a bit and smiled. The face of Kattappa, scribbled crudely with her finger in the slime on the wall of the well, smiled back. All around her were similar drawings of Kattappa. Did Kattappa know she had been caught by Jeemotha? That she was still paying the price for allowing him to escape, and for destroying the Kali statue? It had been months now, since Jeemotha had imprisoned her in this well.

Drawing these images of Kattappa was one of her ways of coping with her situation. Trapped in the bottom of a huge stone well, ankle-deep in water, Ally was slowly losing all hope of escape. Her feet were filled with blisters after months of confinement. Light filtered through the cracks between the wooden planks that covered the mouth of the well. It was a good sixty feet above where she stood. Sometimes, bats squeezed in through the gaps and hung upside down from the planks, staring at her with their cold eyes. They had disgusted her initially, but later, she began to love them. She envied their ability to escape at will the world she was trapped in.

In the initial days of her capture, she had tried to climb the wall of the well, only to fall and injure herself. Soon, she became accustomed to the water snakes creeping over her body, to the buzz of mosquitoes in her ears, and to the numbing pain in her feet. She learnt to sleep leaning against the moss-covered wall. The water had a foul smell, but after a few days, she no longer thought about it. Her captors occasionally lowered a pail into the well with some stale food in it. There was no particular time for it. Hunger gnawed her from the inside.

She dreamed about Kattappa, and about the day when the slave would arrive like the prince of some fairy tale, slay the villains and rescue her. She knew such things only happened in stories. He had most likely forgotten about her existence.

The moon was high up in the sky when Ally heard the noise of a plank moving over her head. The screeching sound echoed inside the well. A couple of bats that were hanging chattered in fear, flapped their wings and vanished. A beam of dull moonlight stretched inside, but failed to reach the bottom. Ahead peered down, and a moment later, the wooden pulley started screeching and the pail started descending, briefly blocking the sky. Someone was coming down using the pulley. She pressed back against the moist wall.

Ally's hands furtively searched for some rock, anything hard to hit the man the moment he landed. Her fingers finally found a rock, fist-sized, and tightened around it. The container swung above her head, scraping against the wall, showering her with mortar. She waited, ready to pounce, gripping the rock tight. A cold breeze brushed past her sweaty skin.

'Put the rock down,' the man hissed.

She froze. It was Jeemotha. He had not come into the well since she was imprisoned. The pail tipped to one side and he jumped down, splashing water on her. He held the swaying pail and stood warily, beyond the reach of her hands. She thought of throwing the stone at him, but knowing how nimble he was, she wasn't sure she would hit him.

'Why? You couldn't control yourself and came to me at this ungodly hour, darling?' she mocked.

'I have better taste than to bed a slave's whore,' he said.

She was about to retort but controlled herself. There was an unusual bitterness in his voice when he said the last two words, as if she had betrayed him. Did he have feelings for her? That would be a chink in his armour which she could exploit. But nothing was predictable about Jeemotha. It could be a trap. She decided to play along, to lure him, to make him think that she was hurt because he had treated her in such a fashion.

'You ... you betrayed me,' she said in a trembling voice. When he didn't respond, she pushed on. 'You threw me to the wolves. That Guha—'

'But for me, he would have skinned you alive. Have some gratitude, bitch,' he said. Again, that note of bitterness.

'I would've preferred that over this life.'

'As if you have a choice.' He laughed sardonically. With a faraway look, he added, 'You betrayed me for a slave. Not that I care.'

She stared at him and then looked away when he turned towards her. She was thankful for the darkness pooling in the bottom of the well, hiding her smile.

'I felt pity for him,' she said.

'And pity turned to love,' he said in a melancholic voice.

'Perhaps,' she said, and waited a beat to steal a glance at him. His hand lashed out and gripped her throat. He slammed her against the wall. Loose stones and gravel dropped down into the water.

Jeemotha started laughing. 'Nice try, bitch. You think I am such a big fool to fall for your coy trick?'

'Nothing wrong in trying,' she said, fighting the disappointment she felt. She smiled despite the pain. He eased his grip and his eyes twinkled with mischief.

'In fact, it is I who should thank you, girl. Your lover boy's act of destroying the Kali statue opened up a new business opportunity for me. These are hard times for honest businessmen, but Kattappa has made me better off. I have been employed gainfully in the past few months.'

'How?'

'Ah, you may perhaps be surprised to know that I raid distant tribal hamlets and sell their people as slaves. They lead a miserable life before that anyway. At least I am putting them to some use. The boys are bought by the bhoomipathis. And the girls and women discarded by the bhoomipathis are sold to devadasis like Kalika. I wonder sometimes—where are the boys disappearing? I never see them working in the farms or households of the bhoomipathis who purchase them. Not all bhoomipathis purchase them, mind you—only Akkundaraya, Guha and, sometimes, Durgappa, the bhoomipathi who mans the great fort at Gauriparvat. I always had my doubts about where these boys are used. Not that it is my concern, but for a merchant, knowing what his client needs his merchandise for is useful.'

'Ha, I could've spared you the effort, pirate. Everybody knows that the boys are used for Gaurikanta mining.'

'That any fool can tell,' Jeemotha said with a snicker. 'What interested me was what happens to these boys later, when they grow up? What is the secret Mahishmathi is hiding? Mahishmathi considers the mining of these stones as being top secret, so much so that they hide these stones inside the Kali statue and conduct a farce religious ceremony to bring it to the palace. So, what happens to these boys when they grow up and are too big to work in the mines? You are wondering how I found out? Akkundaraya talks, if you make him drunk enough. Those boys who don't perish in Gauriparvat are used as galley slaves to transport the stones to Guha's land. Some are used as workers to fill up the statue. And then they are ritually killed so that no one in Mahishmathi city finds out the secret. Killed to the last boy. And your slave's great act has only resulted in more boys being kidnapped. Boys small enough to crawl into the mines. That is what misplaced heroism does to innocents. Anyway, it also offered me a great business opportunity. The panic with which Mahishmathi is reacting interests me. They need Guha and Akkundaraya to bring new batches of stones, and for that they need more children. I did my job admirably and have supplied them with many. What are merchants for, if not for the progress of the nation?'

'Why are you telling me all this?' Ally said, fighting back her tears. Jeemotha was silent for a moment.

Ally stood looking at the ripples in the water. 'You're no longer useful to us, Ally.' Jeemotha's voice was unusually soft. She looked at him, surprised. He averted his eyes and murmured, 'It was Guha's lust that kept you alive so far. Now, a monster called Hidumba has come, and he wants you dead.'

'A monster worse than you?' she asked. He stared at her and then burst out laughing.

'This is something I like about you. Though your sarcasm is blunt, you never give up attempting it,' Jeemotha said. Ally laughed, defiant, as if she wasn't afraid of death. He casually flung a dagger at her. She caught it by reflex. He stepped towards her.

'I am allowing you to live,' he said and paused, as if debating how to put it across.

'You won't do anything for free, for sure,' she said.

'This is the deal. You will stab me and escape. I will tell you where to stab me, so you don't hurt any of my vital organs. You will escape to the south of Guha's land and reach where the Kali statue you sunk rests. You know the place where your slave lover toppled the statue. The Mahishmathi government has brought several divers in to retrieve as many stones as they can from the riverbed, but an expert like you would definitely be welcome. The current has taken the stones a long distance away, and they are fighting hard to retrieve them. They're probably very desperate and you should easily be able to wriggle your way in to join the workforce. And then, you will help me when the time comes.'

'Help you how?' she asked suspiciously

'I will let you know the details later,' Jeemotha said. 'But it involves the Kali statue—the new one.'

Ally knew the pirate had something nefarious brewing in his mind, but she remained quiet. Anything was better than being holed up in the well.

The pirate circled a point under his right rib with his index finger and thumb. She hesitated for a moment. It was easy to thrust your sword when the opponent was trying to kill you. It was difficult to commit an act of violence on someone who wasn't defending himself, even when he had asked you to do it, even when the man asking for it was a low-life scum like Jeemotha. The pirate was getting impatient. Finally, he grabbed her hand and thrust the dagger in himself. Then he gasped and stifled a scream. He started cursing in a low voice. She felt the warmth of blood on her fist and the iron smell of it made her gag. She saw him staggering and then clutching the slimy wall for balance. The water was turning darker near his ankles.

'Are you all right?' she asked.

'Ninteen, twenty, twenty-one …'

She heard him count and that brought her back to her senses. She scrambled into the wooden pail, pulling herself up using the rope and managed to come out of well. Fresh air hit her face and she collapsed to her knees, sobbing quietly. She gulped in a few breaths of fresh air, savouring her freedom. She could see the outline of Guha's mansion in the distance and she started moving stealthily away, towards the compound wall, keeping herself to the shadows. By the position of the stars, she guessed that it was well past midnight. Faint sounds of merriment were coming from the mansion of Guha.

She saw two sentries on their beats at the wall of Guha's mansion. She had to time her exit perfectly. She was about to make her move towards the wall when the entire compound exploded with shrieks and shouts. Something was happening inside the barn. The barn door flung open, throwing a rectangular frame of light that almost reached the bush behind which she was hiding. A plumpish boy ran out, clutching something close to chest. A moment later, two giant men emerged, chasing after him. She saw another child with a large head standing at the barn door, locking it again. When the child barked, 'Catch him!' she gasped. It wasn't a child but a dwarf. She had never seen a face so hideous and evil. So struck was she by the dwarf's appearance that she didn't see the boy rushing towards her.

One of the giants flung himself on the boy, but with a nimbleness belying his frame, the boy got away and started running towards where she was hiding. He was making towards the wall. The other giant tried to catch him, and the boy swerved away. He lost his balance and fell flat on his face. The guards of Guha were running towards them. Ally saw Guha and Akkundaraya shouting instructions. The dwarf had a whip in his stubby hands now. She was terrified she would be caught, but she desperately wanted to help the boy.

'No one has escaped ever from this Hidumba's hands,' the dwarf bellowed, and cracked his whip in the air. He was running towards them, as fast as his misshapen legs could carry him. Ally could understand why Jeemotha had called him a monster.

She could faintly hear Jeemotha's cries from the well, but she was confident that no one else would hear it in the din. She turned her attention to the boy, and saw that the two giants were struggling hard to pin him to the ground. The boy managed to wriggle out of their grasp and began running again. Ally could hear him repeatedly cry out, 'Sivagami akka, Sivagami akka!'

She saw torches being lit by more guards in the distance. She was soon going to be surrounded. The boy ran straight towards her hiding place. One of the giants caught the boy, and in a flash, the boy bit the giant's hand. The giant howled with pain and the boy took off again. Ally saw that he had a manuscript with him.

'Ranga, catch him,' the dwarf bellowed, and the other giant pounced at the boy, pinning him down. Ally didn't think twice. She hurled herself at the giant and pierced her dagger into his neck. The attack was so sudden that Ranga didn't know what had hit him. With a groan, he fell to the side, clutching his throat. He quivered and went still.

The boy was squatting on the ground, holding his book to his heart. Near him, Ranga lay dead. Ally stood up with blood dripping from the dagger. Guha and Akkundaraya were at the gate of the mansion, stunned by her sudden appearance. Hidumba was the first to recover. He ran towards her and the entire guard force followed, roaring with anger, hurling abuses. Thunga, who was in shock seeing his twin dead, was the first to reach her. She slashed him across his face and he staggered back. She grabbed the boy's hand and yanked him up.

'Run, run!' she screamed, and started racing towards the wall, pulling the boy behind her as sticks, stones and arrows whizzed past them. She wasn't sure how she was going to jump over the wall. Alone, she could have managed. But not with the hefty boy.

They reached the wall and stopped. 'Can you climb?' she asked. The boy was panting and puffing. A stone whistled past them and exploded to pieces on the wall.

'Will you tell Sivagami akka that I kept her book safe?' the boy said hurriedly. 'I got it back from the dwarf. I ...' he gulped, clearly guilt-ridden, 'I stole it from him. But it is Sivagami akka's and not his. Can you tell her?'

'What?' Ally asked.

'Sivagami akka,' the boy said again. 'Tell her Gundu Ramu has her book safe.'

Their pursuers had almost reached them by now. An arrow struck her shoulders and she yelled in pain. She pulled out the arrow and blood seeped through her fingers.

'I can't climb. Go, for god's sake, go,' the boy cried.

Before she could do anything, Gundu Ramu ran in the opposite direction, towards his pursuers. She saw them catching him. Soon, they were on him like a pack of wolves. She saw the boy was still holding on to the manuscript, as if his life depended on it. With a sinking heart she understood the boy's case was a lost one. She couldn't fight a hundred armed soldiers single-handedly. Ally stood rooted to the spot, feeling helpless, worthless.

Some of the guards broke away from Gundu Ramu and began heading towards her. Ally saw Jeemotha at a distance. He ran towards the barn door, opened the latch, and flung the door open. After a moment's silence, hundreds of children ran out. Some were as young as three, some were in their mid-teens.

Jeemotha shouted out that the children had escaped. That got Ally's pursuers to turn away from her for a few minutes.

That was enough for her. She leapt onto the wall and scrambled up like a monkey. She toppled down on the other side and immediately started running blindly into the forest. She didn't know who Sivagami was, but she would find her, wherever she was. That was the least she could do to assuage her guilt for not saving the boy from that hideous beast Hidumba. Ally would tell her the boy desperately wanted her to know that he was alive, and he had kept her book safe with him.

SEVEN

Bijjala

Mekhala was lying with her head on Bijjala's lap, holding his hands. She toyed with the mudra mothiram, the official ring of the prince of Mahishmathi. She slowly loosened it from his finger and tried it on hers. Bijjala laughed. 'It doesn't fit you,' he said, as he took it back. 'Besides, this is the official seal of the prince. Not a toy for a woman.'

Mekhala sulked. 'I thought you would be offering me a ring soon,' she said.

'Ah, keep dreaming. You think my father would allow me to marry a traitor's daughter?' Bijjala said, putting the ring back on his finger.

'That is now. But one day, the whole of Mahishmathi will be praising him. There is no hero bigger than my father.'

Bijjala grunted and took another sip from a silver chalice. The drink was strong and tasted awful, but that was what he wanted.

'Hero, *tchaw*,' Bijjala spat. 'If he steps into Mahishmathi, he will be hanged. My father ordered me to drag him back in chains.'

'Then why aren't you doing that?' Mekhala's eyes twinkled and a naughty smile played on her mouth. Bijjala grabbed her and kissed her deeply. She pushed him away.

'Woman, you are disrespecting the future emperor of Mahishmathi.'

Mekhala laughed, making Bijjala madder with lust. She got up and moved away from his reach. She stood by the window and looked out at the mist floating up from the verdant valley. He came and stood behind her, breathing softly into the back of her neck.

'There are many obstacles between you and the throne, my prince,' Mekhala said. 'And only my father can clear your path.'

'Ha ... how is a traitor going to make me king?' Bijjala scoffed.

Mekhala turned towards him and put her hands on his shoulders. 'You don't know my father.'

'Ah, now don't bore me with your old man's story. We have so much to do,' Bijjala said as he tried to kiss her again. She wriggled away, giggling.

'To know me, you should know my father. If you know my father, you will have no doubt that he will one day make you the ruler of Mahishmathi. Neither your brother nor the father you hate can stand in your way.'

'I don't hate my father,' Bijjala said uneasily. He glanced out of the window.

'Scared your soldiers will hear and inform your father? You are a brave man, my prince, so why are you behaving like a coward? To achieve anything in life, you need to be daring, audacious. You need to take risks. That is what my father has taught me.'

'What risk has your father taken? Pattaraya was just a merchant, a sly fox, and now a wanted man who offers empty promises in order to save his life. An unscrupulous man who—'

'Would do anything to succeed.' Pattaraya's voice boomed from outside.

'*Tchaw*, shameless rascal,' Bijjala snapped. 'Is your bloody father listening to what we are speaking about?'

Mekhala laughed aloud. Without knocking, without even a word, Pattaraya walked into the room. Bijjala glowered at him. Mekhala went to sit in a chair in a corner, and got busy peeling a mango. Bijjala stared at the father and daughter, vaguely aware that they were manipulating him. *What did they think he was? A fool?* But Mekhala looked so seductive even in the simple act of peeling the mango that he felt desire bubble up in his veins. When he pulled his gaze back, he saw Pattaraya smiling.

'I always thought the best of you, my prince. Why are you so cross with me?' Pattaraya said, sitting on the bed.

'Like hell you did. I am going to drag you to Mahishmathi soon.'

'You will make a good general to your brother when he becomes king.'

Bijjala glowered at Pattaraya. 'Yes, I hate my brother. And without you rubbing it in my face a hundred times, I know my father was unfair to me when he made my brother the vikramadeva. But how does it matter? I am the first-born. I am the crown prince.'

'You feel entitled because of an accident of birth. I am amused. History is full of entitled fools who realised too late that a lucky accident of birth guarantees nothing in life. You think that because your father is a king, his father was a king, it will go on like that. You think this country is your birth right. No wonder people consider you a naive fool.'

Mekhala giggled, making Bijjala more angry.

'How dare you talk to me like that?' Bijjala slammed his fist in a pillar, cracking the plaster. He flexed his fist to suppress the pain he felt. Mekhala chuckled.

'Son, to achieve anything in life, you need to work for it.'

'What original advice! I've been hearing this inanity since I stopped drinking my mother's milk.'

Pattaraya smiled. 'See how your father and brother have made a fool of you, by sending you to chase after me.'

'For me, the palace and the jungle are the same. I am a warrior,' Bijjala growled, but the doubt had already corroded his mind.

'You have great strength, son. You are an amazing warrior. What you lack is someone who can guide you. Someone like me. Is it wrong on my part to help my future son-in-law become the emperor of Mahishmathi?' Pattaraya said.

Bijjala stared at Mekhala and saw she was blushing.

'You scheming old fool. Just because I have slept with your daughter doesn't mean I will marry her,' Bijjala said and laughed loudly. 'Then I would have to marry half of Mahishmathi.'

Mekhala's face fell. She hurried out of the room, stifling a sob.

'You've hurt my daughter,' Pattaraya said.

'Don't worry. She can stay in my harem when I become king.'

'Without my help, how are you going to become king?'

'Ho, ho—kingmaker the great, now a fugitive beggar. Enough. I have enjoyed your daughter. Now it is time to take you to Mahishmathi.'

'It was here, in this tavern, thirty-five years ago that I became Pattaraya.'

'What were you before? A jackass? I can't tell the difference even now,' Bijjala said and laughed.

'Shall I tell you a story?'

'Do I look like a five year old who cries, "Mama, Mama, tell me a story"?'

'Son, this is your last chance to become the king of Mahishmathi. Hear me out.'

Bijjala shrugged. He sat down on the cot and gestured for Pattaraya to stand up. 'Fine, tell your goddamn story. If I fall asleep, don't bother to wake me up. Keep droning on.'

Pattaraya took a deep breath.

'Nothing that you know about me is true. Not even my name.'

'Who cares?'

'I am the illegitimate son of a merchant.'

'Always knew you were a bastard.'

Pattaraya continued, ignoring Bijjala.

'My mother, God bless her soul, was of low origin. She was a distant cousin of that bear dancer's father.'

'So, you are no Vaishya. I always knew that you are low-caste scum. And to top it, you are related to Skandadasa. Yet, you want your daughter to marry the crown prince of Mahishmathi.'

'Skandadasa was a fool. He didn't know how to come up in life.'

'He became the mahapradhana.'

'A low caste, whether he becomes the prime minister or the king, would be considered as a low caste. It doesn't matter how sincere, intelligent or capable he is. This accursed society would say he reached the position because he won some undue favours. They would invent some fantastic stories about how some God blessed him. If everything fails, they will say he was a high caste in his previous life and was cursed to become a low caste in this one. Take Valmiki, Kalidasa or Vyasa—all born as low castes, and see how they have been appropriated. That is how this goddamn country works. Skandadasa never accepted it. I knew it from the age of three.'

'So what did you do? Bought a sacred thread, wore it, and called yourself a Vaishya?'

'If it were so easy, everyone would've been a high caste by now. As I said, nothing comes free in life. One needs to work for it.'

'Oh, no, not again with that stupid advice.'

'I will tell you how I became Pattaraya. My father was a rich merchant; my mother was his mistress. My father was kind enough to make me a servant in his caravan. I wouldn't say I wasn't grateful for that at the time. It was that or starving to death. I was little better than a slave, toiling from early dawn to midnight for a morsel of food. My quick mind and flair with accounts didn't endear me to my step-brothers, though my father often found my skills useful.

'My step-brothers and their mother made my life miserable. My father started trusting me more and more as his high-born sons were proving incompetent in business, and his family feared they would have to share some of their fabulous wealth with me. They feared my father would pass on the business to this low-born, illegitimate son. By the age of eight, life had taught me not to wait for fortune to shine on me. I had to make my own fortune. No God was going to help me, for gods had forsaken our people long ago. I decided I would chart my own future.'

Pattaraya looked out of the tavern. He was now in a trance, and Bijjala was surprised by the passion with which he was telling the story.

'It was from this tavern that I set out to earn my future. My father's caravan was camping here. One night, when everyone was asleep, I set fire to the camp. My father and his accursed family, about twenty servants, a few horses and camels, all died in the fire.'

'You killed them in cold blood?'

'We make our own destiny. Like Arjuna, who had no qualms killing his kin after listening to Krishna, I did my dharma. Didn't I deserve a share in my father's fortune? And if my step-brothers wanted to deny me my right, isn't it my dharma to fight? Now, won't you fight for what is your right if your father favours your brother over you?'

Bijjala's forehead creased in thought. What the wily merchant was saying made sense.

'I had stolen enough money before committing this arson. And I had stolen one of my step-brother's clothes. The plan worked like a charm. When the charred bodies were found, the dandanayakas concluded that everyone except one son of the merchant had perished in the fire. The tavern owner vouched that the boy who survived was the merchant's legitimate son; he said the boy had slept inside the tavern as he had fever, thus escaping the misfortune. That boy's name was Pattaraya. I not only stole his clothes and fortune, but his identity too. The world thought the bastard, low-caste son had also perished in the fire.'

'You bastard,' Bijjala laughed. 'How did you get away with all that?'

'By knowing how to work with people, Prince. In this awesome country of ours, anything can be managed if you are willing to bribe the right people. Greed is the foundation of our society, and that is a good thing for people like us. I handed generous bribes for the soldiers through the tavern owner, Muthayya—yes, the same old man—and the dandanayakas' investigation was lax. The fire was written off as an accident. As I was the only surviving son, my father's fortune came to me. So did his caste. The tavern owner Muthayya became my friend and guardian.'

'You are such a villain,' Bijjala said, clearly finding the story amusing.

'Villain? I am the hero, Prince. I will be a villain only if I lose this game. And I have no intention of losing. I am the bloody hero in this story.'

'Ah, what have you done that is heroic? Slain a dragon? Rescued some princess?'

'Life isn't a fucking fairy tale, Prince. Life is real. Life is brutal. Life is ruthless. I built my empire brick by brick. No man has built a business empire without any capital. My father's fortune became my capital. My acquired caste became my social capital. Other Vaishyas were ready to open their leather pouches to help an orphaned kid of their caste brethren. Those who wouldn't have bothered to throw their leftover food to me had I remained a starving low caste, became so generous because of my new identity. They were willing to give their daughters in marriage. That is the privilege, that is the social capital, and the smartest thing I did was to hide my real caste identity. Otherwise, I would've sunk. They would've butchered me like Skandadasa, the upstart, the fool.'

'You butchered him, bastard.'

'Ha, ha. I am not casteist. I don't allow such sentiments to stand in the way of my ambition. There is no need for two upstarts in this goddamn country.' Pattaraya laughed.

'I have never met anyone who is as heartless as you,' Bijjala said. Pattaraya's eyes widened in anger.

'Heartless? You call me cold blooded? Had I not done what I did, my mother would've remained a servant, a mistress. I brought her to my city mansion and made her live like a queen. The world thought I was a Vaishya who was so generous that he was looking after his father's old servant. That made me look good in the eyes of society, and I used it to further my business interests. But I didn't do it because it made me look good. I did it because I loved that woman. I was devoted to her. I did everything possible for her. Heroes need not slay the dragon or rescue a princess in distress, Prince. Heroes are those who do these little important things.'

'Everyone looks after their mother well. What's the big deal?'

'And I never forgot those who helped me at the time of my need. Ask Muthayya. I send a generous allowance to him every month.'

'All right. You're a generous man, brilliant, self-made ... anything else? But if you're so smart, why are you hiding like a rat here, hero?' Bijjala scoffed.

'That girl—what's her name ... Sivagami—she spoilt everything. I thought she would be a woolly-headed idealist like her stupid father Devaraya, who got himself killed. I should have killed her before killing Skandadasa.' Pattaraya gritted his teeth.

'The great genius stumped by a chit of a girl,' Bijjala said with a laugh.

'Keep laughing. Do you have any idea why your father spared her? Why the drama of that girl duelling with her foster father was enacted?'

'My father is quirky. Not even God knows why some fancy strikes him and when.'

'Have you heard about Gauridhooli?'

'What is that? Some potent thing one can smoke?' Bijjala guffawed.

'Did you observe the girl giving a small pot to the king in the durbar? Did you observe Parameswara grasp it and hide it? Did you see the shock in the king's eyes when that girl gave him that pot that Skandadasa had handed over to her?'

'No. I was busy hearing that girl accusing you of murdering Skandadasa. I was having fun watching her pleading with my father, refusing the bhoomipathi post, crying, screaming, while my father and Parameswara insisted she do her duty of killing Thimma.'

'And why do you think your wily father was acting as if Skandadasa's murder was of no consequence at all? The maharaja kept insisting that Sivagami should prove her loyalty by executing Thimma. Why?'

'Who knows?'

'They didn't want to discuss the Gauridhooli in the open durbar.'

'What is there to discuss about some snuff powder that the bear dancer was keeping?'

'Everything. You didn't even get the game the king was playing. He was diverting the attention of the sabha and using the girl as a pawn. Somadeva didn't want Skandadasa's death to be discussed. He was playing with the girl's vulnerability, exploiting her emotional turmoil so that the lesser members of the sabha would only think of that, and only discuss that. The girl was asking for a duel, an honourable death for her foster father. The maharaja was toying with her. The Mahamakam was interrupted, the Kali statue didn't come, and he had a crisis at hand. Nothing can influence public opinion better than a spectacle. He was preparing for a spectacle.'

'If you say so.'

'That's why you need an advisor, Prince. You know nothing about the game of power, the deft moves of chaturanga. Your father, meanwhile, is an ace player.'

'So why did you run away? Why didn't you continue to play the game?'

'Who said I am not playing the game? Do I seem like someone who will give up so soon? When your father was moving his pieces, I was preparing my next move.'

'Which was to bolt like a rat.'

'Sometimes, fleeing is good strategy in a game. While your father was playing out his drama, I got enough time to slip away from the durbar and flee Mahishmathi. I knew that once the sabha was over and the king had graciously granted the girl her wish to duel with her foster father, the secret agents of Parameswara would come knocking at my door. I was wrong. There were already two soldiers waiting at my gate when I reached home.'

'I sent them,' Bijjala said.

'I guessed so. They were so incompetent,' Pattaraya said with a smile. 'The fools stopped me and told me the king had summoned me. I invited them inside for refreshments and locked them in a room. I dragged my daughter out, pulled out as much as I could carry from my treasury and dumped everything into my chariot. As I was leaving, I saw cavalry march into my compound. I didn't slow down. Whipping the horses to a terrifying speed, I blasted through the column, scattering the soldiers. Perhaps my chariot wheels ran over a couple of soldiers. Who cares? I remember cutting down a soldier who dared to jump inside the chariot. I reached the river ghat and kicked awake the drunken Bhairava. I forced him to ferry us across the river. I could see soldiers were launching their boats. Though I had a head start, I was sure they would catch up sooner or later. But I know the power of greed. When they reached near me, I scattered a few diamonds in the river and watched my pursuers dive in to fish them out. That gave me sufficient time to escape into the jungle on the other shore. For many days, we wandered in the wilderness, until I thought it was safe to take the forest path to this inn, and from here to Kadarimandalam.'

'Wonderful story. But what am I supposed to do about it? Celebrate your escape with you?' Bijjala said, fuming about how his soldiers had been fooled so easily by Pattaraya.

Pattaraya retrieved something from a bag and slammed it

down on the cot. It was a manuscript. 'This will make you king,' he said.

'What is this? A book of mantras? Black magic?'

'The secret of Gauridhooli. Written meticulously by that fool Skandadasa. I have been waiting all these months for you to find us so I can make my next move. Help me reach Kadarimandalam and I shall make you king of Mahishmathi.'

'What are you blabbering about? If you reach Kadarimandalam, you will be arrested and perhaps hanged there itself. Don't you know my uncle Shankaradeva is the governor of Mahishmathi there? And don't you think—'

Pattaraya raised his hand. 'Hear me out. Don't worry about what is going to happen once I reach Kadarimandalam. I want your help to get there. And I promise you the throne of Mahishmathi in return. You need to do only one thing, and I assure you that it will bring you fame for now, and the crown in the future.'

'Don't talk in riddles.'

'I will make it simple for you, Prince. I want you to kill me and return as a hero to Mahishmathi.'

'What? You've gone crazy.'

'When I say kill me, don't take it literally. I once faked my death and became Pattaraya in this tavern. Now, this is the story you will tell the world. You, the brave prince of Mahishmathi, Bijjaladeva, cornered Pattaraya in a forest inn. The fugitive tried to resist arrest. You were forced to kill him in the scuffle.'

Bijjala stared at him for a moment. 'My father will be furious. His orders are to bring you back alive.'

'Let him be angry with you. Anyway, he prefers your brother Mahadeva to you. Let him rage and shout, but he won't be able to do anything about it. If I am dead, I am dead. And he can't keep you away from Mahishmathi for long, so that the your younger brother's path to the throne is clear. You will reach the city as a conquering hero, dragging my mutilated body. Meanwhile, let me get to Kadarimandalam and arrange to make you the king of Mahishmathi. A time will come when your father will send you to Kadarimandalam. Until then, stay in Mahishmathi and keep a close watch on your brother. Your father is bound to give him an important duty. You will know when it happens. Your job is to prevent your brother from achieving what your father wants him to do. Behave well and be nice to people. I have already briefed Keki. She will guide you at each step. More importantly, keep that girl Sivagami close to you. She will lead you to someplace important, which will change your destiny and Mahishmathi's.'

'That orphan girl? How will she help me?'

'She holds the key. Why did she come to Skandadasa's room when we were questioning him? She must have something precious hidden in that room, or no one would take such an insane risk. Remember whose daughter she is.'

'Some traitor who was hanged long ago, when I was a child.'

'Not just some traitor, but Devaraya. The man who made Mahishmathi what it is today. Devaraya, the man who was most loyal to the king, your father's closest friend. Why did he become a traitor?'

'Maybe he wanted to be a king himself. Who doesn't?'

'Ah, not Devaraya. He was a saint, and a fool. It was rumoured that he found something in Gauriparvat. He brought back an old manuscript; a manuscript that contains something important. It changed him. Maharaja Somadeva tried to get the manuscript after Devaraya's death, but did not succeed. For many years, the search continued, but it has remained unfound. Most probably the girl had it, and it might have reached Skandadasa. Keki told me about the black magic book that Revamma found in the girl's bag, and how she had taken the girl and the book to Skandadasa. The day the girl almost killed a boy in the royal orphanage, remember?'

'Why should I? Who cares about some orphans, whether they live or die.'

'You should, if you want to be king and have any intention of remaining on the throne for a long time. Or you will soon have a people's revolution at hand. The bad thing about revolution is no one knows when it will come, and how it ends. Another lesson for you. Well, she had a manuscript with her, and unless it got burned along with Skandadasa's office in the fire during Mahamakam, and I am sure it didn't, for Pratapa said she threw something over the wall of the fort, she would still have it with her. So, she isn't just another pretty face. Just stay close to her. Seduce her, if possible.'

'That would be fun. It will break my brother's heart.' Bijjala chuckled.

'You can break his neck one day. Just follow what I say and you will find yourself the maharaja of Mahishmathi soon. Sivagami will lead you to the throne. She is an important piece in this game of chaturanga. I can see the future. Trust this grand master of the game.'

Bijjala scowled at Pattaraya. All this was too much for him. He didn't understand what Pattaraya was trying to do. He scratched his chin. 'If I drag your dead body to Mahishmathi, how will you help me from Kadarimandalam? As a ghost?'

'My prince, my prince. You really do need an advisor. What do you need to prove to your father that you killed me?'

'Your severed head?'

'A dead body, son. I shall provide you a body. Strike at its face, chop off the nose, ears and lips. Make it unrecognisable. Claim that, when you saw the traitor, you couldn't control your rage. Then tie the dead body to your horse and drag it all the way to Mahishmathi. By the time you reach the city, no one will be able to determine whose body it is. Be sure to send some soldiers in advance, who will spread the news. Hire a few poets who will sing about your heroics and how you slayed the traitor. Buy out all the poets. Poets are cheap and greedy. If some poets refuse to toe the line, intimidate them, or better, eliminate them. Make a grand entry into the city with the disfigured body of the traitor. The people of Mahishmathi love a show. The great hero returns with the traitor's body in tow: that is the story you have to spread. Bijjaladeva, the man of justice, the man who would slay any traitor without mercy. Give a speech about how you are going to bring good times to all. Talk about how stifled you felt in the palace and how much you yearned to be with the people. Get the poets to write about how bravely you wrestled with tigers and crocodiles. Make up stories and repeat them often. Scream about how no one who is against Mahishmathi is going to be spared. There will be enough fools to fall for it. Nothing sells like nationalism and religion in our country. Offer prayers at all the temples along the way. Talk about our ancient culture and tradition. Fools who have done nothing in life will feel proud that they were born in this goddamn country, though they are living like worms. Be their fucking hero. They will soon be devoted to you, willing to kill and die for you, and to lynch anyone who dares question you.'

A smile finally spread on Bijjala's face. 'All this sounds great. But where will you get the dead body?'

'Dead bodies don't fall from the sky, son. We need to work for that too.'

'Oh, not that advice again,' Bijjala said, but he was grinning from ear to ear.

'Muthayya,' Pattaraya called.

'Bastard! He was the one who helped you!' Bijjala said, horrified. Pattaraya removed a bracelet from his wrist, a gift from Maharaja Somadeva, and handed it to Bijjala.

'And I paid him for it for thirty years. Time for him to earn his pay.'

The old tavern keeper appeared at the door and bowed low. Pattaraya smiled at him. 'The prince wants to give you a gift. Please come in.'

The old man's face beamed with joy. He tottered towards the prince and bowed low. Bijjala placed the bracelet in Muthayya's hand. The tavern keeper looked at it in surprise.

'Swami, this is ... this is ...' His voice was choked with emotion.

'For all the service you did for me, Muthayya,' Pattaraya said, with one hand on the old man's shoulders. Muthayya's eyes filled with tears of gratitude. He didn't see the dagger in Pattaraya's other hand. Bijjala watched Pattaraya slicing the neck of the man who had served him faithfully for three decades. As Muthayya collapsed on the ground, Bijjala drew his sword and started hacking the dead man's face into ribbons.

The return of Bijjala was a spectacular event in Mahishmathi. The singers had preceded the victory march of the prince, and people thronged on either side of the highway to see Bijjala ride in on his majestic horse, dragging a shapeless chunk of flesh behind it. It bore a faint resemblance to a human body. The eunuch Keki, running alongside, kept shouting, 'Behold the fate of the traitor, Pattaraya. Behold the hero who slayed him. Jai Rajakumara Bijjaladeva. Jai Mahishmathi.' The crowd cheered loudly. Boys danced before the procession. Drummers appeared from nowhere and started beating their drums in a frenzy. Women threw flowers on the cavalcade from the balconies of their homes. As instructed, poets sang paeans to the prince, drawing particular attention to his broad chest. Bijjala happily flaunted it.

At Gauristhalam, Bijjala gave a stirring speech; it was something Keki had made him practise for many days. He spoke about going deep into the jungle to catch this enemy of the country; how he had wrestled with crocodiles in the river Mahishi, and tigers in the forest; how he had hiked up the ice-capped peaks of Gauriparvat to crawl into its caves and meditate on the future of Mahishmathi. He talked about his sacrifices for the people—but he also made sure to talk about men he lost on the way. With tears in his eyes, he called the widows of soldiers who had died on the mission. The prince fell at their feet. 'Mothers,' he cried, his voice quivering, his lips trembling with emotion. 'Your husbands were all brave men. I am a sinner. I couldn't save them. Every time a man died under my watch, I wanted to jump into the funeral pyre along with him. The only thing that kept me alive was the thought that I needed to apologise to you. Now that I have done so, allow me to jump into a pyre.'

The crowd was moved to tears. The widows wept and pleaded with the prince not to die. Bijjala awarded the widows generously. The crowd cheered for Mahishmathi and its saviour, the prince. A soldier who had accompanied Bijjala on the mission remarked to a bystander that whatever the prince said was a lie. It was a grave mistake, which the poor soldier realised a tad too late. His desperate cries that he was a member of the party that had gone with Bijjala and he knew the truth better than anyone else was drowned out in the angry shouts of the prince's new devotees.

The soldier tried to apologise as blows started falling on his back, but it was too late. Bijjala watched them lynch the poor soldier, and when he was sure the soldier could talk no more, he ran from the stage and hugged the inert body. 'Without brave men like you, would Mahishmathi be there? Oh friend, nay, brother, why did you leave me so soon?' the prince said, cradling the dead man's head in his arms. The other soldiers stood with their heads bent, not facing the crowd or their hero. The crowd wept with Bijjala, and patriotic slogans rung out loud. Excited bards were leaping up and down, crying hoarse about how great Bijjala was. Keki beamed at the prince, proud of how her coaching had changed him. Pattaraya was right. This bloody country loved a vain fool and relished his theatrics.

In the middle of all the drama, Bijjala made a discovery. His official seal, the mudra mothiram, was missing from his ring finger. He decided to get another one made without informing anyone. Officially, it needed the king's sanction and the approval of the council. But creating a passable imitation was only a matter of paying someone a sufficient bribe. It wasn't as though he used his seal much, anyway. He wasn't his brother, a glorified clerk who was more at ease signing official scrolls and copper plates than on the battlefield.

As the procession entered the palace complex, where all the courtiers waited to receive him, Keki nudged Bijjala and gestured with her chin towards Sivagami, who was standing beside Mahadeva.

Bijjala nodded.

EIGHT

Pattaraya

'Where is my daughter?' Pattaraya asked, but received no answer.

Using Bijjala's official ring to forge his pass, he and his daughter had passed into Kadarimandalam as royal artists. Everything had been fine until he reached the palace gates of Chitraveni. The guards had separated his daughter from him, and as soon as he stepped into the guard room so he could be checked for any concealed weapons, he was bound in chains. *She knows,* Pattaraya thought with a wry smile. *Chitraveni knows.* He was being chained because she was giving him a message that she was angry. She had every right to be angry. He had failed in his mission. Pattaraya racked his brain, trying to find the words that would pacify her wrath.

A woman guard carrying a spear shoved Pattaraya past the pillared verandas with low ceilings. The floor was polished wood, smooth after thousands of years of use. Everything looked elegant, feminine, a far cry from the grandeur and glitz of the Mahishmathi palace. Pattaraya felt a sense of exhilaration as he walked into the Kadarimandalam palace. Nothing had changed since he had last visited. Here was the open courtyard with its jasmine vines, there was the garden of saptaparni trees; it was under the banyan tree that stood at the entrance of the sacred serpent grove that he had confessed his love to her.

He was led to a large door that was carved with serpents interweaving in complex patterns. There were small bells attached to the door. Pattaraya smiled at a memory. He had held her close to his heart and made love to her, leaning against this very door. Almost like those intertwining serpents, he thought with a smile. The door opened and he stepped into the hall. Sunlight filtered down through crystals in the roof, creating exotic patterns on the wooden floor. The walls were adorned with exquisite paintings, and a wisp of fragrant smoke hung in the air.

'There she is,' Pattaraya whispered. As he walked towards her, the only thing that disturbed the perfection of the scene was the rattle of his chains. His heart raced as his eyes drank in her exquisite beauty. She was sitting on a carved wooden swing, swaying gently. Her dark skin, smooth as honey, glowed. Somewhere in the far corner of the room, hidden by curtains that danced gently in the breeze, came the strains of a veena and the soft rhythms of a ghatam. She held an incense holder in her hand, and smoke rose to caress and perfume her curly tresses. As Pattaraya neared, his knees became weak, his throat went dry. She raised her eyes and glared at him.

He collapsed to his knees and said in a voice barely audible, 'Chitraveni, my love.'

There was a brief silence and his shallow breath measured the time. The rhythm of the ghatam flowed in waves. The swing went back and forth, taking her away and bringing her near only to take her away again. He waited for it to come back, carrying his goddess. Pattaraya heard the crash before he felt the pain. Like a cobra striking, the woman he had always loved had struck his face with the incense holder. He lay on his side, panting.

'Get up.'

Pattaraya got to his knees with difficulty, not bothering to wipe the stream of blood that warmed his skin. He held on to the swing for support.

'How do you want to die?' Chitraveni asked.

'On your lap, as a hundred-year-old,' Pattaraya said, gazing into her sparkling eyes.

She glared at him and then, slowly, a smile spread on her lips, revealing her pearly teeth.

'Always good with the comebacks, eh?' Chitraveni said, and Pattaraya's lips strained to smile through the pain. Chitraveni held his hair and yanked his head back. 'And good for nothing else. Not even in bed, you loser.'

Pattaraya knew she relished abusing him. The humiliation didn't matter, as long as it was from her. It had always been like that, since the first time he had laid eyes on her. He was a junior minister in Mahishmathi then, and she, a deposed princess. Kadarimandalam used to follow the custom of matriarchy, and had the kingdom not lost the war on the banks of river Povai years ago, Chitraveni would have been the reigning empress of not only Kadarimandalam, but minor kingdoms like Mahishmathi. Instead, her brother Narasimha Varman now sat on the throne.

She held her feet out for him to massage, and he obliged.

'Tell me how you lost,' she said to Pattaraya, not too unkindly. Pattaraya poured out all he had done and how his plans had been thwarted by a girl. Chitraveni found it amusing that it was a girl who had tripped him.

'When will you men learn not to mess with women,' Chitraveni said with a chuckle.

'All is not lost,' Pattaraya said. 'Unchain me and I will show you something.'

'And let you bolt?'

'Where will I run, Chitraveni? I have no place to go, no refuge other than your lotus feet.'

Chitraveni laughed and snapped her fingers. Before he knew it, the lock was opened and the chain fell down around him in a heap. He hadn't even heard the footsteps of the woman who had walked in, unchained him and disappeared.

'She could've slit your throat just as easily,' Chitraveni said, as if reading his mind. Pattaraya took a deep breath, wondering again at his deep love for this woman. Perhaps it was the deep-seated insecurity, the sense of inferiority he harboured for being from a low caste that made his relationship with her so exciting and fulfilling. He was the lover of the scion of an ancient dynasty. Well, one among many lovers, but still, it was a privilege for a bastard son born to a merchant and a woman of the bear dancer caste. It helped that Kadarimandalam did not care about caste.

Pattaraya placed the manuscript of Skandadasa before her. She took it in her hand and flipped through the pages.

'The complete design of Gauridhooli extraction, my queen. We will neutralise the advantage that Mahishmathi has,'

Pattaraya said. 'I want you to be the queen of Kadarimandalam again, Chitraveni.'

'What makes you think I am not the queen of Kadarimandalam now?'

'Not like this, not imprisoned in this palace with a few servants, with no real powers.'

He saw Chitraveni's eyes moisten as she sat without saying a word. Pattaraya hung his head in shame. When he had first met her—an event that had swept him off his feet—Chitraveni was still the empress of Kadarimandalam. Her mother, the queen empress, had been killed in the war of Povai, and the mantle had fallen on a young Chitraveni. She held on with tenacity in the inner fort with her limited band of followers, while her commander-in-chief, Achi Nagamma, led the battle against the Mahishmathi army on the streets.

Mahishmathi had conquered Kadarimandalam and crowned Chitraveni's incompetent brother Narasimha Varman as king, with Somadeva's cousin, Shankaradeva, as governor, but the war was still being fought. Achi Nagamma declared that until the last woman warrior of the kingdom was killed, they would fight for Queen Chitraveni. The people of Kadarimandalam continued to consider Chitraveni as their ruler. They continued to pay taxes to her, defying Narasimha Varman's order, and they refused to bow down to the Mahishmathi army, preferring death to a life of subjugation. They laughed at the governor Shankaradeva, even daring to spit at him when he walked on the street. At the risk of death women lined up in the streets and laughed at the conqueri army. That was the way the women of Kadarimanda chose to treat Mahishmathi and its arrogant men. The fa were still controlled by women and, for them, a male ruling the country was something exotic, something that happened only in barbarian lands. 'As long as the sun and moon exists, only a woman will rule the home and the country,' declared Achi Nagamma.

Shankaradeva wanted to call for brutal suppression, executions, rape and pillage to teach Kadarimandalam women a lesson. Maharaja Somadeva was wiser. He knew that, after conquering a land, it was better to take the vanquished people into confidence. The butter should not know that the knife was being heated, Somadeva had famously quipped. He chose Pattaraya, at that time a junior minister, to talk sense to the defeated queen and put an end to resistance.

Instead of issuing threats to a defeated monarch, Pattaraya had met her laden with gifts. When he was allowed to meet her in her sabha, Pattaraya had touched his head on the ground in front of her and put her feet on his head in abject surrender. The act was something that the queen hadn't expected from the envoy of the victor.

Pattaraya's tact hadn't gone waste. He was offered the greatest honour for a man in Kadarimandalam. He was invited to Chitraveni's harem. He still remembered the night when he was ushered to her bedroom, the angry and jealous faces of her concubines, the hundreds of devadasas of the Kadrimandalam harem, the men whose lives were dedicated to art, music and love-making. Later, when he had convinced Chitraveni to be prudent and accept Mahishmathi's sovereignty, she coaxed him to talk about himself.

'You are a good man,' Chitraveni had told him, running her long fingers through his curly hair. For no reason he could fathom, he was touched. He had never considered himself a good man. A smart man, yes, a wily man, of course, an ambitious man, no doubt, but a good man, he wasn't. Good was an epithet that was associated with fools—fools like Skandadasa. When she said he was a good man, his entire life flashed in his mind: the murder of his father and his family, the deception he was living including his name, the lies he had told. He still couldn't fathom what had taken hold of him. He couldn't stand the duplicity any more.

Pattaraya confessed to Chitraveni the reason behind his mission. He confessed to the fraudulent life he was leading. He confessed all his sins and cried. Under a low moon, on that still night, they sat on a balcony of the Kadarimandalam palace, exchanging their life stories. It was an awkward beginning of a love affair between the unlikeliest of couples. She was the scion of an ancient dynasty; he, a low-born bastard who had acquired his status through deception and villainy.

Chitraveni wanted to know how Mahishmathi, an irrelevant kingdom that had been an insignificant vassal state under the yoke of Kadarimandalam empresses for thousands of years, had risen suddenly and subjugated the ancient empire. What made their swords unbreakable? What made their arrows so sharp that no armour could withstand them? What made their horses so swift, elephants so fearless, and the iron balls in their catapults so devastating that no fort could survive an assault. How did the valleys of Kadarimandalam suddenly turn so fertile? Those had been shrub-filled wastelands in her mother's time, and Somadeva's ancestors used to beg the Kadarimandalam empresses for sustenance. For generations, men of the Mahishmathi royal family used to be married off to Kadarimandalam princesses, living as one among many husbands. What was the secret behind their sudden rise?

Pattaraya knew there was a special ingredient that went into their weapon-making. He promised her that he would find out what it was. She promised she would marry him if he did. Pattaraya was wily enough to know marriage meant nothing to her. He would be one among many husbands. He made her promise that their first-born daughter would succeed the Kadarimandalam throne. It was on that condition that he promised to deliver Mahishmathi to her. She agreed, and said she would also provide him money and secret agents to carry out the task.

With this secret pact, he was able to convince her to accept the suzerainty without further struggle. Chitraveni ordered Achi Nagamma and her army to surrender and a treaty was signed. Pattaraya returned to Mahishmathi victorious and secured the post of bhoomipathi for this diplomatic coup.

But Somadeva was an astute politician. He kept none of the promises Pattaraya had made to Chitraveni on behalf of the king. With the help of his cousin Shankaradeva, he worked on systematically dismantling the family structure of the Kadarimandalam people. With one royal decree, women lost the rights of inheritance, and the eldest man in the family became its sole heir and head. This was carried out across all social classes. With multiple husbands of erstwhile head women fighting for their share of property and wealth, Kadarimandalam society collapsed. The men wanted the women to be relegated to submissive positions as it was elsewhere. The spirited women fought back. Men often got the help of the state administration, and new laws were made in favour of men. The women's army was disbanded and women were banished from public spaces. Achi Nagamma vanished into the forests bordering Kadarimandalam and Mahishmathi with her band of soldiers, cursing Chitraveni and saying she would win the war against Mahishmathi and ensure a more capable woman sat on the throne of Kadarimandalam.

Mahishmathi relegated Chitraveni to the position of a minor noble and kept her alive only for the fear of a rebellion her death could trigger. Her harem was dismantled, and hundreds of devadasas were hung from the trees.

Using the puppet king Narasimha as his front, Shankaradeva went on a mission to 'civilise' Kadarimandalam. He made the king issue an order that any woman having multiple partners would be beheaded. In a matter of a decade, the centuries-old culture of Kadarimandalam went through a huge upheaval.

Pattaraya was pained at what was happening in his beloved Chitraveni's land. He decided to bring with him to Mahishmathi their young daughter, whom they had named Mekhala. He told everyone in Mahishmathi that Mekhala was his daughter from his first wife, who had died. She was being taken care of by her maternal grandmother, but since that old lady had died, he had to now take care of his daughter himself.

Pattaraya had one mission in life: that his daughter become the queen of Kadarimandalam after Chitraveni. He wanted to ensure that Kadarimandalam would once again rule over Mahishmathi and the many other kingdoms as it had for thousands of years before the sudden rise of Mahishmathi. For him, this was the perfect revenge against a destiny that had placed him at the lowest of the low. He had toyed with the idea of usurping the throne himself, but if he were to win the war against Mahishmathi, the people of Kadarimandalam would never accept a man as their ruler. It was a safer bet to be a kingmaker, rather than a king.

Chitraveni got up from the swing and walked towards the window.

'You say you have the method to make Gauridhooli in this manuscript of yours, but where will you get the stone?'

'They will come at an appropriate time,' Pattaraya said, walking up to her. She threw open the window and took a deep breath. Pattaraya looked at the spectacular sight spread out before them. The glistening palace of Governor Shankaradeva could be seen near the sea, at the mouth of river Mahishi.

'Built with my people's money. Mahishmathi's gift to Kadarimanadalam. Governor Shankaradeva's palace,' Chitraveni said with a sigh.

Dwarfed by the palace of the governor lay another palace from where sounds of merriment and laughter floated by.

'My brother, Narasimha Varman. The fool is having his fun while my people starve. The puppet king of Mahishmathi … That swine sits on the throne from which my mother ruled, my grandmother ruled, my great great great grandmothers ruled. My country is now ruled indirectly by a usurper, an upstart king and his kin?'

'We will regain everything, Chitraveni. I will set up a workshop to make Gauridhooli under this palace itself.'

'Ah,' Chitraveni scoffed. 'And the Gaurikanta stones will fall from the sky?'

'It will reach when it has to, my queen. I have made arrangements.'

Chitraveni stared at him.

'Trust me,' Pattaraya said, planting a kiss at the nape of her neck. She pushed him away.

'I trusted you once and you betrayed me, Pattaraya.'

'I didn't betray you. I failed once, but I will succeed soon,' Pattaraya pleaded. He took a deep breath. 'Give a few more months and Mahishmathi will be in a deep crisis. Already, half its weapons have become useless. The land is turning fallow. If we strike at the right time ...'

A smile flitted on Chitraveni's lips.

'I have waited for so long, I can wait for a few more months. But there is something that can't wait.'

Pattaraya's heart beat quickened. He moved towards her. She pressed her palm on his chest and leaned in as if to kiss him. When he brought his lips towards hers, her dark lips grazed his beard and moved to his ears.

'But there are things that can't wait. I want that bastard Shankaradeva dead,' she whispered.

'I will kill him,' Pattaraya said.

'Do you think it is that easy? The man never leaves his palace. It is guarded by three thousand men from Mahishmathi. He lives a secret life. There is no way you can even reach the governor.'

'Where I can't reach, our daughter can,' Pattaraya said and smiled.

NINE

Shivappa

'I am cold, feverish,' Shivappa cried from the tent. 'Someone please help me.'

He could hear the sounds of merrymaking from outside. It was the night of the new moon, when the leper village indulged in a drinking bout and revelry. It was also the first anniversary of Malayappa's death. Bijjala had returned to Mahishmathi. Twice, Shivappa had tried to sneak out of the leper village, and both times he had been caught by Malla. The old leper didn't know it, but Shivappa had allowed himself to be overpowered and caught to make Malla feel complacent. In the one year that he had lived there, he made sure no one saw him as adventurous or brave. This way, he had been allowed a little freedom to roam around in the village without leaving its precincts.

The leper village had thousands of huts that stretched from the graveyard of the untouchables in the south, to the leper cremation ground in the north. The last sentry point on the path meant for untouchables lay just beyond the leper cremation ground. The northern borders of Mahishmathi officially ended there, and the forests began. The path meant for untouchables followed the river. It wound its way from the Mahamakam grounds, continuing north to the periphery of Dasapattana, past the slave graveyard and through the untouchables' village. It then cut across the graveyard for untouchables, went through the leper village and their cremation ground before reaching the sentry point.

Shivappa desperately needed to reach the slaves' graveyard, which lay between the south end of Dasapattana and the north of the untouchables' village.

Shivappa often wondered why Bijjala hadn't eliminated Kattappa yet. Apart from Shivappa, Kattappa was the only one who knew what Bijjala had done to Kamakshi. That information in the hands of Bijjala's rival would effectively end his dream of becoming the crown prince. Knowing Bijjala, it was a miracle that he had spared Kattappa so far. Perhaps it had to do with Kattappa inheriting the position of their father. As the bodyguard of the king, he was in the maharaja's presence day and night. Bijjala had probably not got the chance to kill Kattappa.

But their father's first death anniversary was a day when Kattappa would be sure to leave the maharaja's side. As per custom, Kattappa had to offer boiled rice, chicken and a pot of toddy at their father's grave tonight. If Bijjala wanted to get Kattappa, this would be the time and place when he could do so without risking anyone witnessing his crime. There was the possibility that Bijjala would send some of his henchmen to get Kattappa. But, knowing Bijjala, Shivappa was sure the prince would trust no one else for such a delicate task.

Shivappa screamed again and finally Malla entered the hut. Shivappa cried, 'I am dying of fever. I am feeling thirsty. Please...' The old leper came up to Shivappa and squatted by his side. He placed his disfigured palm on Shivappa's forehead. This was the moment Shivappa had been waiting for. In a swift move, he covered Malla with his blanket and jumped up from the floor. Grabbing the chair that had served as the 'Vaithalika throne', Shivappa brought it down hard on the leper's head. The chair broke into splinters and the beggar's cry was muffled by the blanket and drowned out by the drunken merriment in the village. Shivappa arranged an unconscious Malla on his mattress and covered him with the blanket. No one was going to miss the old man till the next afternoon.

Shivappa sneaked out of the hut and ran through the village. He entered the untouchables' path and started running south, praying he wasn't too late. As he was crossing the periphery of the untouchables' village, he remembered he was carrying no weapon. Cursing, he backtracked. After a desperate search, he found an axe lying outside one of the untouchables' huts. He grabbed it and rushed to slaves' graveyard.

Unbidden, the guilt of beating a helpless leper to the verge of death overcame him. *It isn't my fault, it isn't, it isn't,* he repeated. *Once I have killed Bijjala, I will be the same old Shivappa again. Kamakshi, I am doing all this for you,* he pacified himself. Memories of his father rushed to him as he spotted the graveyard wall in the distance.

A storm was forming in the east. Shivappa slowed down as he neared the graveyard. A sudden gush of wind rustled the dry leaves around, startling him. Tying the axe to his back with his turban, he scaled the walls of the graveyard from the riverside. He sat on top of the wall, his feet dangling down, and ran his eyes over the graveyard. Thunder rumbled in the distance. He could see a light being held up by someone approaching from the main gate of the graveyard. His heart skipped a beat when he realised it was his brother. He felt an urge to rush and fall at his brother's feet and beg for forgiveness for all the crimes he had committed. Kattappa looked so dignified, so pure, that Shivappa felt worthless.

Without knowing why, Shivappa felt tears flowing down his cheeks. *You don't deserve to be a slave, my brother. You deserve to be our king, the king of the Vaithalikas.* The rain started coming down heavily. The lamp that Kattappa was carrying sputtered for a moment and then the flame went off with a hiss. Lightning flashed across the sky, and the light made Kattappa appear like a tribal god, standing with his head bent, drenched in rain, praying.

When lightning next lit up the sky and the graveyard, Shivappa saw him. Bijjala! He was moving towards Kattappa. His sword flashed in the lightning. Rain fell in sheets. His brother was absorbed in prayer and unaware of the danger. Shivappa jumped down and landed softly on the bed of leaves. Gripping his axe, he ran towards Bijjala. The pounding rain masked his footsteps. Lightning led him towards his prey. Bijjala was almost upon Kattappa when Shivappa reached. He thought of swinging his axe and beheading Bijjala with one strike. But he wanted to look into his eyes when he killed him. He owed that much to his Kamakshi. Bijjala was yet unaware of Shivappa's presence. He raised his sword to kill Kattappa and Shivappa tapped his shoulder.

Bijjala turned, stunned by the intrusion. Shivappa drew back the axe to swing it with full force. Lightning lit the graveyard and, in its ghostly light, Shivappa saw Bijjala's face frozen in a silent scream. Shivappa grinned. It was a pleasure to see the terror on Bijjala's face.

Shivappa had expected Bijjala to fight. Instead, Bijjala took off, screaming. Shivappa's axe missed him by a whisker at the unexpected move. He regained his balance and, cursing, chased after Bijjala. He heard Kattappa shouting, but his words were drowned out in a crash of thunder. Shivappa could hear the heavy footsteps of his brother behind him.

There were only a few feet separating Bijjala and Shivappa now, and Shivappa swung his axe out. He missed, though, and swung his axe again. Rainwater had made the ground slippery, and just then, Bijjala lost his step and fell. Shivappa's axe came crashing down. Bijjala screamed and rolled over. He scrambled up and took off again.

Shivappa now understood why Bijjala was so terrified. He thought he had seen a ghost. For Bijjala and for Mahishmathi, Shivappa was a dead man. Dead and buried. And the prince had seen his nemesis in the graveyard where he was supposedly buried. Shivappa laughed. That made Bijjala even more terrified.

Lightning struck a tree nearby and it burst into flames, filling the air with acrid smoke. The thunderclap that followed was deafening. Shivappa laughed and swung his axe again. It caught a tree, chipping away a chunk of its bark. That was intentional, aimed to torture and terrify Bijjala. He could hear his brother yelling at him.

'No, Anna, no, I am not going to stop. Watch me kill this bastard,' Shivappa hollered. 'He was trying to kill you and I saved you. Now watch how his head is going to be splintered.' Shivappa felt insanely happy.

The chariot came unexpectedly from the left, knocking Shivappa down. The axe flew from his hand as he fell into the bushes.

Keki whipped the horses and the chariot halted besides Bijjala. The eunuch pulled the prince in. Shivappa watched it careen away. He screamed in frustration. He should have guessed there would be help for Bijjala, that the prince would have come in his chariot. He wouldn't have walked. The princes never walked. Why hadn't he thought about that? He had been so close ...

'Shivappa!' he heard his brother scream, murderous rage clear in his voice. Shivappa turned to see his brother standing with his sword unsheathed. His back was towards Shivappa—he couldn't see where his brother was in the dark. When Kattappa turned, Shivappa quickly ducked behind the bushes. Kattappa hollered his name again and swung his sword in rage, cutting leaves from the bush. Shivappa saw his axe lying a few feet away. He grabbed it, crawled for a few feet before getting up and running in the direction in which the chariot had vanished.

Shivappa reached the lepers' village by dawn and went to check on Malla. The old beggar was still breathing, but barely. He looked at Shivappa with terrified eyes. Shivappa made him sit, but the leper could barely stay still.

Angry that his attempt to kill Bijjala had failed, Shivappa started hewing the hard ground inside the hut. The old leper thought Shivappa was digging a grave and fell at his feet, begging for mercy. For a moment, Shivappa was taken aback.

Then he realised the equation between them had changed forever. Shivappa made a gesture of slitting the leper's throat with the sharp edge of the axe and the old man trembled with fear.

From that moment, Shivappa was no longer a captive and Malla his guard. The sense of power that realisation brought Shivappa was astonishing. He felt omnipotent, like a king, by showing Malla mercy. He walked out, dragging his axe. Outside, the sky had started bleeding. In the dull light of the dawn, he saw many drunken lepers lying in various positions all around. The power he felt over them, with the axe in his hand, was exhilarating. He could kill them all if he wished it. He could spare their lives too. It wasn't bad to be a king. Once he had finished off Bijjala, perhaps he should consider Brihannala's offer.

As the sun rose, he swung his axe and started practising the long-forgotten martial art moves his father had taught him. His first attempt at getting Bijjala had failed, but he was no less determined to take his revenge. He would find a way. His brother was unlikely to get permission to leave the king's side until their father's next death anniversary. Shivappa had enough time to plan his move.

TEN

Keki

'Don't be scared, my prince,' Keki said as she fanned Bijjala's face.

'Scared? Who is scared?' Bijjala said, taking a swig of wine from the crystal chalice. He wiped away the beads of sweat that lined his forehead. Keki watched him closely. This was an opportunity. If she played it well, she could get a posting in the Antapura. Who knows, maybe she would replace her nemesis, Brihannala, as head eunuch of the harem.

'Disgusting,' Keki said.

Bijjala's eyes flashed.

'Ghosts, I mean. Disgusting things,' Keki said, pouring out some more wine for the prince. Bijjala grunted and emptied the chalice.

'Keki,' Bijjala said. 'You take me to be a fool.'

'Oh, no, my prince,' Keki said, trying to hide her panic.

'I was surprised by the attack and at that time I thought it was a ghost. Now, the more I think about it, the more I am convinced Shivappa isn't dead,' Bijjala said. 'And that makes me more worried.'

Keki assessed the prince's expression. In a way, she was happy about what had happened. She had warned Bijjala not to go behind a lowly slave. They needed to work hard to change Bijjala's image and make him popular, and such diversions were risky. But Bijjala would not listen. Recent events might open new opportunities for her to make money. She was taking all the risks for Pattaraya, whom she didn't fully trust. If Pattaraya deceived her after everything had been done, she needed something to fall back on. The games these big people were playing could turn in any direction. And it was the small people, people like her, who would be sucked into things in a blink and spat out. While doing Pattaraya's work, it was prudent to do some work for herself too.

After eliminating all possibilities, Keki had also come to the conclusion that Shivappa was alive. To confirm her suspicion, she had gone to the graveyard and dug up the place they had buried Shivappa. She couldn't find a body.

'It would be better we spread the rumour of the ghost, my prince,' Keki said, pouring another drink for Bijjala.

'Why?'

'Imagine if Shivappa is seen by someone else. The entire Mahishmathi army will be on the hunt for him. And imagine if the soldiers or our secret service catch him. What would the slave say to the king about the Kamakshi incident?'

Bijjala stared at Keki. If the maharaja knew what he had done to Kamakshi, he could forget about becoming crown prince.

'You find out where that slave is hiding and kill him,' Bijjala said. 'Don't get me involved.'

'You want me to get killed by that slave? I am no match for him, Prince. And where will I search for him? This city is too big for a poor eunuch to search alone. And we can't involve anyone else.'

'What if Kattappa reveals my secret?'

'If the slave hasn't already revealed your secret to His Highness, he isn't going to do it at all. And if he has already told your father and the maharaja hasn't even asked you about how that orphan girl died, it means her death is of no consequence. You're worrying for no reason, Prince.'

'One can't trust these slaves,' Bijjala said.

'We'll finish Kattappa when we get the opportunity. Let's not chase him and get into trouble. We have better things to do. Now that you've been established as a great warrior who slayed Pattaraya, we should concentrate on building your reputation. People should be saying, Prince Bijjala is the one who should have been made vikramadeva, not that coward Mahadeva.'

'But the threat of Shivappa will always hang over me. What if he comes after me again? How can we get rid of him without anyone knowing?'

Keki agreed the threat was real. Shivappa could make another attempt to kill Bijjala, or get caught doing it: both were a threat to Bijjala. The palace was the safest place for the prince right now, Keki said, and asked for a day to think the problem over.

In a few days, the rumour of Shivappa's ghost spread like wildfire in the city. There were multiple 'sightings' of Shivappa's ghost at various places at the same time. There was high demand for special threads and amulets to ward off the ghost, and astrologers and priests started making much money. There were stories of young women getting possessed by Shivappa's ghost—it was said that they started talking in what they thought to be Shivappa's voice. Soon, stories about Kamakshi's ghost also started floating around. Servants vouched that they could hear the young couple singing on full moon nights and weeping for their lost love.

'I don't understand what you are trying to do, eunuch,' Bijjala complained. He was having his dinner in his chamber and Keki stood fanning him.

Keki smiled at Bijjala and whispered, 'What we need now is to attract Shivappa from his hiding place to somewhere secluded. Only one man can help us do that.'

Bijjala stopped eating. Keki looked around, as if scared someone might be eavesdropping, and said, 'Rudra Bhatta.'

'That fool?'

'My prince,' Keki said, 'he is a great tantric. Master of black magic. Exorcism.'

'Bah, but Shivappa is no ghost.'

'Let the slave think we also believe him to be a ghost. I will bring a few black magicians to the palace and the guards will be sure to spread the rumour around. Your father is going to disapprove, even mock and chide you. That rumour will also spread. Then we will move the black magic outside the palace. I will ensure people hear that you are secretly attending a tantric ritual in a remote temple to get rid of the ghost. Let Shivappa think he will get another chance to corner you alone.'

'Hmm.'

'But there is a problem,' Keki said as she scratched her head.

'What is it?'

'Rudra Bhatta is expensive.'

Bijjala drummed his fingers, deep in thought. Then he turned and said, 'Will it work or are you leeching me?'

'You don't believe this humble servant. Allow me to leave. I shall never show my unlucky face to you ever again,' Keki said, sniffling.

Bijjala unclasped his pearl necklace and flung it on the floor. 'Not a word to anyone.'

Keki grabbed it and pressed it to her eyes. 'Not even under threat of losing my head.'

Keki turned to go and Bijjala yelled, 'Wait, if we spread this rumour and Rudra Bhatta gets caught, won't I be implicated?'

'We will turn it around; we will say we were setting a trap. Let the priest sacrifice a few children to make it real and after we finish Shivappa, we won't spare the priest. The prince lays rest to the rumour by capturing the priest in the act of sacrificing children and will also get the traitor Shivappa.' Keki grinned.

A few days later, Keki was waiting in the shade of the temple gopuram. She had sent word to the head priest through a temple servant and was waiting for Rudra Bhatta to turn up. It was past midnight when he finally arrived.

'I had warned you not to come here,' the priest hissed.

'I got a fortune to share, but it seems someone has attained enlightenment and cares nothing for worldly treasures,' Keki said and started to walk away. Rudra Bhatta ran after her and grabbed her wrist.

'Oh no, not now,' Keki said, fluttering her eyelashes.

Rudra Bhatta let go of her hand, embarrassed. Keki giggled and continued walking. The old priest ran behind her, panting. 'Tell me,' Rudra Bhatta pleaded. After making the priest beg for some time, Keki relented. When she told him what she had in mind, Rudra Bhatta remained quiet for a few moments, deep in thought.

'What if he really is dead and it is his ghost who is after the prince?' the priest asked finally.

'Ah, swami. Enough. Don't make me die laughing. Would you be doing all your mumbo jumbo had you really believed in ghosts? You're not scared of ghosts because you know they don't exist.'

'It's risky.'

'Money doesn't grow on trees,' Keki said.

'What if that slave kills the prince?'

'Then we will all have a royal feast. You'll make lots of money on funeral rites. What if the prince kills Shivappa? Imagine the fortune we would earn.'

'Something is telling me that nothing good is going to come out of this.'

'Don't be so scared. The prince will slay Shivappa. What I need from you is a bloody good show: mantra, tantra, smoke, skull, blood, gore, loud bells, incense, red cloth—you know, the usual stuff. Atmosphere, that is what we want. And only you can create that, swami. Let your learning be of some use to someone.'

Rudra Bhatta thought for a moment and then said, 'I know a place where we can do the tantric puja. I did many sacrifices there a long time back. You know ... even the darkest one.

Absolutely safe place. But what is the guarantee that Shivappa will come there to get the prince?'

'Oh, your Vasheekarana Yantra, the occult talisman can't do the job? How sad.'

'It will work only if the slave is a ghost. You said he isn't dead yet.'

'That is not what you say when you sell those trinkets for a hundred silver coins apiece to desperate men who want to attract other men's wives. And how much do you charge for that mercury blob? Dhanakarshana Yantra—the one that will attract wealth if you keep it in the puja room? Fifty gold coins? It is attracting hordes of money to you for sure.'

'Shut up, eunuch. You're insulting a Brahmin.'

'Apologies, swami. I don't want to be cursed and turned into a frog. I have no intention of hopping on four legs to my home. You're a great man and all your mantras actually work. Now, listen to me. There isn't any guarantee that Shivappa will come for the first puja or the second or the third. We can only hope that he will. But the spectacle needs to go on. The news of it is sure to spread, and it will reach Shivappa one day or another. We need to smoke him out of his hiding hole. By the way, do you mean the Rakta Kali temple?'

'How do you know about it?'

'Ah, swami. You think no one knows about your mischief. I know what you have done there in the past. How many children you've sacrificed. How many women. Why do you think I waited for you since morning? You're the right man for this.'

'You'll get me caught. You don't want me to resume the sacrifices?' Rudra Bhatta was sweating profusely despite the cold of the night.

'I want you to be as authentic as possible. Should I supply the children?'

'The dandakaras will come after me.'

'Oh, don't worry. I will steal them from the untouchables' village or get some orphans. No one cares whether an untouchable lives or dies. I will get a few from the slaves too. These creatures aren't holy cows. They live a miserable life and, maybe, they will be born in a better home next time. We are doing them a favour. What we want is widespread panic. I will start the rumour that Shivappa's ghost is devouring the children, so that people won't dare to come out after dark. More people will come to you for talismans. That is additional income for you, swami. What an easy life you have, I feel jealous.'

'You expect the government to believe it? Are you a fool?'

'Dear Rajaguru, tell me how you got away with your previous human sacrifices, you great tantric?'

'That ... that was long ago. And perhaps the government thought the missing children was the handiwork of pirates like Jeemotha. You know for what ...'

'And why should the government think differently now. There is a crisis. The Kali statue has sunk. We know how tense the government is. We know about the secret order to bring more Gaurikanta stones. They will think that the missing children is the handiwork of enthusiastic bhoomipathis trying to meet their new targets. No one will suspect us. They will conduct a farce investigation to pacify people. Arrest someone or the other and hang a few luckless bastards.'

'I don't want to be that someone who gets hanged.'

'Fine. I will find another man who can do the job. There

is no dearth of priests in this city. Maybe your son Kalicharan Bhatta will be a wiser choice.'

'No ... I will do it. But ... the tantric puja is expensive.'

Keki started laughing. 'Swami, what are princes for? Every puja will make you richer.'

'And you will take on the responsibility of bringing the sacrificial offering?'

'Yes, leave it to me. Now hug me, swami. You can take one more ritual bath to wash away the pollution of touching me. I really need a hug. My head is bursting with all the plotting and planning. Phew!'

Rudra Bhatta reluctantly opened his arms and Keki hugged him tight. 'We are going to be richer. Such princes like Bijjala are Amma Gauri's gift to people like us. Would you care to come with me for a drink?'

Rudra Bhatta shrugged. 'I need something to calm my frayed nerves. But ... but I have a bad feeling about the whole thing.'

'Oh, no, swami. You are a noble man, you have the grace of Amma Gauri in abundance. The mother looks after her favourite children with lots of affection. Now don't dwell on unnecessary things. The night is still young. I know a place where there is good wine and great women. Let our lives be filled with lots of joy and music.'

ELEVEN

Sivagami

It had been a frustrating period for Sivagami. She had been unable to meet Rudra Bhatta. His influence in the government had waned and he kept to himself, shut up in the Kali temple. The junior priests she met evaded her questions about him. They told her the chief priest was undergoing penance and wouldn't talk to anyone. The priest's son, Kalicharan Bhatta, was officiating the rituals in the temple and pujas in the palace. Officially, though, Rudra Bhatta remained the chief priest.

Sivagami heard rumours about Rudra Bhatta's indulgence in black magic, but nothing was substantiated. She also learned that Kalicharan was a secretive man, and it was said that he spent more time with devadasis than the Devi. He was notorious for his bad temper. In his teens, he was caught brewing a highly potent intoxicating concoction in the temple premises. The consumption of his mixture had resulted in the death of two of his friends, but with the help of Pratapa and Pattaraya, his influential father had hushed up the case. Sivagami had dug up all these details from palace administration archives before attempting to meet Rudra Bhatta. She had also found out that Kalicharan was married to the daughter of one of the most prominent officials of Mahishmathi, but the official's name wasn't mentioned. It was as if there was a deliberate attempt to keep the name a secret. She also learned that Skandadasa had once ordered the arrest of Kalicharan, but his crime or what had happened after, had been obliterated from the records.

All this intrigued Sivagami. In the guise of learning about administration, she had spent hours in the palace library, studying the palm leaf archives. Her intention was to get some clue about what had led to her father's death and what was the secret of Gauriparvat. However, there was nothing there that gave her any hint about either. The information on Rudra Bhatta and his son lay scattered among various manuscripts, and she had meticulously joined the dots.

The rumours of children going missing from the untouchables' village reached her in time. For several days, Sivagami frequented the village, much to the scorn of her peers. She wanted to find out more. She was sure she was onto something. The villagers were tight-lipped and treated her with an indifferent respect, but she persisted with the tenacity of a mongoose. It was frustrating not to be taken seriously— no one believed a woman could make a difference. It took a great effort from her to build a rapport with the women of the village. Every visit was an eye-opener for her. She had never seen the brutality of the social system up close. What struck her at the untouchables' village was the passive stoicism of the distraught mothers. She had expected them to be angry. Instead, they blamed their fate on some previous life.

She soon learned about children being taken away from villages beyond the borders of Mahishmathi. She was told that they were kidnapped during raids by pirates. Some women had migrated to the city from their tribal hamlets, fearing such incursions. But what was happening now was different. There was no attack or violence. Children were simply disappearing.

Every day, she would return home, frustrated that she was making no progress in finding out why children were disappearing, or why the administration was indifferent about it. Before she stepped inside, she would bathe to wash off the pollution from having visited the homes of the untouchables. She felt ashamed of this ritual bath, but she was uneasy if she didn't do it. *The thought of pollution by fellow human beings runs deep in all our veins,* she would justify to herself. But it didn't make her feel any better. *One day, I will end all this*, she promised, knowing full well that it was an impossible dream.

After another incident of a child going missing, she decided the time had come to confront the priest. If he wasn't directly involved, he might be able to give her names of other priests who did black magic. At least it would be a good excuse to meet Rudra Bhatta.

Sivagami rode through the busy streets and reached the Kali temple. She waited in the temple premises until the temple closed for the afternoon. She mounted her horse and entered the Brahmin streets behind the temple. Ignoring the hostile gazes that followed her, she rode to the huge mansion of Rajaguru Rudra Bhatta. She rode past the gate, dismounted and pulled at the rope tied to a bell at the door. A young priest opened the carved door, saw her and immediately tried to shut it. Sivagami put her arm out to prevent him from shutting it.

'Rajaguru Rudra Bhatta will not see anyone till next amavasya,' the priest said and slammed the door shut, giving her barely enough time to save her fingers from getting crushed.

She banged on the door and called out, 'Open, open! I need to speak to the rajaguru urgently. I have the mahapradhana's orders.'

After a few minutes, the door creaked open a bit and a woman peered out. 'Father-in-law is asking for the order,' she said.

Sivagami fumbled. She had no such order with her. Her bluff had been called by the wily priest. Hiding her frustration, she walked away. She decided to wait for the priest to emerge from his house. The day was amavasya, the new moon day, and if the priest was indulging in occult practices, this was an important day for him. She decided to follow him when he left the house.

She waited near the water troughs for the street cows. Vajra drank water from the trough and she sat on the wayfarers' platform under the huge banyan tree. She could see the hostility in the eyes of the people who walked by—the Brahmin agrahara was beyond the jurisdiction of all bhoomipathis—but she ignored them. The temple opened for evening prayers and more devotees walked by. She sat, wishing she had found some other place that would have been less conspicuous. A bhoomipathi sitting in the wayfarers' resting place was bound to get tongues wagging.

Street-lighters lit the lamps. A few children came up to look at Vajra and stood chatting animatedly until their mothers smacked them and dragged them to their homes. Slowly, the streets emptied out. Vendors covered their wares and pushed their carts home.

She sat alone, deep in thought, wondering about Mahadeva and his strange love for her. Did she love him? She flung a wilted banyan leaf up in the air, saying if it landed on the greener part, she loved him, and if it was the lighter side of the leaf, she didn't. She did this over and over again, and whenever a leaf fell to indicate she loved him, she smiled, chided herself for her weakness, and tossed the leaf again. She was feeling silly and drifting into a dream, when she heard the priest's gate creak open. A chariot rumbled out. The priest was riding the chariot. *Unusual for him,* thought Sivagami. She checked her sword and walked to Vajra.

She mounted the horse and started following the priest's chariot at a safe distance. Rudra Bhatta never looked back. Not even once. *This is also unusual,* thought Sivagami. A strange fear gripped her.

Sivagami slowed down when she heard a hum. As she turned a corner, she saw that a group of people were rushing towards her, carrying sticks and stones in their hands. They appeared so suddenly that she had to pull hard on the reins to stop Vajra. The horse neighed in protest. A lean, pale man with a receding hairline stood before her with a staff in his hand. He had sacred ash smeared on his body from head to toe. Behind him stood many men with sticks, kitchen knives and pestles.

'Get down, woman,' the man snarled at Sivagami.

Sivagami felt blood rush to her face. She was more angry than scared now. Her right hand curled around the hilt of her sword and she sat ready to draw it at the slightest provocation. The horse's ears twitched nervously.

'No official dares to enter on a horse in this agrahara. This is a holy street,' an old man in the crowd cried.

'I am warning you, move away,' Sivagami said, as she nudged Vajra. The horse took a few tentative steps towards the crowd. Sivagami drew her sword out and rested it on her shoulder. The crowd backed away, but their leader stood his ground. She swerved and tried to dodge him, but he caught hold of the horse's reins. Vajra panicked and reared up. The sharp horseshoe caught the man's right thigh as he did so, and he was thrown into the crowd. He howled in pain. Sivagami snapped the reins and Vajra took off, racing through the crowd that scattered in fear. Sivagami knew what would happen if they caught her—a council of five senior Brahmins, headed by Rudra Bhatta, were the judge and jury here.

As Vajra galloped away, Sivagami worried about the man who had been hurt. They raced through the narrow streets and Vajra's hooves smeared the holy rangoli designs of many courtyards. Just as she was about to reach the royal highway, the crowd reassembled from nowhere, blocking her way.

The first stone landed on her shoulder, drawing a gasp from her. Soon, stones were flying past her, some finding their mark, some hitting Vajra's posterior and some whizzing past too close to her head. She was in full gallop, fleeing for her life. She could hear the crowd screaming and hurling abuses at her. A woman jumped out from one of the side alleys. Sivagami almost ran over her. Vajra neighed in pain and protest as she pulled hard on the reins. The woman fell on her knees, scrambled up and ran towards the crowd, flaying both her arms.

'Stop, stop. For God's sake stop,' she cried. The stone

pelting stopped. Sivagami turned back in surprise. The woman was standing as a shield between her and the angry crowd.

'Gomati, you shameless woman,' the leader of the mob yelled. 'That bitch almost killed me.'

The woman refused to move.

The man limped to her and screamed, 'You are insulting your husband. You are spoiling my honour, our family name, our decency. How dare you come out like this and stand in the middle of the street, half naked? Don't you have any shame, woman?'

The woman didn't budge. She didn't yell back. Her eyes were filled with tears, and she was so frail that it seemed like a good gust of wind would blow her away. But she stood, her fists clenched with determination, her chin held high, defiant.

'That woman has no right to enter our street, daughter. Move away,' an old man who held a stone in his hand, said.

'I called her,' Gomati said.

There was a confused murmur among the crowd.

'What are you talking about?' her husband hissed.

Gomati threw back her head, looked straight into his eyes and said, 'Do you want me to say it in public? Do you want me to say why I called her?'

The man's eyes flared in anger. He grabbed his wife's hair and, in a flash, Sivagami's sword was at his throat. The crowd gasped.

The man's grip loosened. Without a word, he slunk away into the crowd. In minutes, the rest of the crowd had dispersed. Sivagami dismounted and touched the woman's shoulders. Surprising Sivagami, the woman fell at her feet.

'Help me, Amma,' she cried, holding Sivagami's feet and refusing to let go despite Sivagami's ardent requests.

'My father-in-law is evil beyond your imagination. I suspect, no, I am sure, the missing children are being sacrificed. And my father-in-law Rudra Bhatta is doing the tantric puja for some important person.'

Sivagami listened, stunned and disgusted. This was the opportunity she had been waiting for.

TWELVE

Mekhala

Mekhala stood at the rear entrance of the palace of Shankaradeva. The old maid who had brought her was pleading with the guard to let her in.

'She is my granddaughter. My daughter got widowed and has come to stay with me, swami. This is my only grandchild. Give her a job, swami.'

Mekhala stood a little away, toying with a strand of hair, hoping she would come across as shy. The old maid's job was to somehow place her in the staff of Shankaradeva. From there, Mekhala had to work her way into the governor's inner circle. Not an easy task, not a task she wanted to do, but she had no choice. If it was what her father wanted, she would do it. She would do anything for him. But it pained her that her father had asked her to do something so abhorrent.

She missed her father already. Before she left, Pattaraya had kissed his daughter's forehead and said, 'Go forth and win, my daughter.' She had been able to sense his fear for her. Her mother, the one she had not seen for years, and for whom she had no love, stood by with a scornful smile.

'At her age, I was the crown princess of Kadarimandalam. Would you stop being so protective of her, Pattaraya?' Chitraveni had snapped.

Mekhala wanted to lash out. At her age, she wanted to say, Chitraveni had already lost the war and become a prisoner confined to her old palace. But Mekhala didn't have the courage to talk back. Born and brought up in the ethos of Mahishmathi, the morals of Kadarimandalam were shocking and overwhelming for Mekhala. She had slept with Bijjala because her father had told her to do so. She had liked the haughty prince too. That was how men were supposed to be, she felt. But in this mission, she could sense her father's apprehension, and that made her jittery.

'I haven't killed even an ant in my life, Nanna,' she had said when they were parting.

'You needn't kill anyone, daughter. I will do it for you. Your mother would do it for you. Your job is only to worm your way into his inner circle and understand his weaknesses, learn the lapses in security and how the palace can be stormed.'

'But I am scared,' Mekhala had said.

Her father had hugged her, kissed her forehead and said, 'If you feel you are in danger, remember that your father will always be there for you.'

Now, as she was ushered into a room where an important-looking man sat, her courage drained away. The office and the demeanour of the man made her feel sure he was the governor.

'This is no place for a woman to work, devi,' the man said politely. Mekhala stood with her head bowed, wondering how she was going to seduce him. She had not expected the governor to be so young.

'We are starving in the village, swami. I will do any work—cleaning, washing clothes, cooking ...' Mekhala said.

'I'm happy that our women in Kadarimandalam are accepting that the real place of women is in the kitchen. It means our governor's policies are working. Earlier, you would be in my position and I would've been begging you for a job. Ha, how times have changed—for the better. Mahishmathi has liberated Kadarimandalam men.'

'You ... you're not the governor, swami?' Mekhala asked, crestfallen.

The man burst out laughing. 'I am just a captain—Nayaka Kumara. I'm in charge of security here. I am here,' he said, reaching down to put his palm a few inches from the floor, 'and the governor is here.' She looked at his palm raised above his head and her heart sank. He was just a lowly officer. Had she been in Mahishmathi, as a senior bhoomipathi's daughter, a nayaka wouldn't even have dared to stand before her.

'We are like worms, swami. We live below the ground and you are all big officers,' Mekhala said. 'We are hungry, swami,' she added.

'Hmm,' the captain said, suppressing a smile. 'You are a beautiful girl. I don't want to send you away disappointed. Let me see what I can do for you. You can start by cleaning the stables.'

Mekhala's face fell. Carrying horseshit on her head wasn't something she particularly looked forward to. The captain laughed and said, 'Don't worry. I won't send a pretty girl like you to clean the stables. You can clean our security offices. Happy? Now you won't starve.'

She bowed deep in gratitude. He came up to her and stood close to her. Too close for her comfort. She braced herself. He said, 'Girl, there are different kinds of starvations. I too am starved.'

The man grabbed her and kissed her on her lips. She winced as his hands groped her and tried to push him away.

'I want to go,' Mekhala said.

'You aren't going anywhere, girl. If you try to escape, well, there is always the moral police. I will have to report you to them. They don't like immoral girls like you. They will stone you to death. But if you behave, you don't have to worry. This Nayaka Kumara will protect you. You stay here and feed me. You will not starve, nor will I.'

Suddenly, he caught hold of her hand. 'That is an expensive ring,' he said suspiciously.

Mekhala's heart skipped a beat. But from the way the captain was looking at it, she deduced that he hadn't realised it was the official seal of the prince of Mahishmathi.

'That was given by my lover,' she said shyly.

'You have a lover?'

'Not anymore. He jilted me and went off in a merchant ship. I haven't heard from him in the last five years,' Mekhala said.

'Ah, let the sea dragons get him. Let the typhoon sink his ship.'

Mekhala's eyes filled up.

'*Tchaw, tchaw*, don't cry, girl. I am there for you,' the captain said, pulling her closer. She acted sufficiently placated.

'What did you say your name was?' he asked, lifting her chin.

Mekhala scrambled for a name. For all the planning she had done, she had missed this basic thing. 'Menaka,' she blabbered the first name that came to her mind.

The captain laughed out. 'Ah, the apsara. If you're Menaka, I am sage Vishwamitra. Now seduce this hermit.'

After a few months of satisfying the captain's hunger, Mekhala was nowhere closer to achieving what she had set out to do. Leave alone meeting the governor or learning about the chinks in the security of the governor's palace, she barely saw any sunlight. The captain confined her to his working and living quarters.

Mekhala still knew frustratingly little about Shankaradeva, except that he was a recluse and rarely moved out of the palace. When she tried to find out something more about him from Kumara, he said, 'The governor never gives an audience to anyone. I haven't even seen him once. Why are you so obsessed with that old man? Am I not good enough for you?'

She laughed and didn't bring up the governor for a few days.

A week later, she said, 'It is strange how so few—how many are there, you said?—ah, two dozen Mahishmathi soldiers and an old man in his seventies is controlling the populous Kadarimandalam. Don't you feel ashamed that Mahishmathi can enslave your country so easily?'

The reaction was not what she expected. Kumara flared up. 'Kadarimandalam people were savages, living under the thumbs of their women. Mahishmathi brought us enlightenment, liberated and civilised us and taught us the worth and strength of man. Now the haughty women of Kadarimandalam know their place. There is some morality now in the depraved society.'

'But I heard that the king Narasimha Varman is the governor's puppet. That way, the governor is shielding himself. Zero responsibility and total power. And none of the morality codes are applicable to the puppet king who has a harem of thousands.'

Kumara stared at her. Mekhala realised her mistake, but it was too late.

'Who are you? You don't talk like an illiterate village girl.'

'I ... don't you know, swami, that there are no illiterates in Kadarimandalam? I was educated until the authorities found out about it and stopped it, saying women shouldn't be literate. I'm sorry,' Mekhala said, her eyes filling. That always worked with the captain and fortunately she had the ability to summon tears to her eyes at will.

'Good thing for you. See what a little bit of education has done to you? I am a large-hearted man, but had you said this to anyone else, you would've become bird feed by now. Have you heard about Chitravadha?'

Kumara spent the rest of the afternoon explaining to her the various ways of torture in Chitravadha with a relish that sent shudders down Mekhala's spine. She acted sufficiently chastised and scared, drawing a compliment from Kumara that she had started behaving more ladylike.

As the days went by, she felt she was wasting her time with Kumara. She had to find a way to reach the reclusive governor. A few times, through a window, she saw the governor's procession leaving the palace amidst great pomp. The governor's chariot was drawn by sixteen horses and glided with gold, but it was completely covered, and she never caught sight of the governor. When she mentioned it to Kumara, he said, 'That shows how smart he is. Many times, there is no governor inside, or there is a dummy there. There were many assassination attempts on him in the earlier days, when that accursed woman Achi Nagamma was yet to be driven into the forest. Now, by travelling in the covered chariot, no one except the closest aides, who are Mahishmathi soldiers, will know whether the governor is really inside the chariot or not.'

The next few weeks were spent observing the governor's movements. She was soon able to identify a pattern. Mekhala found that the two dozen Mahishmathi soldiers who formed the inner circle when the chariot moved behaved differently on certain occasion than others. The difference was subtle, but she could see that they were more relaxed sometimes. Mekhala reasoned that the inner circle knew when the governor was inside the covered chariot, and when he was, they were more alert. That knowledge made her feel exhilarated. It made her hopeful that her plan would succeed.

The captain's living quarters was a part of the residential complex by the palace gate. There were multiple walls with their own gates, and living quarters attached to the gates, before one reached the governor's palace. Mekhala had to time everything right, and had to do it while avoiding the ever-alert security. After three aborted attempts when she lost her nerve at the last moment, Mekhala decided to take the plunge on the next available opportunity.

The day came before she was fully prepared. She observed there was tension in the air; the captain had left the house before dawn. The leader of the governor's security guards made multiple visits to the main gate and, from experience, Mekhala knew that this indicated that the governor would be inside the closed chariot. When she heard the horn blaring, announcing the departure of the governor from his palace, she hurriedly pulled out the things she had been collecting over the last few days. She had made a crude rope using the captain's old turbans. She slung it over her shoulder and ran out. Mekhala squeezed through the narrow gap between the boundary wall and the rear wall of the captain's quarters. She made a lasso and threw it up. After a frustrating seven tries, the lasso caught a stone. She tugged it to test its strength a couple of times, and then started scaling the slippery wall.

Hang on, hang on, Mekhala told herself as she climbed. A house fly buzzed around her face, sometimes landing on her cheeks, other times on her forehead or nose. A chameleon sneaked out from a crack in the wall. Mekhala watched it advancing towards her, its reptilian eyes focused on the house fly. It stood with one webbed foot clasping and unclasping the air, staring at her with its cold eyes. Its colour changed from the mossy green of the wall to the dark grey of the roof. 'Don't jump on me, don't jump,' she wanted to scream at it. She heard the last but one gate being opened. He would be at the main gate at any moment.

The fly settled on the tip of her nose. The chameleon's long tongue lashed out and gobbled up the fly. She screamed in terror. A soldier who was pacing the wall stopped in his tracks. Mekhala saw with rising panic that he was coming towards where she was. She could hear horse hooves and the rattle of the chariot. The governor was here and would cross the gate any moment now. The soldier squatted on the wall and peered down into the gap. Mekhala lashed out and poked his eye. He screamed in pain and fell back. She clambered up and rolled onto the edge of the wall. The soldier she had poked was lying down, holding his eye. She leapt over him and ran towards the gate. She could hear the soldier screaming for someone to catch her. As she ran, she came face to face with two soldiers who were taken aback to see a woman racing towards them. Before they could react, she shoved them to either side and sprinted to the gate. It was creaking open and the chariot was making its way through. She leapt from the twenty-foot wall and crashed through the roof of the chariot.

For a moment, everything went blank for Mekhala. Dazed, she attempted to stand up, holding on to a seat inside the chariot. She swayed, and as her eyes adjusted to the darkness, she saw an old man cowering in a corner. The light from the cracked roof illuminated his bald head. His turban lay uncoiled on the floor, among the splinters of the roof. Mekhala was about to ask for his help, when the door of the chariot swung open and Nayaka Kumara's face appeared. 'Your Excellency ... Menakaaaa!' Kumara screamed when he saw her.

Mekhala's quick reaction would've made her father very proud. She turned to the frightened governor and said, 'Save me from this man. He kidnapped me from my village and has kept me captive.'

The captain's abuses and screams were drowned in the melee as the elite Mahishmathi guards captured him and dragged him away. Mekhala was arrested by the guards, but she was sure the governor would call her soon. They threw her into a cell and double-locked the door. At sunset, a guard pushed in some puffed rice in a coconut shell for her to eat, and left.

That evening, she munched on the puffed rice and watched the Chitravadha of Captain Kumara through the high window of her cell. The gory details that the captain had fed her about the infamous Chitravadha were true to the last bit. *The bastard was telling the truth,* Mekhala thought, as she ate the last of the puffed rice. She watched the soldiers take what was left of Captain Kumara from the cage and feed their guard dogs. Two servants scrubbed the cage clean and carried it away.

Later in the night, Mekhala was questioned by various officials, and she stuck to her story that the captain had kidnapped her from her village and her name was Menaka. She pleaded with them to let her go. The officers grew frustrated that they weren't able to find anything incriminating on her—no weapons, no poison, nothing that could've harmed the governor—and they reluctantly decided to release her.

Mekhala panicked. All her efforts would be wasted if they merely threw her out of the governor's palace without her even getting an audience with him.

On her father's advice, she had been saving the ring of Bijjala for something important that her father had in mind. She had hidden it in the captain's manuscript of *Devi Bhagawatham*, knowing full well that he would not touch any scripture. As she was accompanied by a Mahishmathi officer to the deceased captain's room to pick up her things, she deliberately caused it to fall down. The officer stared at the ring in shock. He snatched it from the ground and the Gauripadmam diamond in it glinted in the sunlight.

'Where did you get this from?' he asked.

Mekhala snatched it from his hand and cried, 'That is the engagement ring my lover gave me. He is a big official in the government. Not the government here, but in the capital of Mahishmathi.'

As she had expected, the officer marched her to the governor's office. Two officials stood guard next to her as she waited outside the closed doors of the governor's office, while the officer briefed Shankaradeva about the unusual development.

Mekhala was summoned in and the officer walked out. She entered the vault-like room which had thick curtains and a lone lamp burning at the far end. The governor was sitting cross-legged on a cushion with a writing table before him. The sound of the cloth fan above the governor, that was pulled by unseen servants from another room, gave a sonorous creak. Mekhala reminded herself to walk as seductively as possible. She cursed the low lighting in the room. The golden hue of the oil lamp would give a honey-coloured tinge to her smooth skin, but how would he notice her beautiful eyes? She practised her most dazzling smile in her mind as she walked up. The man kept staring at her, but to her disappointment, there was no lust in his eyes.

Shankaradeva put the ring on his desk. The diamond in it caught the light of the lamp and throbbed, throwing off an eerie blue hue, unsettling her.

'Where did you steal this from?'

She was taken aback by the question. Mekhala summoned her tears, but strangely her eyes were dry. So was her throat.

She was frozen with fear. The man with the hawk-like nose looked like some ancient judge, stern and unmoving. Her charm had no effect on him. She gulped and the man repeated his question in a quiet voice.

'I ... I was offered marriage and I gave everything to him,' she sobbed, covering her face with her palms so that he wouldn't see her dry eyes.

'How did you meet him?'

'He is a big officer in the Mahishmathi army, he said. He had come in search of some traitor or other ... Pat ... Pattadhara ... or something,' Mekhala said.

'Pattaraya?' the governor asked.

'Maybe. I don't know the traitor's name. But I fell in love with him and he said he would marry me. He presented me this as a token of his promise. He went away. I came in search of him and got trapped by Captain Kumara who offered a job in this palace and then made me a prisoner. He raped me,' Mekhala cried.

'Do you know the position of your ... er ... lover who gave you this?' Shankaradeva asked.

'I have no idea, swami. He gave his name as... Krishna. But I am planning to go to Mahishmathi. If you could give me back my ring, I shall take it around and ask everyone. Someone would recognise the ring and lead me to my lover.'

Mekhala saw the look of horror on Shankaradeva's face and suppressed a smile. Her plan was working. They wouldn't want a village girl roaming around in the city of Mahishmathi with the prince's ring, claiming he had jilted her. This was the time to strike, when the iron was hot.

'But swami, will my lover accept me now? Even if I find him? I have been raped. He will cast me away. He is a big officer, and who would want a woman who is spoilt like me? He will never marry me now. I have nowhere to go, swami. Give me a job here. I shall serve you well,' Mekhala said, and paused before adding, 'I shall serve you in all possible ways. I have nowhere to go. Show mercy on a poor jilted woman.' *Hopefully the old man would get the hint,* she thought.

Shankaradeva nodded and pulled a rope dangling above him. A bell clanged outside and the officer walked in. Shankaradeva put the ring in a drawer and closed it. He said to the officer, 'Take this girl to King Narasimha Varman's harem.'

'No!' Mekhala screamed. Her carefully built plans had come crashing down.

Shankaradeva said, 'I have done more than you've asked for. You will be one among thousands of women in the harem, but you will be a woman of the king. What more could you ask for?'

THIRTEEN

Kattappa

'Kattappa destroyed the Kali statue. This slave is a bigger traitor than his brother,' General Hiranya said as he placed a sheaf of palm leaves before the king. Parameswara stood behind the old general.

Kattappa waited, tense, knowing and dreading what was about to come. He was in the chamber of Maharaja Somadeva for his customary tasting of the king's food before the maharaja could eat. Kattappa waited for the punishment. He would most probably be hanged in the morrow. He would die a dishonourable death. He had failed his father. He had failed himself. He choked with emotions and bit the tail of his turban to stop himself from breaking down. He felt the cold hand of the general on his shoulder. Kattappa pulled himself up and stood erect, the customary stoic expression back on his face.

'Your Highness, allow me to deal with him my way—' General Hiranya said. The king raised his hand and cut him off.

'Who killed that girl?' the king asked Kattappa. The abruptness of the question from the maharaja took him by surprise. He knew his shock had given him away. Kattappa froze.

'We are sure it wasn't your brother,' Parameswara said.

'Tell the truth, was it my son Bijjala?' the maharaja asked.

Kattappa remained silent.

'Give me permission to take him to my chamber, Your Highness,' Hiranya said, holding Kattappa by the scruff of his neck. The king stopped him with a gesture.

'Speak, son,' the king said, caressing the hilt of his sword. The smile on his thin lips hadn't vanished, but Kattappa saw that it didn't reach his eyes. He stood, barely breathing. His mouth was set in a firm line, his eyes had a faraway look. There was a swoosh of air and he felt the coldness of steel on his neck. He closed his eyes, but other than that, not a nerve twitched, nor a hair moved.

'It is an order,' Somadeva said.

Silence.

The slave remained standing with his eyes closed, not wanting to face his king, yet unwilling to go against the ancient code of honour. No slave would reveal his master's secret. He would take Bijjala's secret to the grave. He waited for the sword to fall. A hearty laugh filled the room and he opened his eyes in surprise. The king's arms were on his shoulders. Somadeva pressed him to his chest, like a father would a son. Kattappa's first impulse was to tell the king that he shouldn't have touched him. Now the king would have to bathe before having his dinner. But he was choked with emotion.

The king led him to his ornate chair, encrusted with diamonds and pearls, and covered with smooth silk. Somadeva sat in the chair and gestured for Kattappa to sit beside him, on the floor. The slave squatted on his haunches and crossed his arms over his shoulders in the traditional gesture of abject surrender.

General Hiranya was staring at the scene with unmasked displeasure. Maharaja Somadeva ran his fingers over the bald head of Kattappa, like one would with a dog, and said, 'General, I would've been surprised if he had given away any secret. He is the son of Malayappa, who served me his entire life. If I had half his honour, I would've been the most righteous king. But then, I wouldn't still be king or have even lived this long, isn't it? You can either have honour or the throne.' The king laughed out loud.

'But the statue of Kali ... There is a crisis ... Perhaps Your Highness hasn't grasped the seriousness of the situation ... please ...' General Hiranya said in an agitated voice.

'Wait outside,' Somadeva said with a sarcastic smile. The general bowed deep, a tad too deep, before turning on his heels and marching outside with deliberate footsteps. The king chuckled at the display of such impotent rebellion. Mahapradhana Parameswara bowed and left without being asked. The king clapped his hands and the servants started serving his meal. When Kattappa stood up to taste the food again, the king stopped him.

On the low table before Somadeva, on a large golden plate in the shape of a banana leaf, the royal chef started spreading the dinner for the king. Spiced turtle meat, peacock leg roasted and marinated with pepper and ginger paste, seer fish fried and marinated with virgin coconut oil and ground cardamom, exotic nuts from the barbarian lands across the eastern sea, ripe mango boiled in coconut milk and tamarind extract, jasmine-flavoured rice, cakes made of millets, ladies' finger fried in mustard oil, payasam made of bamboo shoots and jaggery, dried dates brought from the desert lands of the West, ficus pickled in honey—the chef kept on serving various courses to the king. The king's dinner could have fed a hundred slaves, and Somadeva ate less than what Kattappa had tasted—he would pick a small portion of each dish, chew it with a frowning face, and push it away.

The aroma of the food was making Kattappa hungry. He could feel the king's piercing eyes on him. He gulped.

'Eat,' the king said, holding the peacock leg in front of Kattappa's face. *Should he touch it and risk polluting it?* Kattappa hesitated. But the king was waiting for him to take the meat. Kattappa took a deep breath, bit off a piece of the meat without touching it with his hand, and started chewing it. The king was amused. He turned the leg to the other side as Kattappa finished chewing. 'Eat, eat,' the king said.

The words of Shivappa came rushing to him. *They treat you like a dog and you're proud of it.* Kattappa stopped chewing.

'You eat exactly like your father,' the king said kindly. 'He relished roasted peacock too.'

Kattappa stopped breathing. He couldn't imagine his proud father squatting before the king and eating leftovers like a pet dog. But he knew the king was telling the truth. Why roasted peacock, his father would have eaten a rock if his master had offered it to him. A teardrop, more from helplessness than anger traced its way down his cheek. Kattappa felt the soft hands of the king on his bald head. He sat like a statue, holding the piece of peacock meat between his teeth, squatting on his haunches before his master.

'Son, did it hurt?' The king touched his neck; it had swollen up from Hiranya's grip.

A wave of gratitude and emotion rushed through Kattappa's veins. No one, not even his father, had ever asked him that. A slave's wound was no one's business, not even the slave's. And he knew why his father would have eaten a rock for this man. His master was kind, his master was compassion personified. His brother, as usual, was wrong. He looked at his master with tear-filled eyes.

The king smiled and said, 'Son, you're working too hard. You hardly get any rest. You can take a few days off from this duty.'

Kattappa started sweating. Was his master angry with him?

'Don't worry. I am not displeased with you,' Somadeva said, as if reading his mind. 'I'm not angry that you didn't answer my question about Bijjala. I know my son was responsible for that girl's death. I know you had to kill your brother to save my son, and the girl was your brother's lover. By not betraying your then master, even in the face of my ire, you've made your father proud. Until I call you back, you're free. If anyone stops you, tell them you have my permission.'

The king lifted the hand that had been caressing Kattappa's head. A servant immediately rushed up with a bowl and a golden pitcher of water. Somadeva washed his hands and wiped his mouth with the silk cloth that the servant handed to him. He took a palm leaf, scribbled something, and pressed his royal insignia ring to it after dipping it in lac. With trembling hands, Kattappa received the official order proclaiming him as a free man until further orders. His eyes clouded with tears as he watched the king walk away.

Kattappa stood up, not knowing what to do with his new-found freedom. The fear of Bijjala crept up from nowhere. Now that he would no longer be the king's shadow, Bijjala was sure to get him. He wasn't afraid of Bijjala killing him. It was the fate of slaves to be killed by their master. He was scared that he would die before he fulfilled the promise he had made to his father on his deathbed. He had to hunt down his brother. If Bijjala caught him before that ...well, he would deal with that when it came. Now that he was free, was he willing to fight Bijjala if required? Kattappa wasn't sure. Slowly, the sense of freedom was sinking in. He was a free man. Kattappa pronounced the word 'free'. He choked on the piece of leftover meat the king had given him. Kattappa stood up to his full height and spat the piece of meat into the plate the king had used. The servant who was clearing the table looked at him in surprise.

Kattappa walked away, not bothering about the servant's reaction. *I am a free man,* he thought. *For a few days, I will walk with my head held high.*

When he opened the door, Hiranya stepped forward, barring his way. Kattappa looked straight into the general's eyes. Then he gave a curt bow, side-stepped the man, and continued to stride away.

'Hey!' the general yelled out.

Kattappa stopped and turned on his heel. He stood with his arms on his waist and waited as Hiranya walked up to him. The general stood inches before Kattappa, glaring at him.

'Slave, where the hell do you think you're going?' Hiranya hissed.

'I have His Highness's orders. I am a free man until he tells me otherwise,' Kattappa said, trying to suppress the jubilation he felt at being able to talk to the general like an equal. He held the palm leaf with the king's insignia like a shield before him. He had had enough of talking to people with his arms crossed over his chest, and his gaze turned down towards his toes. He could almost hear Shivappa's laughter at the exhilaration he was feeling at being free. *Didn't I tell you, Anna, that you can never suppress the urge to be free? Man is born free. He must die free.* Unbidden, Shivappa's words came to his mind. Kattappa fought the urge to smile, fought the surge of affection he felt for his younger brother. The glint of a smile, which flashed for a second—even that would have seemed rude to the old general.

'What ... what do you mean?' the general fumbled.

Kattappa turned on his heel and walked quickly down the corridor. There was a full moon in the sky, and the breeze carried the heady fragrance of champaka flowers. A small owl fluttered past his head and soared high in the horizon. *Free*—Kattappa wanted to scream at the owl. *Free*—he wanted to yell at the clouds that swirled above, playing hide and seek with the moon.

The soldiers watched the slave walking through the corridors of the royal palace with his head held high and the hint of a smile on his lips. He walked past the fort gate, surprising the guards there. Had he not been filled with thoughts of his freedom and his brother, he would have definitely observed that no one was trying to stop him. He would have wondered why not one guard had asked why a slave was taking the main fort gate. And he would have sensed the presence of the man who was shadowing him.

FOURTEEN

Somadeva

Hiranya felt like he was going to explode with rage. He looked away and said with remarkable control of his frayed nerves, 'I can't fathom the reason behind your action, Your Highness. We are staring at a disaster. I have explained to you our situation, and yet …'

There was an uneasy silence. Parameswara stood with a calm expression. Somadeva grabbed the general's hand and made him sit in a chair by the window. He sat down by his side and didn't let go of Hiranya's hand. The king looked at the general and smiled.

'My dear Hiranya, my faithful servant and my dearest friend—nay, my brother. What would have I been without men like you? What is bothering you?'

'I told you what is bothering me, Your Highness,' Hiranya said.

Somadeva sighed. 'Do you think it isn't bothering me? But there is no need to panic. We are trying to recover the stones from the riverbed. You are aware of that. We have cordoned off the area in Guha's land, and we have our best divers on the job.'

'Half the stones would have reached the southern seas now.'

'We have to make good with what we have. Whatever we are able to recover will be filled in the new Kali statue and brought to the city and then we will resume our production.'

'That won't be enough.'

'We have ordered maximum mining at Gauriparvat.'

'That means ...'

'Unfortunately, we have no choice.'

'The pirates and slavers are ruthless. And with so much at stake, they will go to any extent to make a killing,' Hiranya said.

'Senapati Hiranya,' Parameswara intervened, 'we can't help that. Greed is a great driver of commerce. The entire empire is built on greed.'

'What guarantee do you have that they won't lay their hands on resources in Mahishmathi. After all, children—'

'Have no fear, Hiranya. No one would dare to touch the children of my citizens,' Somadeva said.

'It will only be the children of tribal villages outside the borders of Mahishmathi,' Parameswara said.

'I know you are asking yourself whether their lives don't matter. I have asked the question myself many times, friend,' Somadeva said. 'But a ruler has to think about the greater good. Does it bother you when you lose soldiers on the battlefield?'

'It does. It hurts like hell,' Hiranya said.

'So does this, my friend. Yet, you persist, you give orders for attack, you don't pause to mourn for your comrades. You don't stop fighting to cry for those who are slain. Why? Because you know that their sacrifice is for a bigger cause. It is the same way, my friend. We have brought prosperity to countless people, and this is the price we pay for it. It hurts, but you get used to it.'

The general looked beaten and depressed, grappling with the enormity of the problem they were facing. *Men like him are great in the battlefield, but in times of peace, in times of crises that require strategy and cunning to navigate, such men turn useless,* thought Somadeva.

'Forgive me, Your Highness. But I hope you have heard—'

'About the rumours of children missing from the untouchable colony?' Somadeva asked. Hiranya nodded.

'Ah, and the stupid thing about the ghost of that slave roaming around devouring children?' Parameswara shook his head in dismay.

'Perhaps the pirates are trying to make easy money. Someone is taking a calculated risk. If they get bolder, they may try to kidnap children from other parts and it may end in an uprising. I am worried about that,' Hiranya said heatedly.

'It isn't the pirates. I'm sure of it. There is some mischief going on,' Somadeva said, 'but I don't want a scandal. Not now. For heaven's sake, we just had a failed coup. I don't want to trigger another one.'

'That slave Your Highness freed could have given us some clues.'

'Kattappa, poor man—he is just a tool who was used by someone wisely,' the maharaja said. 'But he will lead us to whoever is behind all the bizarre things happening here. Someone is plotting the destruction of Mahishmathi.'

'Maybe it's the girl you made bhoomipathi. Devaraya's daughter.'

Maharaja Somadeva laughed aloud. 'Oh, no. Perhaps she does harbour hatred towards me and my regime. I am used to such hate. That doesn't bother me. What is a chit of a girl going to do against me? Someone more sinister, someone who is a match for me, is playing a dangerous game. He or she is in the shadows, moving the pieces with amazing dexterity, and effectively using people who have a grouse against my regime. Sivagami could be a pawn in his or her game, just like Bhutaraya was, or Thimma. I am indulging that girl, Sivagami. And to add to my amusement, my fool of a son has fallen head over heels in love with her. I have let it be. One day, that will also come in handy. But no, she isn't the master player.'

'Then who is it?' Hiranya asked.

'Ah! It could be anyone. A master player would not reveal themselves so easily. And that is what I love about this game.'

'One false throw of the dice, one false move, and whatever we have built over decades will collapse like an anthill stomped by an elephant,' Parameswara warned.

Somadeva chuckled. 'Even masters make mistakes. And in the game of chaturanga, skill alone does not ensure victory. One needs luck too. There are too many things that can go wrong. We play as it comes. Now I have made another move. I have set free Kattappa and I have got my best spy to track him. But the spy will report not to me but to my son, Mahadeva. It is a part of Mahadeva's training.'

'But why is that slave so important?'

'I believe Kattappa's brother isn't dead. All these "sightings" of the ghost are nothing but the imaginations of our superstitious people. Some wily people are using this superstitiousness to their advantage. I don't care about such minor things. But I do care that Shivappa is alive.'

'Why should the mighty empire of Mahishmathi be bothered about a young slave?' Hiranya asked, his eyes wide with surprise.

'My dear Hiranya,' Somadeva said in an amused tone. 'Are you still not seeing it? The person who is plotting against Mahishmathi isn't vying for my crown, but to make my empire splinter into small kingdoms. Malayappa would've been the king of the Vaithalikas had he not surrendered to me. Malayappa is dead, may his soul attain moksha, but his sons are still alive. The brothers are being used as a rallying point for the scattered tribes. Bhutaraya made the mistake of not declaring Shivappa their leader, for he was hungry for the position himself. Now that he is dead, there are only two potential leaders for the Vaithalikas: Kattappa and Shivappa. Kattappa is loyal to Mahishmathi. That leaves Shivappa. The boy is important to whomever is playing this game against Mahishmathi. Our enemies are weakening us in a well-planned manner, or chance has played into their hands.'

Hiranya and Parameswara looked at him uneasily. It was the first time they had seen Somadeva worried.

The king sighed. 'They gave us a big blow by sinking the Kali statue. They have pushed us into a corner, and I am sure our desperate situation will encourage more tribes beyond Mahishmathi to revolt. As you correctly envisaged, our economy and trade is in the doldrums. Internal strife is increasing. Our weapons have turned brittle. Gauridhooli production has stopped. Now imagine an uprising in Vaithalika lands, cutting off the path from Mahishmathi to Gauriparvat. Imagine the Vaithalikas declaring independence, with Shivappa as their ruler. We are not a homogeneous nation, Hiranya. We are a collection of various jaatis, kulas, tribes, villages, religions ... Our people have been citizens of Mahishmathi for perhaps one or two generations. They have belonged to their jaatis, tribes, language groups for many thousand years. When it comes to loyalty, which do you think will win? So, we need to get Shivappa.'

Hiranya stared at the king. 'Why not launch an all-out hunt for him?'

'For now, the Vaithalikas think he is dead. The rumours of his ghost are working to our advantage, and I am also using it. That will keep their morale low. If we carry out an official manhunt, word will spread that Shivappa is alive. Besides, we don't want to be the ones caught doing something against Shivappa. The brothers hate each other, and I have let loose Kattappa on his brother. My loyal dog Kattappa will do my job for me. That is how you play the game. With Shivappa out of the reckoning, it will take a lot of time for the Vaithalikas to regroup. By that time, I would be able to bring all the Gaurikanta from Gauriparvat and resolve the crisis.'

After a moment, Hiranya bowed deep. 'Your Highness, I am short of words to praise your brilliance. You are the master player.'

Somadeva laughed and Hiranya joined in. But Parameswara's forehead remained creased with worry.

As the two senior officials bowed to leave, Somadeva said,

'Parameswara, you were speaking about some guru who wants permission to set up an ashram.'

'I rejected the permission, Your Highness. We have enough trouble, and we barely know anything about this guru.'

'Allow him to set up the ashram,' Somadeva said.

Parameswara's reluctance was clear.

Somadeva laughed. 'You worry too much, my friend. Let the guru come. What better way to make people forget about their government's failings? Give them religion—it's an age-old technique used by rulers. Let the guru come and teach my people how to laugh, breathe or stand in contorted postures. Use him to our advantage. Use him as a diversion. He can regale my people with stories about rebirths, snake women, moksha, heaven, hell, prophets, direct communication from God or whatever nonsense this sly man sprouts. As long as he restricts his activities to the—what is the word, no, not religious, the other word that has become so fashionable now, ah, spiritual—as long as he restricts himself to the spiritual realm, let him do his nonsense.'

Parameswara still didn't look convinced.

'What is his name?'

'Guru Dharmapala.'

'I thought it would be more impressive name. This guru seems green behind the ears. Let him come. A diversion would be good.'

'The mahapradhana doesn't seem to be pleased,' Hiranya said.

'Ah, grumpy old man. A good man, but he has his days. Leave it. I know what I am doing. Would you two care to share some gold liquid with me?' Somadeva asked.

'Your Highness is being too kind to a humble servant,' Hiranya said.

'Ah, stop talking nonsense, Hiranya. Our friendship started long long ago, before I had this crown.'

'Then we were adventurers.'

'Ah, those were the days. We built an empire. You, Parameswara, Thimma, Devaraya.'

Hiranya stood silent. Somadeva stared at the wall. The lamp was flickering, and their shadows danced around.

'A king has no friends,' Somadeva said in a soft voice.

When the offer for the drink wasn't repeated, the old friends of Somadeva bowed and left silently.

The king continued to stand still, staring at his own flickering shadow.

FIFTEEN

Shivappa

Shivappa froze in fear. At the entrance of the leper's village, by the banyan tree, he saw a familiar figure. Kattappa was dressed in rags, but his disguise didn't fool Shivappa. How did he get time away from the king's service? And how had his brother known that he was hiding here? Perhaps Kattappa was just combing every nook and corner of the city and had reached the lepers' village as a last resort. Regardless, his brother's presence terrified him. Shivappa acted nonchalant as he felt his brother's eyes bore into him. He stooped even more, curled in his fingers tightly and limped to Malla's hut.

Perhaps, just perhaps, he had managed to fool his brother. Shivappa tried to settle his frayed nerves by telling himself that no one would be able to see through his disguise from such a distance. For the past few weeks, Shivappa had been on edge. There had been a few newcomers to the village, and to Shivappa's suspicious eyes, they looked like spies in search of someone. He had therefore grown out his hair and beard, wore rags, and limped about with a blanket around him, even on the hottest days.

There was always a group of beggars living under the banyan tree, waiting for permission from the village head, Sundari, to set up their own hut inside the leper village. Sundari called herself the queen of the village and ran the leper colony like a tyrant. Any newcomer had to wait for her permission before even entering the village.

The lepers from the village survived by foraging for food in the city garbage, but they had no permission to enter the city during the day. Every night, the lepers would march into the city with Sundari leading them.

That night, Shivappa was a part of the twenty-member gang led by Sundari. He was agitated. He knew he had to flee. But flee where? The leper village had given him protection and anonymity so far. He was angry that even that was being taken away before he could avenge his Kamakshi's death. He thought of attacking his brother before Kattappa attacked him. But that would be inviting attention to himself.

As the lepers from the village walked, the few who were yet to gain admission into the village followed them at a distance of more than thirty feet.

The rains hadn't relented for the past three days, and the roadside drains were overflowing. Most of the street lamps had gone off in the brisk wet wind that blew from the jungle beyond the river.

Shivappa was careful to stay in the centre of the gang. Sundari walked, tinkling a bell so that no one in Dasapattana would have the misfortune of seeing them. He caught a glimpse of Kattappa walking among the seven outsiders every time he stole a glance. As they entered Dasapattana, Shivappa turned to take their count once again. There were only six in the trailing gang.

Shivappa's heart skipped a beat. He quickly scanned the area for Kattappa. He saw that his brother had joined the main group of lepers and was limping towards him. Shivappa frantically looked around for an escape route.

The rain came down with a sudden fury, and Shivappa thanked his stars. He was barely able to see his own gang members, let alone the followers. Shivappa slipped away into a side street and started running. He ran without looking back. Rain lashed his face as he jumped over puddles and rivulets of muddy water running down the streets. He could see a few homeless families huddled under lamp posts, shivering in the rain. They cowered in fear as he passed. He roared at one family, making them scurry away like rats. He was sure they would help spread the rumours of the ghost that prowled the streets.

Shivappa saw the building that had been dear to him a long time ago. Revamma's mansion. His heart became heavy with sorrow. He stood looking at it, fighting a thousand memories and panting as rain washed over his body. A concert of toads from the bushes rose over the fury of the rain. A flash of lightning lit up the background and the mansion looked like a crouching beast. Thankfully, there were no palanquins or chariots on the road. A few branches of the banyan tree under which he and Kamakshi had made love lay bent and broken. For a moment, he wished he was the same old boy who had dreamt of running away with Kamakshi to some faraway land, and not a broken rebel running for his life. Or a ghost prowling the deserted streets. He looked around. There was not a soul on the road. He wiped his face with his palm and went up to the gate.

At the last minute, he decided to walk around the wall and enter the compound from the back instead. The street to the right looked slushy with mud and fallen leaves, so instead of the usual clockwise route, he turned to the left. And froze.

There was someone at the far end of the street. He quickly darted behind the pillar by the gate and waited. The man was keeping to the shadows, sometimes even walking through an overflowing drain to do so. Shivappa waited with bated breath. The figure reached the far end of the orphanage compound wall, hesitated as if indecisive, and then turned towards the rear of the compound. Shivappa stealthily followed him. He reached the left edge of the compound and peered around the wall. The man had reached the farthest end and was looking to his right. Had Shivappa taken his usual route, he would have come face to face with the man. Lightning flashed in the sky and, in its light, Shivappa saw the profile of the man. He cursed. Kattappa was following him like a shadow.

Shivappa retraced his steps. He knew Kattappa wouldn't wait in his position for long; he would come in search of him very soon. He decided to jump the compound wall of the mansion from the main street itself. He had avoided it because the chance of falling into the hands of dandakaras on night patrol was high. But left with no choice, he scrambled up the slippery wall. When he had managed to perch on top of the twelve-foot wall, he heard footsteps. His brother had completed the round and was coming to the front gate.

Shivappa jumped into the compound and landed softly in the mud. He ran towards the open veranda and peered through the keyhole. A small light was burning in a corner, and he could see, sprawled on the floor, a man with only a strip of cloth covering his groin. A few pots of palm toddy lay scattered about and the man's dhoti was lying by his head. The man was giggling and seemed to be singing.

Suddenly, there was the loud peal of a bell above Shivappa's head. Startled, he ran in a panic, not knowing where to go. He crashed into a huge copper vessel placed outside to collect rain, and it rolled down the courtyard, clanging loudly as it did so. Shivappa crouched behind the tulsi plant in the courtyard as the door creaked open. The man who had been lying drunk looked out of the door, mouthing expletives. He stared at the bell hanging from the roof beam and wagged his finger at it.

'Shut up ... slup up ... no singing here ...' he slurred and giggled. The pealing of the bell stopped. 'Ahh ... good boy. Now get down from the roof. Come, come, jump down,' he coaxed the bell. It rung again then and the man rushed inside and slammed the door shut. When the sound of the bell died away, he opened the door and peeped out. Again, he waggled a finger at the bell. Then he saw the copper vessel lying on its side in the courtyard.

'Oh, sweetheart, why are you lying there in the rain? I will take you inside,' the man said, swaying on his unsteady legs. Just as he stepped out into the rain, a window on the first floor flung open. Shivappa, hiding behind the tulsi plant, cursed under his breath. An enormous lady was peering out with a flaming torch in her hand.

'Thondaka, you ass. Drunk again. Go to sleep!' she screamed.

'Who is that talking from the sky? God? Oh ... you ... the devil herself ...'

'Ayyo ... your mother is the devil?' Revamma yelled.

'That is what I said, right?' Thondaka laughed.

'Wait there, you good-for-nothing donkey. Getting drunk and not letting anyone sleep. I am coming down now.'

'Come down,' Thondaka spread his arms wide. 'Jump. I shall catch you. Come on, jump, you devil,' he screamed. Revamma threw her torch at him. It swirled through the air and briefly lit up the place where Shivappa was hiding. The torch fell a few feet away from the tulsi plant, flared for an instant before it went out with a hiss and darkness spread again.

'Hey, someone is there in the courtyard,' Revamma cried.

'Yes, there is,' said Thondaka. 'It's me.'

'Fool, there is someone else.'

'That's you. And you are the fool. The old woman has lost her senses. Going senile, I think,' Thondaka said and giggled.

'Idiot! Look behind the tulsi plant. I saw someone crouching there.'

Thondaka staggered to the tulsi plant and cried, 'There is no one here.'

The bell rang again. Thondaka weaved his way to the gate and opened it. He blinked at Kattappa standing outside.

'Hey, were you the one crouching behind the tulsi plant just now?'

Kattappa didn't bother to answer. He shoved Thondaka to one side, ran in and began looking here and there for his brother. From the balcony, Revamma hurled abuses. When she saw that it had no impact on Kattappa, she yelled at her son, 'Donkey, throw him out.'

Thondaka blinked uncomprehendingly. After a minute, he

went towards Kattappa on unsteady legs and said, 'My mother wants you to go.'

'Shh. There is a ghost here,' Kattappa said.

'I know.' Thondaka giggled and pointed to the balcony.

'No. I saw it come from the graveyard. I am a black magician who is searching for it. It is the ghost of that dead slave, Shivappa. He has come to take revenge on you all. His lover Kamakshi lived here and you killed her.'

Thondaka gulped in fear. 'I killed no one.'

'Tell that to the ghost. But it won't believe you. The ghost is sure you killed Kamakshi.'

'What am I supposed to do now?'

Revamma, meanwhile, was shouting at the top of the voice from the balcony. 'Is it your mama, you ass? Has he come to arrange a wedding for you, idiot? Throw him out. Or run and find a dandakara and get him arrested.'

Heads were now popping out of the windows in the orphanage.

'If you see the ghost, don't make it angry. But you should come and tell me,' Kattappa said.

'Are you sure it is here?' Thondaka looked around fearfully.

'Who do you think was hiding behind the tulsi plant?'

'Wasn't that you?'

'I was outside the gate and the gate was locked. But someone was hiding behind the tulsi plant and your mother saw.'

'Shivappa?' Thondaka said with a shiver in his voice.

'And is Shivappa dead or alive?'

'I went for his burial and put a fistful of mud in the grave.'

'So who was hiding behind the tulsi plant?'

'Wasn't that you?'

'Your mother is right. You are a donkey.'

'But how can the dead Shivappa be hiding behind the tulsi plant?'

'Think, if you can,' Kattappa said, trying to control his exasperation.

After a moment's silence, Thondaka started crying in fear.

'Amma, Shivappa's ghost is here. It was he who was hiding behind the tulsi plant.'

'I am coming down there to break your thick head if you don't throw out that slave,' Revamma said, and vanished from the window.

Kattappa retreated, and by the time Revamma came down and knuckled Thondaka's head, he had left. Revamma took out her anger by kicking around the empty toddy pots and hurling a half-filled one at Thondaka before stomping into the mansion. The inmates hooted and whistled all through her performance, and that didn't seem to please her. She went back to her bedroom, lamenting her fate for having such a worthless son, and cursing the thankless inmates of the orphanage who were making fun of her misfortune.

One by one, the windows on the top floors were closed. Struck by inconsolable grief for losing half a pot of toddy, Thondaka was fighting a losing battle with the earth that was drinking up his nectar. He had licked whatever remained on the ground when the words of Kattappa finally sunk in. He stood up and stared at the tulsi plant. He didn't dare go near it. A street dog howled and then yapped from somewhere far away. Thondaka ran inside. The door was ajar. He slammed the door shut and stood panting, eyes shut tight. He started reciting the various names of Arjuna, the talisman to conquer fear, which he had learnt when he was a child. He slowly opened his eyes once he had recited all the twelve names of Arjuna, and his heart jumped to his throat.

In front of him was the ghost of Shivappa. He was standing with his back pressed to the wall.

'You ... you are dead. You don't exist. I don't believe in ghosts. Ha ha ha ha,' Thondaka laughed and promptly fainted.

When he regained consciousness, he was lying on his back in the attic of the mansion. Staring at him, from a hand's distance away, was the ghost's fierce face. Thondaka wanted to cry for his mother. He felt a wet warmness spreading between his legs and the thick smell of urine filled the attic.

'You shall worship me,' the ghost commanded Thondaka. 'When the palace drums strike midnight, you shall come here with food and water every night.'

Thondaka nodded. Then a doubt assailed his simple mind. 'Ghost swami,' he said, 'what food do you people eat? It will be difficult to bring blood and all.'

'Bring whatever you eat, or else I shall eat you,' the ghost said, suppressing a smile. 'And if you talk to anyone about me living in your attic ...'

'Aren't you already dead. So how can you "live" in the attic?'

'Shhhh.' The ghost placed a finger across Thondaka's lips. 'When I talk, you listen. No questions. Never tell anyone I exist here.'

'You are a ghost. You don't exist,' Thondaka said helpfully.

'Yes, I don't exist, and if you open your mouth, you also won't exist. You will inform me about whatever is happening downstairs, who is coming, who is going—everything. Every night, when the palace drums strike midnight—'

'I shall come with food and water for you, swami,' Thondaka said with folded hands.

It was a good hideout for Shivappa, and he prayed he wouldn't be found before he had taken his revenge. A loose word from the fool Thondaka would ensure not only his death, but his brother's too.

The next night, through a crack in the attic wall, he saw Kattappa prowling the street in front of the orphanage. There was also a dandakara at the gate of Revamma's mansion, acting on her complaint about a slave's intrusion the previous night. Seeing the dandakara, Kattappa walked past Revamma's mansion, but Shivappa saw him turn back and stare at the house before turning the corner of the street and disappearing.

'Hey, who are you?' The shrillness of the voice startled him. He turned to see a girl standing there with a broom.

Shivappa relaxed. He said with a smile, 'I am a ghost. A bhuta. But don't be afraid. I am a friendly bhuta.'

The girl frowned at him. 'Who is afraid of ghosts? In the stories I have heard, they have always helped people.'

Shivappa laughed.

'Namaskaram, bhuta,' the girl said. 'I am Akhila. Will you help me?'

That was the beginning of an impossible friendship.

SIXTEEN

Neelappa

'You're sure the fool is there?' Brihannala asked Neelappa.
'Please don't call our king a fool.'

Brihannala laughed at the pain in Neelappa's voice. 'I'm sorry. All respect to your king.'

They were sitting by the river, near the slaves' graveyard. The world was quiet around them except for the drone of crickets. The night was crisp and cold.

Neelappa said, 'I was there with Sivagami last week. We were visiting Akhila, to persuade the girl to live with Sivagami. The girl is adamant. Revamma's home is as appealing as hell, but the girl hates Sivagami so much that she prefers to live in the orphanage rather than with her sister.'

'Spare me the sob stories of Thimma's family. Tell me how you found out that Shivappa is hiding there.'

'The girl talked. You know I have a knack of dealing with girls,' Neelappa said and grinned, showing his gap-filled teeth.

Brihannala chuckled. 'The ever-affectionate grandpa.'

'Who can tell many stories.' Neelappa smiled. 'So, while Sivagami was arguing with Revamma, I talked to Akhila. The girl had come to me when I was standing by my chariot, attracted by the horse, and we became friendly. When I remarked that the orphanage looks like a haunted house, the girl got excited and said she had seen a ghost there, but it was a good ghost. The ghost lives in the attic, she said. Only Thondaka, the son of Revamma, seems to know the secret, for she has seen him sneaking food and water up to the attic. She was very proud of her ghost friend. I challenged the girl to prove her claim. The girl was miffed and stomped away. I waited. After sometime, I saw the small attic window open suddenly and a face peered out. It was only for the blink of an eye. Probably the girl tricked him into looking out. And I saw Shivappa there before the attic window was snapped shut.'

'Bloody balls of the holy bull!' Brihannala said. 'So he has been hiding in Dasapattana after giving Malla the slip, and we have been searching for him all over the city.'

Neelappa nodded.

'His luck won't hold for long,' Brihannala said. 'The girl may blurt out the secret to someone else.'

'His luck has already run out, I fear,' Neelappa said. Brihannala frowned.

'I saw him.'

'Who?' Brihannala asked.

'Who else? His brother—Kattappa. I saw him in the vicinity yesterday night.'

Brihannala swore under her breath. 'See our luck! Our entire plan depends on these two idiots.'

'Only you can find a way to help us, swami,' Neelappa pleaded. 'The future of the Vaithalikas depends on you.'

Brihannala sat deep in thought. She ran a tight network of spies. No one knew the complete operation, no one knew who was a spy, double spy or a traitor to the cause. Sometimes, she would sacrifice one or two spies to mislead the Mahishmathi guptacharas, the spy network that reported directly to the mahapradhana or, perhaps, the king himself.

'The king knows I am somehow involved. He is no fool. I know he knows I am involved. And he knows that I know he knows,' Brihannala said and laughed. She threw a pebble into the river and watched it sink down.

'Both of us are waiting for the right opportunity to strike, like a cobra and a mongoose. The king is the cobra, ha, a king cobra, with the poison that can kill an elephant. I am the mongoose, lithe, small, furry and unimposing. But do you know that it is the little mongoose who emerges victorious in every fight it has with a king cobra? In evasion lies its victory; getting the cobra to strike and moving away in the blink of an eye is the mongoose's forte. I will give your people freedom. That is the dream of Achi Nagamma.'

'You aren't even a Vaithalika. Why are you taking such an insane risk for a forgotten people? Do you love us so much? Neelappa asked.

Brihannala laughed and said, 'The age of kings is coming to an end. It will be the people who rule the world.'

She looked at the confused face of Neelappa and continued, 'What does the mongoose do after slaying the king of snakes?'

After a moment's thought, Neelappa said, 'It slices its dead enemy into many pieces, like a ritual.'

'The mongoose never wants to be king. Yet it fights, for it resents anyone being a king.' Brihannala smiled. 'Understood?'

Neelappa stared at her and slowly nodded his head. He understood what Brihannala was implying. She wanted to cut Mahishmathi into pieces.

Brihannala stood up and walked to Neelappa. He placed his hand on Neelappa's shoulder and said, 'You once owned Gauriparvat. Great injustice has been done to your people. I am a humble servant of dharma. My aim is to restore dharma and give back what once rightfully belonged to you.'

Neelappa nodded. Brihannala continued, 'After the failed coup, the Mahishmathi army ravaged forest villages, pillaging, raping and killing Vaithalikas in the thousands. Somadeva is trying to teach your people a lesson. In Shivappa, lies your hope. We need to get him out of the city safe. If Kattappa or Mahishmathi's spies get Shivappa before we can, you can forget about regaining Gauriparvat for your people.'

'Shall I eliminate Kattappa?'

'And have the whole Mahishmathi spy network on our back? Remember, Kattappa is the personal slave of the king. The king has set him free for a reason. No. We need to stick to our original plan. Get Shivappa out of Mahishmathi.'

'But how?' Neelappa asked.

'Damned if I know,' Brihannala said. 'I wish I had enough people under my command.'

'Good will win over evil, swami. And there is no one more evil than Somadeva,' Neelappa said.

'I don't know about that, Neelappa. I don't know who is evil in this bloody game. I can only hope our cause is just, and the belief that good will win over evil is right. But I am too bloody cynical to think the world follows any logic. It is a bloody jungle. The fittest survive. The strongest rules. The wiliest win. That is the way of the world. You have grown grey enough to know that.'

'You are being too pessimistic,' Neelappa said.

Brihannala shook her head. After a pause, she said, 'You're right and I am wrong. For the young and gullible, we need to tell the clichéd story of good versus evil. We need to assert that we are the good and the other side is the evil. And to prove that, we need to win this time, Neelappa. All of us have suffered so much that we need some victory to keep our faith intact. Win, and we shall be hailed as the good. Lose and we are damned.'

'Amma Gauri will show a way for her beloved children,' Neelappa said, folding his hands in obeisance towards the distant Gauriparvat. A crescent moon shimmered above the peak. When Neelappa opened his eyes after his prayer, he saw a movement in the river. He squinted his eyes and saw someone was swimming across the river with smooth, silent strokes. He shook Brihannala who was immersed in her thoughts, and pointed to the approaching figure, which was swimming towards the shore, but some distance away from where they were. Brihannala and Neelappa rushed towards where they thought the swimmer would come ashore. But when they reached the spot, they couldn't find anyone.

'Where has he gone?' Neelappa asked.

'Not he, but she,' Brihannala said, peering at the footprints on the mud. She started following the trail.

'Anna,' a voice called out softly.

Brihannala turned around. 'Ally?'

Ally stepped out from behind the bush, where she was hiding. For a moment they stared at each other, and then

Ally rushed into Brihannala's arms. She hugged her close and started crying on her shoulder. It was a disconcerting sight for Neelappa to see Brihannala's tears. He averted his eyes.

'It breaks my heart to see you like this,' Ally said, half crying and half laughing.

'Why? A woman's outfit doesn't suit your brother?' Brihannala asked, looking down at the glittering saree and jewels.

'I have never seen you without your beard.'

'It would appear odd if the king's eunuch had a beard.' Brihannala ran her fingers over her smooth chin. Neelappa moved away, allowing the two a little time to themselves. He knew Ally wasn't Brihannala's blood sister. But they were all children of Achi Nagamma. All of them. Now that the rebel Bhutaraya and his followers had perished in the failed coup during Mahamakam, Achi was the undisputed leader and the mother figure for the revolutionary movement. She was the incarnation of Amma Gauri—so believed the tribes of the jungle.

Later, when Ally had finished telling her story and how she had brought down the Kali statue using Kattappa, Brihannala exclaimed, 'At last, Kattappa has done something useful in life.'

Ally's face fell, and Brihannala's keen eyes didn't miss it even in the dull moonlight. 'Don't foster any crazy thoughts in your fickle mind, girl,' she said.

She laughed the comment away, but Brihannala's gaze bore into her. She changed the topic. 'Who is Sivagami?' she asked.

Neelappa gave a start when he heard Sivagami's name.

'Why do you want to know?' Brihannala asked.

'I have a message for her. From a young friend. I want to tell her that he is alive and her manuscript is safe with him.'

'Manuscript? What manuscript?' Brihannala asked, suddenly alert.

Brihannala and Neelappa exchanged glances. 'You have the book with you?'

'No, the boy wouldn't give it.'

'And where is the boy?'

Ally narrated how she had met Gundu Ramu and how the dwarf, Hidumba, was taking hundreds of children to Gauriparvat. Brihannala cursed and fumed. When she calmed down, she said, 'Initially, my idea was to send you away. But now I think you should inform Sivagami about the boy. If I have read her correctly, she will move heaven and hell to reach Gauriparvat now, if she knows the boy is alive. And that will open a window of opportunity for us.'

'But how do I go undetected into the city?'

'I will get you an entry token. There are enough girls coming from the countryside, dreaming about a life in the city. Everyone thinks they will one day become like Kalika in her heyday. The rich and cultured Nagaravadhu, the bride of the town, the darling of the nobles. Most end up in questionable devadasi homes. Getting into the palace harem may be tough, but placing you in one of the devadasi homes is something I can arrange without much difficulty. Find Sivagami and tell her about that boy—what is his name again?'

'Gundu Ramu.'

'Tell her about him. Tell her the grave danger he is in. Tell her about her book. And then leave the bloody city and go to the place you were assigned. You had no business coming here and risking the mission. You are supposed to be where they are rebuilding the Kali statue.'

'Is this how a brother treats a sister?' Ally retorted hotly. 'Asking her to stay in the home of devadasis?'

'Have you forgotten your lessons? Morality is for fools. We are doing everything possible for a greater cause. When men are ready to give their lives for the cause, you worry about such silly morals?'

'I ... I can't.'

Brihannala glared at her.

'Are you in love with that slave, you fool?'

Ally looked down at her feet.

'You didn't come just to pass on a message about a boy to Sivagami, did you,' Brihannala said, peering at Ally. 'You came with the hope that you will meet your lover.'

Ally turned her face away, defiant.

'He is a bloody slave, Ally, a dog of the king of Mahishmathi. A fool who wants to kill his brother ...'

Ally's fingers curled at the hilt of her sword.

'Stop calling him a fool,' she said angrily. 'There is no man nobler than him. He is the scion of the Vaithalika tribe. He is the king, a living God, my Kattappa.'

They stood glaring at each other. Neelappa tapped the shoulder of Brihannala, who tried to wave him away. Neelappa grabbed Brihannala's wrist and dragged her back.

'She will destroy everything,' Brihannala hissed.

'Hush,' Neelappa said, as he pulled Brihannala away so they would be out of Ally's earshot.

'I am no one to advise you. But I feel you are missing a great opportunity here. Your anger is making you blind to it.'

'What do you mean?' Brihannala asked irritably.

'Why not use her to get Shivappa out of Mahishmathi?'

'But she is madly in love with that stupid slave Kattappa.'
'Use that too,' Neelappa said.

Brihannala stared at him. Then her face relaxed and a smile spread on her face. She slapped his forehead and said, 'You're right. I got carried away. I will talk to her and make her understand. As you said, perhaps this is how Amma Gauri is showing she is with us.'

Brihannala returned to Ally and Neelappa followed closely. Brihannala took a deep breath and said awkwardly, 'I am sorry, dear.'

Neelappa moved towards the riverbank and sat looking at the river Mahishi flow by quietly. He could hear the soft sobs of Ally and the cajoling words of Brihannala. Neelappa sat feeling numb. The face of Kattappa haunted him, and he tried not to think about the fate of the slave. When his eyes drifted to the distant Gauriparvat, he clenched his fist to his chest and whispered, 'Amma Gauri, forgive me for what I have done.'

SEVENTEEN

Sivagami

For some reason Sivagami couldn't fathom, Neelappa had been excited and humming some mantra the entire day. As they turned towards the street that passed by the river, she saw a massive ship coming down the river Mahishi. It was much bigger than anything she had ever seen. It had multi-coloured sails and a dragon-faced prow. It was garishly painted, with the intention to impress the onlooker with its myriad colours and intricate design. She could see that there were more than two hundred oars on just one side—there were probably more than six hundred galley slaves to row this giant of a ship.

For some time the ship sailed parallel to their chariot before it gathered speed and overtook them.

'What is that?' Sivagami asked Neelappa.

'You didn't know? I had told you about it. Today is the day he is coming,' Neelappa said in an excited voice.

'Who?' Sivagami asked, but Neelappa was craning his neck to get a better view of the fast-moving ship. He cracked his whip and the chariot picked up speed. By the time they were nearing the dock, the street was filling up quickly with an excited crowd. The ship horn blared, and people craned their necks to watch as the landing platform was lowered onto the dock from the ship's deck. Suddenly, men and women wearing red appeared in the crowd and formed a protective chain by holding hands. Neelappa was standing on his seat now, trying to get a better view.

'He has come, he has come,' Neelappa finally cried excitedly. The crowd surged forward. Sivagami could hear the volunteers chant, 'Jai Guru Dharmapala', as they struggled to keep the crowd at bay.

A path was cleared, and a procession started progressing towards the palace. First came elephants with diamond-studded caparisons. It was followed by horses, camels and a few exotic creatures like horses with stripes. Sivagami saw another creature with the face of a deer, but its neck was longer than a camel's neck, and it was spotted like a leopard. The men and women dressed in red were now dancing on the streets, as others beat out a rhythm on drums and cymbals. They were singing a chorus that went:

Guru Dharmapala
Jaya Satyachara
Chitanandaroopa
Namami thvameva

Soon the crowd picked up the chant. Sivagami saw a holy man walking barefoot behind this exotic procession of singers and dancers. He had dark hair and a flowing beard; his right palm was raised in benediction. As the holy man was passing Sivagami, an old woman fell at his feet. He picked her up by her shoulders, wiped away her tears, hugged her, and whispered something to her. Then Guru Dharmapala manifested a golden mango from thin air and gave it to the woman. The woman was in ecstasy and she broke out into happy sobs as disciples led her away from the guru. Soon, men and women pushed and shoved to fall at the holy man's feet and take his blessing.

Neelappa pleaded with her to permit him to go and get the blessing of the guru, and when she gestured her consent, he rushed to fight and shove his way forward.

Guru Dharmapala manifested various things from thin air, sometimes holy ash, sometimes strings of pearls, ladoos, mangoes, a Shiva Linga, garlands and flowers, and threw them high in the air. Sivagami saw Neelappa fighting with other people to catch the guru's prasad.

A train of men with skin the colour of ebony and well-chiselled bodies trailed behind the guru carrying various boxes and baskets. The fragrance of exotic perfumes spread in the air as they stood waiting patiently for the guru to move forward. Even the finely woven muslin that covered the boxes couldn't hide the splendour and radiance of the gifts the boxes contained.

As the guru finally began walking, raising his hands to bless everyone, he turned towards Sivagami, and seemed to freeze for a moment. Then he smiled at her and the procession resumed. Neelappa came up to her holding a rudraksha chain in his hand. 'The guru has blessed me,' he cried as he took the chain to his eyes before putting it around his neck. He turned to Sivagami and asked her whether they could proceed. She didn't hear him. She was deep in thought. Something about

Guru Dharmapala worried her. She was sure she had seen him somewhere before, but couldn't recollect where.

As they headed home, Sivagami's thoughts moved to how people were so easily fooled by gurus and men who claimed they were avatars of God. From a distance, she could see the frail figure of Gomati standing at the gates of her home. Sivagami jumped out of the chariot and gestured for Neelappa to leave them alone. Gomati waited until Neelappa had moved the chariot some distance. She looked around fearfully and then whispered in Sivagami's ears, 'Next Tuesday night.'

Sivagami took a deep breath. The time to trap Rudra Bhatta had come. She climbed back into the chariot, and as they entered the courtyard, a figure stepped out of the shadows. Neelappa pulled the reins and the chariot screeched to a halt. Vajra neighed in pain. Something came flying at her and Sivagami instinctively ducked. It fell on the chariot floor and rolled as the figure vanished back into the shadows. Sivagami saw that it was a scroll and picked it up.

'Should I chase her?' Neelappa asked.

'Her?' Sivagami asked in surprise.

'It looked like a woman, daughter,' Neelappa said.

'It seems she had a message to deliver.' Sivagami moved to the light of a torch to read the scroll.

'Gundu Ramu is alive and he has your manuscript. Save him before they kill him. He is in Gauriparvat.'

Her hands trembled. A sense of overwhelming misery washed over her. Guilt, shame at not pursuing the trail of Gundu Ramu weighed her down. Had she given up on Gundu Ramu too soon, mourning for his imaginary death and moving on with life? The boy hadn't given up on her. Sivagami wished she had asked Neelappa to chase the messenger. Who had her Gundu Ramu? And why was he in Gauriparvat? She must reach him before anything happened to her dear friend. The mysterious Gauriparvat that had caused the death of her parents had now in its grip another one dear to her.

EIGHTEEN

Kattappa

'Not even a dog would drink this,' Malla said, flinging the pot of toddy at Kattappa's face. Without a word, Kattappa picked up the shards of the pot. The old leper lay down on the damp ground, muttering curses.

It was with great difficulty that Kattappa had got admission into the leper village. He'd had to gift Sundari the necklace the maharaja had given him.

Kattappa desperately wanted to barge into Revamma's mansion to check if his brother was there, but was unable to do so without raising suspicion. He found out from other lepers about the mishap that had happened to Malla, and about the young man he had been guarding. Anyone else would've fled the place the moment he knew what he had come for wasn't there anymore. But not Kattappa. He felt duty-bound to serve Malla, as the poor man was made invalid by his brother. He was carrying the burden of all his brother's sins, he felt.

Since Shivappa had left the village, Brihannala had stopped paying Malla, but the leper was used to the easy life now. He sensed that Kattappa felt bad about his state for some reason, and started exploiting his vulnerability by exaggerating how he was tortured by Shivappa. For Kattappa, it was a blotch on his family and an insult to his father's memory that his younger brother had exploited a helpless old leper. He stayed put in the leper's colony, serving the beggar during the day, and slipping away at night to keep a watch on Revamma's mansion.

One hot afternoon, as Kattappa was going to fetch water from the river, he was surprised by someone he had been struggling to forget. She was walking towards him, dripping wet. He guessed she had swum across the river. She stood before him, coy, smiling, twisting her hair with her fingers.

'Ally,' Kattappa whispered.

He watched her eyes fill up with tears, a smile light up her lovely dark face. He saw her clothes were in disarray, the water drops shining on her shoulders, and he averted his eyes. When he had met her last, he was a slave bound in chains, and she had freed him. She had made him do something terrible, the import of which he was aware of only when he had reached Mahishmathi.

Later, Kattappa would wonder about the anger that had gripped him at that time, the sense of deep injustice, the compassion towards his fellow slaves who were barely out of their teens and who were being driven like cattle. How different was it from the anger his brother harboured about slavery? And that anger had prompted him to act against his beloved Mahishmathi. How different was he from his brother, whom he wanted to kill? In his mind, he had always justified his action by saying that he had destroyed the Kali statue because the woman who freed him had ordered him to do so. He owed it to her. He hadn't strayed from the path of his dharma.

Now, when he saw Ally in the flesh, his shoulders stooped with guilt, for he knew that it wasn't a sense of duty to the woman who had freed him that had made him do that ignoble act against his king, his country and his Goddess. It was kama, desire, and not dharma, righteousness, that had lit his path. Anger bubbled up. Why couldn't she just leave him alone?

Kattappa stood frozen, looking into the distance. Her proximity seared him. She noticed the way he was holding his fingers and took his palm in her hand. 'Kattappa, what happened to you?'

He pulled back his hand from her grip, and as he did so, it brushed against her bosom; he felt as if he had been singed.

'I am not a leper. It's a disguise,' he blurted out, and felt like an idiot. She looked at him with surprise and then burst out laughing. From the hut, Malla uttered another obscenity and the wind carried it to them. Kattappa felt embarrassed and Ally laughed again. His gaze slipped from the dimple that formed in her smooth cheeks to her bosom and he quickly looked away. She smiled at his discomfort and reached out again to hold his hand.

'Nice disguise,' she said, and her eyes sparkled. He gulped, feeling irritated that his anger had melted away, cursing the helplessness he felt. He was sweating, his face burned and blood pounded through his veins.

'Why ... why are you here, devi?' he asked, gathering courage. His fingers were entwined with hers. His, gnarled and with calluses, and hers, long and smooth. In answer, she leaned against him. The fragrance of champaka flowers in her hair, the smell of the river on her shoulders ... he closed his eyes, not sure the sound of the pounding heart was his or hers. When her lips locked with his, he grabbed her with an animal passion. The pot slipped from his hands and broke. His arms went around her narrow waist. Ally became like the creeper entwining a fig tree. Like jasmine, she blossomed, intoxicating the slave with the fragrance of life. Not too long back, he had rejoiced that he was a free man. Now he understood that a man is never free. But these chains didn't hurt. They burned with a pain so sweet that he wished he would be charred to death and be reborn again. And again.

Later, when they lay on the grass, watching the sun painting the sky orange, immersed in a deep silence, listening to the buzz of the dragonflies, he felt a lightness. He had told her everything that had happened in his life, and she had poured out her heart. He turned towards her and said, 'I don't believe that you came here to find me.'

'You're a free man now. You can choose to believe or not believe,' she said with a smile.

'No, you are teasing me. I am no fool to think that a beautiful woman like you would come so far to meet a slave. You weren't even aware that I was free. You are lying, devi.'

'I love it when you call me devi. No man has made me feel so important. No man I've met has made me feel so respected.'

The mention of other men pricked him and he lay back on the grass. A flock of birds arced through the sky.

'Jealous?' She giggled, tracing his lips with her forefinger.

'Why should I be,' he said with vehemence, and added after a pause, 'devi.'

She burst out laughing and he scrambled up. He'd had enough of being treated like this. He stomped away and she ran back behind him, calling his name. She hugged him from behind and he froze in his tracks. She bit his earlobe and he pushed her face away.

'You're right. I didn't come to meet you,' she said. His face fell. It was as he had guessed, yet it hurt.

'I came for my father,' she said softly. The way she said it made him turn towards her. Her lips trembled, her eyes brimmed with tears and he felt his heart would break. *It is silly, you can't be this soft, this mad, you fool,* he told himself.

'Devi,' he said, and lifted her chin. She smiled through her tears and hurriedly wiped them away with the back of her hand.

'My father has leprosy. He was chased away from our tribe when it became known. My mother took another man and I was cast away like an unwanted puppy. I found another mother, Achi Nagamma, who is the mother for all those who have none. But I always missed my father. I was searching for him and came to know he is dying. His name is Malla. Do you know him?'

'I ... I know him,' he said, and she grabbed his hands in excitement.

'Oh, Amma Gauri.'

'He lives with me,' he said, pleased with the impression he was making. She hugged him and sobbed on his shoulder.

'I don't know how to thank you, Kattappa,' she said, her body shaking with emotion. He showered her with kisses. He felt like a saviour, like a prince in some fairy tale, who had brought his princess a precious gift.

Later, much later, he would recall these words again and again. Why didn't he catch the lie at the time? Why didn't he ask how she had found out Malla was living there? Why had she come exactly at the time that he was living in disguise?

As expected, Ally didn't get permission to enter the village, despite Kattappa telling Sundari that she was Malla's daughter. From experience, Kattappa knew that anyone entering the lepers' village without permission entered it at the risk of their lives. It took only one cry from Sundari for other lepers to rush out of their huts and pounce on the intruder with sticks and stones.

Though there were no walls around the village, outsiders could come up only to the banyan tree that stood a hundred feet away from the first row of huts. The dusty mud path wound its labyrinthine way through rows and rows of huts. The village ended a few hundred feet from the riverbank. The path continued through the riverside towards distant countryside, beyond the cremation ground for lepers and vanished into the thorny forest that stretched to the north. The last hut of the village, bordering the cremation ground, was that of Malla. The more the disease progressed in a leper, the more north, towards the cremation ground, his accommodation moved.

Kattappa had learnt this uncomfortable truth and he didn't know how to tell Ally. The poor woman was devastated enough that she couldn't meet her father. What perplexed Kattappa was what Malla had said when Sundari asked him whether he wanted to see his daughter. The grumpy old leper had become livid and said he didn't have a daughter. He had no one. He cared for no one. When Kattappa tried to reason with him, the old man became abusive and was soon in the grips of a debilitating fit. Sundari ordered Kattappa to take the leper back to his hut and warned him not to mention the old man's daughter again. When Kattappa told this story to Ally, she burst into tears. For the past few days, she had been living by the river, waiting for permission to enter the village and see her father.

Kattappa didn't know how to pacify her. Ally said it was all her mother's fault. Her mother had abandoned her father for another man, and not allowed him to enter their home when he contracted leprosy. The old man carried the grudge and she couldn't blame him. She sobbed on his shoulder, and they ended up making love in the grass. She seemed to feel better after that, but Kattappa could sense the deep anguish in the soul of the woman he had started loving with all his heart.

He tried his best to reconcile Malla and his daughter, but the old leper persisted with his denial of ever having been married or siring a daughter. Kattappa often lost his temper and ended up cursing him, saying Malla deserved the disease for he was so heartless. Later, he would feel guilty for the harsh words he had uttered to the invalid leper and serve him like a dutiful son.

'Beware of that woman who claims to be my daughter,' Malla warned him in one of his sober moods. That made Kattappa so angry that he didn't return to the hut that night. Instead, he spent it under the stars, on the softness of Ally's lap.

Running her fingers through his thick curly hair, she said in a soft voice, 'Kattappa, would you do something if I ask you? Could you please sneak me into the village? I want to see my father once.' She paused and then added, 'Before he leaves me.'

Kattappa scrambled up. Choking with emotion, he said, 'Devi, I will take you now.'

'Now?' she asked, smiling.

In answer, Kattappa grabbed her wrist and started walking to the village. They could hear someone singing. The village had gone hungry—the king was going somewhere and because the streets were full of soldiers, the lepers didn't have permission to forage in the city for leftovers. It meant hunger, but it also meant a night spent together in the village. The untouchables came with liquor and left it by the banyan tree. The lepers would later repay them by doing some work. If there was no food, there was always music. There was fire. There was the open sky and the breeze, the song of the night bird and a hundred stories to retell. To the world, they were lepers; but for them, every man and woman, they were the heroes of their tales. Like little flowers that bloomed even in rotting garbage, their hope blossomed in such nights. They might wither in the sun of the morrow, but who cared for tomorrow, when today was here. There was no tax for dreaming, even in Mahishmathi; at least, not yet.

When Kattappa and Ally sneaked up to the hut of Malla, the old leper was sleeping on the dirt floor. His mouth was agape and his ribs rose and fell gently. Ally sat by his side and cried. Songs of merriment flowed in through the door of the hut. Kattappa could feel her sorrow, and wished he could envelop Ally in an embrace and kiss her sadness away. He chided himself for the profane thought. The meeting was sacred, one filled with piety, guilt and love of a daughter for her father, and he was defiling it with such thoughts.

He was reminded of his father and tears filled his eyes. There was so much misery in the world. He was a lucky bastard, he thought. Not that he didn't have his share of unhappiness. But his fate was nothing compared to that of the lepers he lived with. It was nothing compared to that of the woman he loved. 'Look at those who are less fortunate, and you will always be grateful to God who has showered you with so many blessings,' his father would say.

The scorn of his brother popped up in his mind. 'To be grateful to God, one needs to see more and more misery and thank him that we aren't that miserable. What a wonderful God!' his brother had said and laughed at his father's words. Kattappa gritted his teeth in frustration. His brother had corrupted his mind. The image of his father lying dead on his lap flashed in his mind, and the anger returned.

Ally broke the spell. She touched his shoulder and gestured that they should go. When they had sneaked out of the hut, they saw that a fight had broken out among the lepers, and the vilest abuses were being flung about. The songs were forgotten. The nightingale had flown away, and the crescent moon had hidden behind clouds. The dream had burst like a bubble and life—cruel, indifferent, miserable life—had rushed in to fill the space.

When they had reached the graveyard, Ally turned to him and said, 'If I ask you something, would you promise to do it?'

He gazed at her, hurt that she had to ask.

'My father does not have many more days left,' she said, looking at the river.

He wanted to protest that it wasn't true to pacify her, but he wasn't used to deception, and he had never been able to lie easily. *Yes, sure,* a voice said, *you lied to the whole world that your brother had died, and he paid you back by killing your father.*

'When that happens, I don't want him to be burnt in a leper's cremation ground. I want to take him to our village and give him a proper burial as per our tribal customs. Would you help me do that?'

Kattappa wanted to say he had a big task to do, a word to keep, a promise given to his dying father to fulfil. After that, he was ready to go to the ends of the world with her. But when he looked at the tears on her cheeks and the hope in her eyes, he nodded. She hugged him tight and showered him with kisses, and he prayed that her father wouldn't die before he could get Shivappa.

'Where is your village?' Kattappa found himself asking her. When she told him, his face was creased with worry.

'That would require crossing the river.' What worried him was that they had to cross the city too. The village lay deep in the south.

'Can you arrange a boat?' Ally asked.

'We can get one if we reach the dock. Bhairava will help—he is the only one who will ferry people like us. But reaching the dock will be difficult. How would we transport ...' Kattappa hesitated. He took a deep breath and said, 'Every caste has their own graveyard or cremation ground, Ally. The body of a leper can't be taken through the city. If the soldiers find out, there will be hell to pay. They would seize ...'

'We could use the untouchables' way.'

Kattappa nodded, but he was still worried. How could he tell her that he was being watched? He had seen the spy sitting by the entrance of the village, under the banyan tree, waiting for Sundari's permission to join the lepers. He would just have to find a way to divert the spy.

NINETEEN

Gundu Ramu

'Oaf, watch where you're going!'

Gundu Ramu turned to see the dwarf smack Thunga's head with the back of his palm. The giant gave a sheepish grin. The slash Ally had made had dried to an ugly purple scar across his face.

The cart swayed dangerously. A quarter foot to the right and the cart would have hurtled down the rocky cliff. His heart almost leapt out of his mouth. *I shouldn't lose the manuscript, I shouldn't lose it,* he repeated to himself. But as the cart steadied and resumed its tortuous path, he felt perhaps it would have been better had it ended like that. Gundu Ramu was living his worst nightmare. Behind the cart stretched a huge train of children on foot, climbing up the mountain. They were shackled to each other and the clang of the chains as they dragged themselves uphill echoed all around, disturbing birds in the sparse bushes that grew on the cliff face.

Most of the children who had tried to escape from that dreadful farm—Gundu Ramu didn't know the name of the place—had been captured, and the rest were hunted down and killed. They had travelled for many days in Akkundaraya's ships before being dropped at a grassy plain. From there, they had been trekking up hills for countless days.

Hidumba was standing on the cart with his right leg resting on Thunga's shoulder. Gundu Ramu was in the back of the cart, his hands and feet tied with a hemp rope. A fly buzzed around Gundu Ramu's nose and sat on his forehead. He shook his head and it flew up, only to come back down to land on the tip of his nose. He wished they hadn't tied his hands. It itched and pained everywhere. He was terrified at the unknown fate that awaited him.

Gundu Ramu didn't know where they were taking them, and what they were going to do with him. The mountain path seemed to stretch endlessly, climbing higher and higher, and the crisp breeze made him shiver. Used to the sweltering plains, he was finding it hard even to breathe. He could see the distant mist-clad peaks and a hint of snow at the top of Gauriparvat. The valley was covered in mist, and Mahishmathi appeared so distant and far. What would Sivagami akka be doing? The thought of Sivagami brought a lump to his throat. Would he ever meet Sivagami again? He had to escape somehow.

Hidumba had read correctly that the boy was a coward and feared physical pain. He also knew that he had led the escape attempt of the boys from the barn, though he couldn't figure out how he had managed that. Like a bully who takes pleasure in hurting hapless victims, Hidumba found that hurting Gundu Ramu was a source of merriment. He often gave dark hints about what he was going to do to the boy once they reached his place, and the terror that the boy's face reflected was a good source of amusement for the dwarf.

However, the dwarf had underestimated the power of love and sense of duty the quiet, unassuming boy had. People often called Gundu Ramu a fool. It hurt him when people did so, but he had learnt to ignore the taunts and act as if it didn't matter. His akka had asked him to keep the book safe and return it to her, and nothing in the world was going to stop him from doing that except his death.

Gundu Ramu raised his head to assess the chances for escape. The first thing he needed to do, was free his hands. The cart had stopped by the mouth of a tunnel. A small waterfall trickled by its side, and Thunga was filling his water skin. One of the horses snorted. Both horses seemed restless. They were stomping their hooves in great agitation. Hidumba clucked his tongue impatiently. The children behind watched with listless eyes.

'Fool. Don't waste the entire day pissing into your water skin. We have to cross Narakapatala before sunset.'

Gundu Ramu knew this was his chance.

'I want to pee,' Gundu Ramu whined.

Cursing Gundu Ramu, Thunga flung the water skin into the cart and came to untie the boy's legs. Gundu stood up and indicated his hands. Thunga looked at his master.

'Will he run away?' Thunga asked.

'Does he run with his hands, bastard?' The dwarf rolled his eyes. 'You should have untied his hands and not his legs.'

'Should I tie his legs again?'

'Leave it. Where can he run now?'

Thunga untied Gundu's hands, and the boy jumped down from the cart.

The road was narrow with a sheer cliff on the left, and dropping to an abyss on the right. The cart wheels were almost at the edge of the road. A steep rocky hill, with the road boring a tunnel through it, lay before them. The dwarf was right: there was nowhere to run.

As he was passing urine, Gundu watched the mist swirling in the valley. When the mist shifted, he thought he saw a glimpse of Mahishmathi city, appearing like a smudge near the horizon. That was enough for him. It may take days, but he would reach there somehow.

'Are you going to flood the valley, son of a bitch?' the dwarf asked in his usual crude and abusive way. No one had spoken to Gundu like that before, not even Uthanga or Thondaka. *Amma Gauri, show me a way,* the boy prayed. As if in answer, the air filled with a low rumbling sound. The horses started stomping the ground in panic and neighing. Gundu Ramu turned towards his captors and saw them looking up, towards the hills. Their faces were filled with terror. The forest path was silent. The horses went quiet too, as if frozen in fear. The rumble grew, and the ground started shaking. It was as if a giant snake were tunnelling its way underground. The hill before them appeared to vibrate. The trees on the cliffside leaned to one side, trembled and collapsed. Cracks appeared in the forest path. Rocks dislodged from the hill ahead and came tumbling down. Gundu Ramu screamed in terror as a boulder the size of an elephant rolled down the hill. The dwarf and his giant guard stood transfixed in horror. The boulder hit the rock that was above the tunnel entrance, spun in the air over their heads and crashed a few feet behind the cart. It rolled down the cliff, smashing trees and crushing shrubs on its way and vanished into the mist that was crawling up. When the dust settled, the air carried the pungent smell of rotten eggs. Everything was still.

Gundu Ramu was the first to recover. Death had passed by them by a hair's breadth, but he was too young to be disturbed by the near death experience, or to contemplate the unpredictability of life. He took his chance. He sprang forward, aiming to slide down the path the boulder had cleared. That it may end on some precipice, he didn't consider. He had one aim—to reach Sivagami somehow. He didn't see the lasso looping above his head. It was only when he felt a brutal jerk and fell backwards, that he was aware of the tightening noose round his neck. Everything went blank for a moment. When he opened his eyes, the hideous face of Hidumba was staring at him.

'Sleazy son of a whore, aren't you?' Hidumba grinned, tightening the noose. Gundu Ramu's eyes bulged in pain and fear. The dwarf yanked and dragged the boy towards the cart.

'Each time it gets more severe,' Thunga said in a fearful tone. 'Amma Gauri is angry. The mountain has become unstable. This is the seventh earthquake in the last three days. We should do a sacrifice to pacify Amma Gauri.'

'Shut up!' Hidumba said angrily. He jumped into the cart and, pointing to Gundu Ramu, said, 'This filthy son of a bitch has too much fat. Let's make him lean.'

Thunga lit two torches and tied it to the sides of the cart. He went to Gundu and tied the loose edge of the lasso rope to the cart. Hidumba snapped his fingers and the cart jerked forward, pulling Gundu Ramu along.

'Run, fatso, run, run. You want to run away, I shall make you run all the way,' the dwarf hollered. 'I will make you cough up your mother's milk today.'

If Gundu Ramu slowed down, the noose around his neck would choke him to death. He had no choice other than to run to keep up with the cart.

The cart entered the musty darkness of the tunnel. Behind him, Gundu could hear the fearful cries of the other children. The tunnel echoed and amplified their screams. A few bats flew past, over their heads.

Hidumba yanked Gundu Ramu and now the boy was running by the side of the cart, panting and puffing. The yells and laughs of the dwarf and Thunga and the terrified screams of the children echoed inside the tunnel. There was hardly any space between the wheel and the wall, and Gundu was running in this narrow gap, his shoulder scraping against the rough wall. Rocks protruded here and there, and the tunnel floor was uneven and slippery. The torches often touched the sides of the tunnel, throwing off sparks. The musty air was now thick with the smoke from the torches, making it difficult to breathe. Gundu Ramu was choking, terrified to death. There had to be some way to escape, something he could do, he kept telling himself. He was scared he wouldn't last for long. He tried to loosen the noose around his neck, but even a moment's slowing down only made it tighter. He could see daylight at the end of the tunnel, like the eyes of an angry beast. The air began to get lighter, and he could feel a slight breeze. His palm brushed against the pin of the wheel.

As the cart left the tunnel, Gundu Ramu pulled the pin off the wheel. The path at that point led to a steep downward slope and Gundu saw the wheel he had set free bouncing away in front of the cart. The next minute he was hurled high in the air as the cart swerved and crashed on the wall on the right. Splinters of wood spun in the air. The rope that held him snapped. The horses slipped and fell down the abyss, dragging Thunga along with them. Gundu didn't know how, but he was hanging on the edge of cliff, his legs dangling down into the abyss. The rope had coiled around his torso and was mercifully caught in some shrub. Pain shot up from his legs and blinded him for a moment. He screamed, half in fear, half in relief. There was no trace of the cart or the two men. The train of children stood watching them in fear and surprise. He pulled himself up, inch by inch, back on to the path. Mist had rolled up the mountain, veiling the road and the sun.

He lay on the path, crying, feeling sorry for the men who had died, the poor horses who had been killed for no fault of theirs, when he heard a faint cry. He sat up, wiping away the blood that trickled down his forehead. He called the children for help, but they stood frozen, their frightened eyes fixed on something. The voice was indistinct, coming through the mist. He limped towards it and stopped when he saw it was the dwarf. He was pinned under a broken wheel, his misshapen legs twisted under it grotesquely. Gundu Ramu was torn with indecision. The dwarf was pleading for help, crying he would die if he were left alone. Gundu weighed his options. Hidumba had been cruel to him, but Gundu Ramu didn't have the heart to leave a hapless man. He lifted the broken wheel up and hoisted the dwarf on his shoulders. Then he turned towards the way they had come. He would limp towards Mahishmathi, even if it took a year. He would give the manuscript back to his Sivagami akka.

'Hey, hey, boy, where are you going? This way, this way,' the dwarf pummelled Gundu Ramu's face. The boy winced but continued walking towards the tunnel.

Gundu Ramu heard a whistle. He looked up and saw that the dwarf had a bamboo whistle in his mouth and was whistling a tune. Gundu Ramu ignored it until he heard the flap of wings. He looked up and his eyes widened in shock. A giant eagle was above his head, flapping its wings, its talons a few feet from his head. He tried to run to the safety of the tunnel and there was a searing gash on his forehead before he could blink. The bird rose only to dive back almost immediately. The dwarf was laughing hysterically.

'No one escapes Gauriparvat, boy. No one escapes alive when Garuda pakshis stand guard.'

The bird was diving towards them again. Gundu Ramu turned hurriedly and the dwarf whistled another signal. The bird changed course at the last minute and hovered before them. Its cruel eyes sent shivers down Gundu Ramu's spine. Hidumba laughed and hit Gundu Ramu's head.

'Fast, fast, fast. You play any trick, you son of a bitch, and the bird will scratch the eyes off your face. He will be hovering above us, watching you. Now fast ... to Gauriparvat.'

With the heavy load of Hidumba and a heavier heart, Gundu Ramu started his climb to Gauriparvat. He heard the eagle flap its wings and rise high. He knew it would be there, above him, watching him like an angry god. The boy limped up the mountain, scared even to think about the fate that awaited him on the holy mountain. The train of children followed behind them.

TWENTY

Keki

'That's the girl I was talking about,' Keki said to Rudra Bhatta, pointing to Akhila.

They were in Revamma's mansion. In another corner of the hall, Revamma was sitting on a mat and Akhila was massaging her feet. The old woman was fanning herself with a woven palm leaf fan.

'I saw the girl hiding some food in her bundle,' Keki said. 'Revamma barely feeds the children enough. If the girl has saved some food despite that, it is to give to someone. And last time I was here, the fool Thondaka was blabbering about ghosts and I heard sounds in the attic. I think I can guess who that ghost is.'

'Are you sure?' Rudra Bhatta asked.

Keki smiled at Rudra Bhatta. 'I will show you.'

'If you are sure Shivappa is hiding here, why don't we just bring Bijjala here?'

'I have explained it to you many times, swami. We can't

risk drawing attention to ourselves. We need Shivappa to come to us.'

'What is the guarantee he will come, eunuch?'

'If she has been feeding him, he will come. These slaves have such weird notions of gratitude.' Keki smiled.

'How much is that witch Revamma asking for?'

'A thousand sovereigns.'

'That is too much,' Rudra Bhatta fussed.

'It is actually low. She doesn't know the girl won't come back. She thinks it is for something else. Otherwise, she wouldn't have agreed at all,' Keki said.

'What will you say when the girl doesn't come back?'

'We will pay for her silence. Maybe add another couple of thousands. So many children go missing.'

'But the girl is Thimma's daughter.'

'Serves the traitor right.'

'That girl Sivagami may create a ruckus. I don't know why, but she is on my back. I have a bad feeling about her. What if she wants to blackmail me about the death of Skandadasa?'

'She has more secrets to hide than us. Don't worry about a chit of a girl. Maybe we can find a way to put the blame on her for the missing child.'

'No one will believe it, Keki.'

'Oh, I am not a fool to claim that she killed her. We will say the little girl committed suicide or ran away because she was sad about her own foster sister killing her father. The thankless foster sister never cared for her and the poor orphan was driven to despair. Had Sivagami loved Thimma's daughter, won't she have taken her to live with her? Say this enough times, and people will start hating Sivagami.'

'Still. I have a bad feeling about the whole thing,' Rudra Bhatta said, his forehead shiny with perspiration.

'Swami, I have thought it through. Now let me tell you why this is doubly sweet for me. Don't you remember how I became what I became? How I lost my manhood?' Keki said.

Rudra Bhatta was uneasy. He knew the reason, but Keki didn't know it was Rudra Bhatta who had given the scriptural clearance for the punishment. Rudra Bhatta was acting as per the Dharma Shastras: Keki had raped a young girl and the punishment for rape was castration.

Keki had been a dandakara, and had fled after violating the girl. He was caught by soldiers, and they took the culprit to Thimma, the commander of the armies. Had they taken Keki to Dandanayaka Pratapa, Keki might have got away with a few lashes. Pratapa tried to get Keki into his custody, but Thimma was adamant. The soldiers had caught him, and not the dandakaras, and it was the army that would decide the punishment.

Thimma, being a man of law and principles, had asked Rajaguru Rudra Bhatta to suggest the punishment as per the Dharma Shastras. And Rudra Bhatta had suggested the milder punishment. Instead of being beheaded, Thimma ordered Keki to be castrated and dismissed from service. Keki had raged, saying he was punished only because he was a low-level dandakara. Bhoomipathis and other nobles raped and pillaged and no one said anything. There was truth in his allegation, but there was no doubt that Keki in another life had been a rapist. And he had got the punishment he deserved.

Keki always maintained that injustice was done to a poor man and she—he started referring to himself in the feminine gender after the forced castration—was determined to take her revenge. Many times, Rudra Bhatta wondered whether the eunuch's friendship with him was a part of Keki's ploy to get him in trouble. But associating with Keki had so far always resulted in profit. Unlike Pattaraya, who made many big promises but who almost got him hanged, Keki was honest in matters of money. No cheating in robbery was her motto.

Keki gestured for him to stay behind and went up to Revamma. 'Amma, a thousand is too much.'

'Oh, is it? Do me a favour. Walk straight, walk through the gate, take a left, walk for four hundred paces, take a right and then walk for two thousand paces and stop right there.'

'What?'

'The fish market is there. You can bargain to your heart's content.'

Keki laughed. 'Amma is in such a happy mood. This is why I love coming here. You make me laugh and forget all my worries.'

'Get lost.'

Keki turned back to Rudra Bhatta and shrugged. Revamma spit a stream of betel juice into a spittoon and smacked Akhila on her head. 'Massage properly, you devil.' The girl shuddered but started massaging with more vigour.

'Tell that Brahmin that he should learn not only to take but also to give. Grown fat with all the offerings made by people. Never seen a bigger miser. He is the head priest and he comes here to bargain for two copper coins,' Revamma said and spat out another stream of betel juice.

'It is for a godly purpose, Amma,' Keki said.

'I believe in only one God. Lakshmi—the goddess of money.'

'You look like Lakshmi, Amma. So divine and graceful,' Keki simpered.

'Get lost, you monkey.'

Keki looked at Rudra Bhatta, who nodded after a moment's hesitation. Keki respectfully placed a cloth bundle down. Revamma grabbed it and weighed it in her hand. Then she opened the strings and started counting the coins.

'Do you think we will short change you, Amma?'

'Of course you will, monkey. You are the type who would steal an eyeball when one winks. One has to be extra careful while dealing with you.'

'I was a dandakara once, Amma,' Keki said.

'That reminds me to count these thrice to be sure,' Revamma said.

Keki touched Akhila's shoulder and the girl cringed.

'Daughter, shall this akka take you to a place?'

Akhila shrank from Keki's touch. She looked at Revamma in fear. 'Go,' Revamma barked, without taking her eyes off the coins she was counting.

Akhila ran outside. She heard Revamma telling Keki, 'The girl's your headache.'

Akhila didn't know where to run. She could hear Keki calling her. 'Daughter, sweet pumpkin, come to Keki akka. Daughter, come, come.'

Akhila stumbled through the veranda. She tripped over Thondaka who was lying drunk, sprawled on the ground. Thondaka cursed, turned to the other side and continued to snore. Akhila had hurt her elbows. She sat crying, looking at the bruise that was forming. Keki came up to her with a smile that sent shivers down Akhila's spine.

'Why are you worried, daughter. Akka is taking you to a puja, sweet pumpkin. Don't you want the blessing of Amma Kali? See that grandpa? The one with a pot belly, he is a great wizard. He can make even the dead come alive. Don't you want to talk to your father? Your mother? He can make them talk from heaven. Come, come. Do you know, sweetheart, that even a prince is coming to attend this puja? He wants to speak to his dead ancestor and that grandpa there has promised that he will be able to. He is a great wizard, did I say that before? Come, come.'

Akhila hesitated. Keki smiled. It was working. The girl was hooked. It worked every time. The lure of a chance to speak to deceased parents always worked with children. That was how she was able to supply children for the sacrifice.

The blow came from nowhere. Keki fell back with a cry, holding her bleeding forehead. The girl—still holding on to the toddy pot with which she had hit Keki—seemed as surprised as the eunuch was. Akhila recovered from the shock quicker than Keki. She leapt over Thondaka and ran. Keki cursed and followed her. Akhila ran up the wooden stairs leading to the attic, crying for Bhutanna—ghost brother, the name she had given to Shivappa.

Shivappa, who had been watching the scene through the gaps on the attic floor, panicked when he heard Akhila running up. He could hear Keki yelling. Soon the eunuch would come up and his cover would be blown. But he couldn't leave the girl who had become his friend to the clutches of Keki. There was no time to think. He lay flat on his chest on the floor and slowly opened the attic trapdoor a little. The girl saw and rushed up, crying his name. He reached out and grabbed her hair as soon as she was within reach, and pulled her in. Keki wasn't far behind and her fingers almost got hold of Akhila's ankle. When the girl was lifted up, Keki cursed and jumped up in an attempt to catch her. Shivappa slammed the trapdoor shut, hitting Keki's face. She tumbled down the stairs and lay unconscious. Through the gaps in the wood, Shivappa watched the inmates of the orphanage rush towards Keki. He bolted the door. Akhila was crying, holding her head.

Shivappa could hear the commotion downstairs. Soon, they would be pounding the attic door. They would barge in and find him. The girl had ruined everything. She had ensured his death. A sense of helplessness grasped him. Why did the girl run up? He felt a lump of hatred rising up from the pit of his stomach. But watching her sob made his conscience stir.

'It hurt, Bhutanna,' she said between sobs.

Shivappa planted a kiss on her forehead. 'There was no time, dear. Forgive me.'

Akhila wiped away her tears with the back of her hands and said, 'It's all right. I am used to being hurt.'

The matter-of-fact way she said the words broke Shivappa's heart. He took her hand in his and said, 'Why did you bring such evil people to your Bhutanna?'

The girl told him about the puja where dead people came to talk to the loved ones they had left behind.

'But I don't trust that … that thing. Keki … I could sense she was lying. Her eyes were like that of a wolf,' Akhila said. Shivappa nodded, but he was listening to what was happening downstairs. There was now silence on the floor below, and it worried him. He peered through the gap in the floor and saw that Keki was slowly regaining consciousness. Revamma and other inmates were standing around her. Keki stood up slowly, wobbled on her legs and fell back down. She sat with her back leaning against a wall.

'There is someone up there,' Keki said. Shivappa felt his heart stop beating. He gestured for Akhila to keep quiet.

'God. God is up in her heaven,' Thondaka said, holding his palms in a gesture of prayer. Keki muttered an expletive and rubbed her forehead which had a bump the size of a lemon now. The inmates were whispering something to each other, which Shivappa couldn't catch.

'The girl has run into the attic,' Revamma said. 'She is a devil. She only must have slammed the door on you, eunuch.'

'No, there is someone else,' Keki insisted.

'Someone else indeed. Wasting my time. Bloody eunuch. Thondaka, go and see who is there.'

Thondaka cried, 'No, no. Not me. You go and look.'

'I will slap you with my slippers, donkey.'

Thondaka was terrified now. 'There is a bhuta living there.'

Revamma slapped her head with her palm. 'I don't know what to do with such a stupid son. Ghost, indeed. I will flay you alive.'

She advanced towards her son and he fled crying, 'I can't go. The ghost of that slave Shivappa lives there. He will gobble me up.'

The whisper among the inmates had now become louder. Shivappa could hear what some of them were saying. 'Yes, we have heard footsteps in the night.' 'I have seen it flying from roof to roof.' 'I was once chased by the ghost and I chanted the Gauri mantra to frighten it off. It bared its fangs, roared and vanished in a puff.' 'I have seen it crawling out of the well.'

'That girl Akhila is a witch. I have seen her sneaking into the attic often.'

'Quiet!' Revamma shouted, and the voices died down.

Akhila said to Shivappa, 'You made me promise that I should come for your help only when it was really required. Bhutanna, help me. Now they want to take me away for some puja. I am scared.'

'Shh!' Shivappa snapped. Unfortunately, his voice rang out loud and clear in the silence. Everyone's eyes turned up. Shivappa's hands trembled. He could hear Keki, Revamma and Rudra Bhatta arguing with each other about who should go up and check. He thought frantically for a way out. Should he fight them all? Someone would come up at any moment.

Akhila seemed oblivious to what was going on. Her thoughts were still on Keki and the puja. 'That eunuch even said a prince is coming to the same puja,' she said. 'He wants to talk to his dead ancestor. Is it possible to do that, Bhutanna?' Akhila asked.

Shivappa turned sharply. 'What did you say?'

'A prince is coming for the puja.'

Shivappa no longer cared what was happening downstairs. Here was the opportunity he was waiting for.

'Where is the puja?' he asked, trying to keep the excitement from his voice. Akhila was confused.

'I ... I don't know.'

Shivappa put a reassuring hand on her shoulder and said, 'Listen, daughter. You go along with the eunuch for the puja.'

'I am scared, Bhutanna. Something evil is going to happen.'

'Nothing will happen to you, dear. You have my word. Don't you believe this Bhutanna? Trust me. You go with them without any protest. I am there for you.'

Akhila nodded after a moment's hesitation. He placed his palm on her head and said, 'Promise. Trust me. I will be there for you.'

The girl hugged him and he felt a prick of conscience. He was sending the girl into the jaws of danger. 'I will be there,' he repeated, more to reassure himself. 'Now be a good girl and go down.'

Akhila nodded and opened the attic door. A hush fell when she started descending the stairs. Shivappa picked up his sword and slung it over the shoulders. He knew he didn't have much time. He heard Revamma slapping Akhila and the girl crying. *Oh God, I hope I have done the right thing*, he thought. He pushed away the guilt he felt into a dark corner of his mind. He could hear the loud arguing.

'You go. You are the tantric. You know how to catch a ghost.' Revamma's voice could be heard above the loud protests of Rudra Bhatta.

'I am the rajaguru. A senior official. And you want me to crawl into your dusty, dirty attic to catch some ghost? How insulting,' Rudra Bhatta shouted back.

Good, thought Shivappa. With them busy arguing down there, he would get a few precious moments. Then he heard the footsteps. They were soft, careful ones. He knew it was Keki, sneaking up while Revamma and Rudra Bhatta fought.

Quick, quick, quick. Shivappa frantically looked around for a way out. He removed a roof tile and tried to crawl out onto the roof. But the gap was too small. Another one had to be removed. It slipped from his hands and crashed down, but he managed to crawl out onto the roof. He sat panting outside, sweating in the afternoon sun.

Keki had seen Shivappa's legs vanishing through the hole. She picked up the broken tile from the attic floor and smiled. *The fly is trapped in the web I wove,* she said to herself, feeling smug. She looked up at the hole in the roof through which Shivappa had vanished.

Rudra Bhatta came up then. He had lost the argument with Revamma. 'There is no ghost here. All stupid, superstitious people,' Keki said. She nudged Rudra Bhatta, who was looking up at the hole in the roof, and winked at him.

'The prince will be waiting. Let's hurry,' Keki said loudly, and as they left the attic, she stole a glance towards the hole in the roof. There was no trace of Shivappa, but Keki was sure he would come to the puja. 'Our good times are coming,' she said to Rudra Bhatta as they climbed down the stairs.

Shivappa had heard Keki, as she had expected. He was frustrated that he didn't know where the puja was happening. He had given his word to Akhila that no harm would befall her. He scrambled down to the edge of the roof and jumped to the mango tree on the rear side of the orphanage. He skirted the compound wall and saw the chariot parked there. An idea bubbled up in his mind. It was crazy, but doable. It was perhaps his only chance. He looked around to see if anyone was there, and then ran to the chariot. He crawled under it and then hurriedly untied his dhoti from his waist. He tied himself to the underside of the chariot. His face was inches away from the ground. It was going to be a rough and bumpy ride. But it would take him to his destiny. He waited for Rudra Bhatta and Keki to come with Akhila and take him to his enemy.

Shivappa didn't know that he had been seen by a spy posted by Brihannala to keep a watch on Revamma's mansion. The spy ran to meet his master. When Brihannala heard what he had to say, she sent word to Neelappa. She also sent the spy with a message for one of the beggars who roamed around the untouchables' village. The beggar, Trivikrama, seemed blind, but he found his way to the lepers' village without much difficulty. He was one of the ace spies in Brihannala's network. Ruthless and quick, he was feared and respected among the assorted revolutionary groups hiding in the forests of Mahishmathi. Trivikrama took a place among the other beggars under the banyan tree at the entrance of the village. He sat facing the setting sun, keeping a safe distance from another beggar who had only one leg.

Trivikrama started singing in a voice so loud that it carried through the village. To everyone else, it was an old song about a king going away for a hunt. But to Ally, the words had great significance. She was sitting beside Kattappa, watching the sun set by the river. The space between the wall of the lepers' cremation ground and the river offered them some privacy. When she heard the lines, 'The king has left his palace', repeated thrice, she knew the time had come to do the thing that she had always dreaded.

TWENTY-ONE

Neelappa

Leaning against a lamp post and panting from exertion, Neelappa rued how age had caught up with him. Brihannala didn't care. No one cared. Who cared for a slave, anyway? But Neelappa was no one's slave. *No, you are a slave to a great cause. You are a slave to freedom,* he thought. He laughed, but it rang false. A small cog in a huge wheel on a speeding chariot—he was nothing more than that. The charioteer was unknown and the destination unclear, yet it carried him, rattling through the uneven pathways of life.

The spy had informed Brihannala that he had seen Shivappa sneaking out through the roof of Revamma's mansion and crawling underneath Rudra Bhatta's chariot.

The street-lighting wagon came rumbling through the lane, carrying a wooden barrel of oil and a pile of cloth-wound torches. Neelappa moved to the shadows, waiting for the lamp lighters to finish their work. The lamp lighter placed a torch in the designated hole after dipping it in the oil barrel. He lit the torch and went to light the next pole. The flickering light from the torch cast pale circles of golden light that dissolved into the thick lake of shadows beyond its rims. Neelappa kept to the dark as he headed to the rear of Revamma's mansion and climbed the wall. Panting with effort, the old man landed like a cat on the other side. He could hear the loud chants of the evening prayers from the courtyard.

Rudra Bhatta was chanting some prayers and the children were repeating them. Neelappa saw Keki standing, leaning against a pillar, a bored expression on her face. Akhila was standing near Rudra Bhatta, her eyes closed in prayer. Her face was pale with fear.

Neelappa circumvented the house, keeping to the compound wall, and then darted towards the chariot in the front courtyard. He crept into the saddle seat and nudged the horse. It started ambling forward. The loud chanting drowned out the rumble of the chariot wheels. The moment the chariot entered the street, he whipped the horse to gather speed. He could hear Shivappa struggling to get free: perhaps he had guessed that it wasn't Rudra Bhatta riding the chariot. Instead of taking the forest path, the chariot was heading towards the royal highway.

From the royal highway, the sound of cymbals and drums broke the silence of the night. The cries of 'Guru Dharmapala, Jaya Satyachara' filled the air. Neelappa turned the chariot towards the sound and reached the main avenue of Dasapattana.

A procession led by Guru Dharmapala was winding its way through the streets. The devotees were dancing and singing, and a huge crowd was following them. A person walking beside Guru Dharmapala caught his attention. Prince Mahadeva. Neelappa smiled at the sight. The prince appeared to have become enamoured by the guru, and was walking like a commoner. The guru, on his open palanquin, carried by four able-bodied monks, was showering his blessings on the crowd that thronged on either side of the main street.

A cart stopped behind Neelappa's chariot, and the cart driver rang the bell in fury, abusing Neelappa for blocking the way. Neelappa apologised and pointed to the horse, 'My mare has developed a limp,' Neelappa replied sheepishly.

'Move to one side, old man. I wonder why the rich allow such senile people to drive their chariots,' the cart man shouted.

Apologising profusely, Neelappa jumped down from his seat and led the horse by its reins to the side. The cart squeezed through the narrow thoroughfare and joined the cortege. A group of excited children passed by, playing on palm leaf whistles and toy drums.

Neelappa peered under the chariot and saw that Shivappa had managed to partially untie himself. Neelappa said, 'My king, we are now in a crowded street. The moment people see you, they will lynch us to death. Please co-operate with this humble slave.'

He didn't get an answer, but smiled when he saw Shivappa had stopped trying to untie himself. It was fortunate that this had happened today, when there was such a big crowd on the streets. It made Shivappa's escape impossible. Neelappa led the chariot into the crowd that was flowing towards the ashram of Guru Dharmapala. They were going for his spiritual talk on amavasya day. The guru had gathered a huge following with his witty speeches, down-to-earth manners, the ability to manifest sacred ash and trinkets out of thin air, and his capacity to provide answers for all problems under the sun.

Neelappa allowed the chariot to drift along with the procession for some time till it approached the river port, near which was situated the ashram. A few minutes later, Neelappa nudged the horse to take a slight left turn, into a narrow street. The intricately carved wooden door of a huge storage house creaked open as the chariot approached, and he led the horse into it.

As soon as he stopped, Shivappa freed himself, rolled down on the floor and ran towards the door, but it shut a moment before Shivappa reached it.

'Easy, Your Highness,' Neelappa said as he walked towards Shivappa. He slowed down when Shivappa drew his sword. The boom of drums from the procession outside echoed inside the storage hall, its emptiness amplifying the sound.

'Open the door,' Shivappa growled.

As if on cue, the door creaked open and Shivappa turned on his heel. Brihannala entered the warehouse and the door shut again. Shivappa rushed towards Brihannala, who stood with her arms across her chest. Shivappa stopped short a feet before Brihannala and said in a menacing voice, 'Move.'

'Your people need you. We are taking you to where you're needed.'

'A girl's life is in danger. Upon Amma Gauri, I will cut off your head if you stand in my way,' Shivappa said and raised his sword.

Neelappa saw the movement of Brihannala's eyebrows. He knew what it meant. *A sin, a mortal sin to hit the king,*

Neelappa thought as he sneaked up towards Shivappa with his unsheathed sword.

'But didn't you see this?' Brihannala said, holding out something in her hand. Shivappa could not make out what it was and leaned forward, sensing Neelappa's presence behind him a tad late. He turned, swinging his sword, but Neelappa was quicker. With all the strength he could muster in his seven-decade-old hands, Neelappa brought the hilt of the sword down on Shivappa's forehead. He watched with horror as his king swayed and then collapsed to the floor, unconscious.

'Forgive me, Your Highness,' Neelappa said as he knelt beside the prone figure of their king and checked his breath by keeping two fingers under Shivappa's nostrils. With tears brimming in his eyes, the old man asked, 'Swami, have I killed our king?'

'You're a model citizen, old man,' Brihannala chuckled, as she hoisted Shivappa's unconscious body on his shoulders. 'All citizens should imitate you. Any leader who behaves like a mule needs this kind of a smack on his head to bring him to his senses.'

Neelappa struggled to keep his tears in check as he staggered towards the rear end of the warehouse, which opened out onto the wharf. Brihannala followed, carrying Shivappa on her shoulders, and placed him down near the door.

Brihannala and Neelappa waited, hoping Ally would come soon, the tense silence thickening between them. The future of the revolution hinged on the next few moments and how Ally and Trivikrama, the spy he had sent to her, would handle Kattappa.

TWENTY-TWO

Kattappa

Kattappa was mesmerised by the mellifluous voice of the beggar. When the song stopped abruptly, he turned to Ally to comment about it, and found she was missing. 'Ally, Ally?' he called out.

He looked around, but could not see her. She liked to play this game of hide and seek with him, and he assumed this was another instance. 'If I catch you, you will regret it, come out,' he teased her. There was no response. Night was falling now, and dread filled his mind. Had she left after kindling the fire of love in his heart? He checked every bush, behind every tree, calling her name. Except for the croaking of frogs, the night was silent and indifferent to his pleas.

At that moment, Ally was sneaking into Malla's hut. The old leper was awake, and when he saw her entering the hut, and saw what was written on her face, he started trembling with fear. 'Kattappa, Kattappa, son ...' the old beggar tried crying out, but his voice was too weak. Ally clasped his mouth shut.

'Sorry, Malla,' she whispered, looking at him with all the compassion she could muster. 'This is a liberation for you from this miserable life,' she said as she curled her fingers around his neck. The leper thrashed his legs about as he fought for breath. Even this wretched, disease-ridden life was precious to him. He didn't care about being lucky in his next life. He clung to his present one with all the will he could muster, but he was no match for the determination of a woman who was willing to do anything for what she believed was a great cause.

By the time Kattappa reached the hut, Ally had finished wrapping the body of Malla in his own mattress.

Kattappa saw her lying limp on the covered body. She was whimpering, 'Father, father.' While he was happy to have found her, Kattappa's heart broke seeing her crying. He knelt beside her and she threw herself on him and sobbed. 'I felt it in my bones. I rushed and was lucky to reach on time,' she sniffled. 'He didn't suffer much in the end. I loved him so much. If only I could take him to our village …'

'Devi,' Kattappa said in a hoarse voice. Tears had made his vision blurry. 'Devi, I promise I shall help you take him to your village. I shall find Bhairava and ask him to ferry us to the other side.'

Ally hugged him tight and wept.

Kattappa's chest swelled with pride. He was being a man to the woman he loved. He would do anything for her. Kattappa shed a few tears for the abusive leper that he had served for a few months, and then left her sobbing beside the body.

Kattappa went to Sundari's hut. Behind the hut was where the leader of the leper gang kept her handcart, which she used to carry what they foraged from garbage bins. Kattappa knew Sundari would be furious when she found out that the handcart was missing. His stay in the leper's village would end with this act. Kattappa wrapped his turban on the rickety wooden wheels of the handcart so they wouldn't rattle and pushed it to Malla's hut.

'You must take your father to the river dock in this,' Kattappa said. 'I have some urgent work to do first.'

'What are you going to do?' Ally asked, surprised.

Kattappa didn't answer her question. 'Push the cart to the dock through the untouchables' way,' Kattappa said and took off. As he expected, when he passed the banyan tree, a lame beggar who was sleeping under the banyan tree at the village entrance got up. Bhanu Gupta was the spy Maharaja Somadeva had ordered to keep an eye on Kattappa, and he was one of the king's best guptacharas.

The sense of urgency in Kattappa's stride made Bhanu Gupta suspicious. He started following Kattappa stealthily, using his stick as a crutch and hopping behind the slave at a safe distance. When Bhanu Gupta found it difficult to keep up with Kattappa, he cursed, bent down, and untied his left leg. He flexed his knee twice, and then rushed to catch up with Kattappa with the strides of a trained soldier.

The 'blind' beggar Trivikrama was watching them. When he was sure that both the lame beggar and Kattappa had moved out of sight, he went towards the river. He plunged into the swirling darkness of the Mahishi river. With clean strokes, he started swimming downstream, towards the lepers' cremation ground. Ally was waiting for him there.

'He ran away, Trivikrama,' Ally said when he emerged from the river.

Trivikrama grunted in reply. 'I don't think he is going to come back. He is being shadowed by Mahishmathi's spy.'

Together, they pushed the handcart with the dead body of Malla through the wild, pothole-ridden untouchables' path, towards the dock.

As Kattappa ran through the labyrinth of Dasapattana's streets, he realised that the king hadn't freed him because he felt pity on him—he was just the means through which they would find Shivappa. Kattappa wasn't on Shivappa's trail, but the spy wouldn't know it.

Taking the body of a leper on a boat meant for ferrying passengers could land him in trouble. Lepers were supposed to be cremated within a few hours of their death. He had time only till dawn, which was not very far. Kattappa had to shake off the spy and reach the dock on time.

He was careful not to look behind as he ran. Any such move would alert the spy that his prey was aware of the hunter's presence. Kattappa swerved to the right, entering a narrower street consisting of the thatched houses of the poor. The sounds of merriment floated in from a distance. It appeared that some procession was winding its way through some part of the lower city of Dasapattana. The houses looked deserted. Perhaps the inhabitants had gone to take part in the procession.

Kattappa reached a dark alley and stood undecided about which way to take. The street forked at that point, and both paths were crowded with houses leaning towards a putrid canal that carried the city waste from upper Mahishmathi. He could sense the presence of the spy a few score feet away, hiding in the shadows. Kattappa took a left, towards the royal city, and when he was sure he was out of the line of sight of the spy, he slid into the canal.

Rodents scampered away as Kattappa crouched in the bushes, ankle-deep in the slush of the canal, waiting for the spy to appear. In a few moments, the spy came up and paused. Kattappa knew the man had seen him take a right, and as expected, he headed towards upper Mahishmathi, away from the river.

Kattappa waited for a few minutes before wading through the stinking drain water towards the river. He passed the huts of leather workers, some of whom were drinking arrack by the canal.

As he made his way through the canal, a few dogs from the leather workers' village started barking. Soon a pack of them started running parallel to the canal, barking into the darkness. Kattappa knew they had smelled him. People may ignore the dogs, but their barking was sure to alert a trained spy. He would return soon to investigate, and it wouldn't take him long to figure out the path Kattappa had used. Kattappa began to run through the shallow canal.

As the canal neared the river, it widened, and more canals carrying dirty water joined it. The water, putrid and stinking, rose to his chest. In the dull light that fell from the carpenters' alley, it was difficult to figure out the correct path to the river. He let himself float for some time. The pack of dogs continued to follow him, barking and running alongside the canal. Mercifully, the canal emptied into the river at that point, and Kattappa was sucked into a whirlpool.

Moving from the sluggish canal, the cold, rushing water of the Mahishi caught Kattappa by surprise. It had probably rained in Gauriparvat, for the water was flowing swiftly, he thought. He swam upstream, hoping to get to the untouchables' way.

Kattappa climbed on to the shore when he thought it was safe. He looked around to see whether the spy had followed him. Satisfied that he was alone, he started running towards the untouchables' village, hoping to meet Ally midway. He spotted her near the bend in the river, where seven palm trees stood in a line. Ally was pushing the cart with great difficulty.

'We have to be quick,' Kattappa said as he began pushing the cart as well. They walked in silence. After a few minutes, Kattappa suddenly gestured for Ally to stop. He tip-toed towards the palm grove and drew his sword. He looked around and then ran back to catch up with Ally.

'I thought someone was following us,' he said.

'You're paranoid,' Ally said, looking behind her shoulder. Trivikrama was the most well-trained spy in Achi Nagamma's army, and it was unlikely that he could be easily traced by Kattappa. It was a miracle that Kattappa had even sensed his presence. Ally felt a surge of irrational pride in Kattappa's skills.

As they were turning a corner, Kattappa grabbed Ally's hand and they halted. A man carrying a torch was approaching them.

'Who goes there?' cried the man.

'A poor man carrying yam to the market, swami,' Kattappa replied. Ally gripped Kattappa's arm in panic. The man came up to them and Kattappa's blood froze. It was the spy he thought he had managed to escape from.

'What is in this?' Bhanu Gupta asked, poking the bundled up body of Malla. Kattappa reacted quickly. He picked up the man by his waist and slammed him on the ground. He stunned the man using marma vidya, the martial art technique which he had used on Shivappa the previous year. The man collapsed in a heap. Kattappa dragged him to the bushes on the side.

'Is he dead?' Ally asked.

'Just unconscious. He will come out of it soon,' Kattappa said as he checked the man's pulse. He then got up and began pushing the cart towards the dock. Ally looked back to see whether Trivikrama was following, dreading what was to come.

As they reached the dock, Kattappa exclaimed, 'Ah, we are in luck. Bhairava is there.'

Instructing Ally to stay behind, Kattappa walked up to the dock. A lone torch hung from one of the wooden piers, throwing off a dull circular patch of light. A few steps down the ghat, the old boat of Bhairava was moored.

'Bhairava,' Kattappa called, but Bhairava was drunk and out cold. Kattappa was focused on trying to wake him up, and he didn't notice Ally pushing the cart towards a warehouse near the docks. She knocked on the door and kept an eye on Kattappa as the door creaked open. Ally pushed the cart inside and Brihannala and Neelappa quickly replaced the dead body of Malla with that of the unconscious Shivappa. Ally had just made it back, when Kattappa turned. He said helplessly, 'The drunkard is not waking up.'

'Can we take the boat?' Ally asked.

Kattappa hesitated. 'That would be stealing.'

'Please, Kattappa...'

Reluctantly, Kattappa nodded and climbed up the ghat steps. He lifted what he thought was Malla's body, staggered down the steps, and placed it gently on the boat. 'Never thought the old leper would be so heavy,' he said.

Ally stood on the ghats without moving. In the flickering light of the torch, he saw tears in her eyes. Kattappa smiled, holding out his hand to her. 'Don't worry, I shall take you and your father across to your village and return.'

Ally closed her eyes and a teardrop escaped. She could sense Trivikrama crouching behind her, like a cobra about to strike. Any moment he would lash out and kill Kattappa, and she didn't want to see it when it happened. Kattappa was untying the rope that moored the boat, and Ally saw him stiffen for a moment. Everything that happened after that was a blur for Ally. She saw Trivikrama leap up above her head with his dagger in his hand. In a flash, Kattappa had drawn his sword and flung it at Trivikrama without even turning around. Ally muffled a scream as Trivikrama landed at the feet of Kattappa—his dagger had only made a scratch on Kattappa's right thigh. The spy shuddered once and then lay still, face down, Kattappa's sword plunged deep in his back. Blood spread out on the ghat steps and merged with the flowing water of the Mahishi river.

Kattappa ran up to Ally. 'Are you all right, Ally? Are you all right?' he asked, wiping away the blood that had splattered across her face. She was trembling all over. When she nodded, Kattappa knelt before the body of Trivikrama, slowly pulled out the sword, and washed it in the river. When he turned back, his cheeks were wet. Ally touched his shoulder, but he fell on his knees before the inert body of Trivikrama and touched the feet. 'I am sorry. I have never raised my sword against a Mahishmathi soldier. Forgive me.'

Ally wanted to tell him that Trivikrama wasn't a Mahishmathi soldier, but a revolutionary, an enemy of the state, and Kattappa had not broken his vow to serve the country till his last breath. But she stayed silent, feeling miserable for her duplicity. She gently touched his shoulder and Kattappa stood up, quickly recovering his composure.

'We should leave immediately,' Ally said. Kattappa nodded. 'What to do with him?' Ally asked. 'Should we take it too and drop it somewhere deep? Leaving it here would be dangerous.'

'Let it be there. Let the poor soldier that this sinner killed get a proper funeral. I don't want him to be eaten by the fishes of Mahishi.'

'You're crazy,' Ally said. 'Throw the body into the water. No one will know. There are no witnesses.'

'There is one.'

'Who?'

'My conscience.'

Ally took a deep breath. She was uncomfortable leaving the body of Trivikrama on the ghats. Ally stole a glance at the warehouse door. She hoped Brihannala would take care of it. Ally stepped into the boat and Kattappa rowed it towards the middle of the river. The boat caught the current and started moving swiftly.

'Ally, I want to say something ...' Kattappa's voice trailed away. Ally was looking beyond Kattappa's shoulders, at Brihannala and Neelappa sneaking out of the warehouse and rushing towards the ghat. She saw them fling two bodies into the river—Malla's and Trivikrama's—and then disappear back into the shadows.

'Ally?' Kattappa said, and she shuddered. She couldn't see his face in the darkness, and she didn't want to see it either.

'Devi, I hope we never see each other again.'

A sob rose in Ally's throat. His words, so innocently said, took ominous form in her mind. Brihannala's instruction had been to kill Kattappa the moment Shivappa was loaded in the boat. She had failed, and probably sensing her dilemma, Trivikrama had come to finish her task. She was responsible for the death of one of the most efficient spies in their movement. Yet, she was feeling guilty for what she was doing to Kattappa.

Kattappa's voice cracked. 'It isn't that I don't love you, devi. It is because I love you so much that I don't want to see you again. I have gone against my oath, and I have killed a soldier of Mahishmathi. I don't deserve freedom. I don't deserve this life at all. Once I leave you and come back here, I need to find someone and do an important thing. Then I will surrender. They will hang me, but it is all right if I can do that one thing before I die.'

'What is that?' Ally asked, dreading the answer.

'Kill my brother Shivappa,' Kattappa said, with an intensity that made Ally shiver. Between them lay Shivappa, wrapped in the mattress of the leper, unconscious, unmoving. At the feet of Kattappa lay the future of Ally's people.

There couldn't be a bigger betrayal, thought Ally, than what she was doing to her Kattappa. There were only a few moments in her life when she hated the revolutionary army that she had been dedicated to since childhood, but nothing came close to this. She felt broken inside.

Kattappa rowed furiously and the boat glided through the water. *How will I, Amma Gauri, how will I?* Ally pleaded. *How will I thrust a sword into his back?*

TWENTY-THREE

Rudra Bhatta

Rudra Bhatta impatiently paced the veranda of his home. Some idiot had taken his chariot from Revamma's mansion in Dasapattana. His son Kalicharan had gone to find his chariot or borrow or steal one if he couldn't find it soon enough. Rudra Bhatta couldn't even complain to a dandakara as he didn't want to explain what he was doing in Dasapattana. He knew Keki and Bijjala would reach the Rakta Kali temple soon, with the girl to be sacrificed, and Rudra Bhatta was worried he wouldn't make it there in time.

Just then, Gomati, his daughter-in-law, walked out of the house.

'Where are you going at this time?' Rudra Bhatta snapped at her.

'There is a spiritual discourse at Guru Dharmapala's ashram,' Gomati said.

'You are going alone? Without your husband?'

'I know the way,' Gomati said.

'You ... you ...!' Rudra Bhatta exploded in rage.

'The guru says we are all free souls and no one is bound by any relationship. I shall go, for I am free,' Gomati said with a smile.

'Woman ...' Rudra Bhatta's lips trembled in anger. 'You ... you ... how dare you? You are my daughter-in-law. If people see you there ... in that imposter's place, what will they think of me? Go inside. Go, go!'

'I will wait for my husband to come then. I shall take him too.'

Rudra Bhatta was livid. He pointed his finger to the door and said, 'Go inside now!'

Gomati stomped inside and slammed the door shut. Rudra Bhatta's mood worsened. He was being questioned in his own home. He was being disobeyed, disrespected. All because of that guru Dharmapala. Rudra Bhatta hated the newcomer. The new guru had taken away most of his patrons, and only a few old faithfuls approached him with their horoscopes or to do some occult puja or the other.

Rudra Bhatta seethed with jealousy and indignation. He had held the Mahishmathi nobles in his grip through his knowledge of the ancient scriptures and his colourful interpretations. He had become rich by offering secret occult pujas. There was always demand for the shatrusamhara yajna, a sacrifice to destroy one's enemy, or dhanakarshana yajna, to attract money. Now Dharmapala was selling amulets from his ashram, which he claimed gave the same effect as an elaborate sacrifice.

His son Kalicharan's wayward habits had drained most of Rudra Bhatta's wealth, and now all of the rajaguru's hopes were pinned on the generous reward Bijjala had offered if they caught Shivappa.

Everything had gone smoothly so far. As expected, no one bothered about the disappearance of a few street urchins of low birth. As if it were a new thing for Mahishmathi to miss a few children, Rudra Bhatta smirked. Where had his fool of a son gone?

He rushed to the gate when he heard the sound of a chariot and saw his son riding it.

'I found the chariot near the ashram of that new guru. Some fanatical devotee of the guru might have taken it to reach the ashram fast.'

Rudra Bhatta cursed the guru heartily. The man would die like a worm, he would be beaten to death like a dog, the priest said.

'I have arranged the things you wanted, let's go now,' Kalicharan said.

'Your wife was being rude to me,' Rudra Bhatta said as he climbed into the chariot.

'I will deal with her once we are back, Nanna,' Kalicharan said, but that didn't improve his father's mood.

The chariot took a sweeping turn on the broad streets of the agrahara and rattled towards the Rakta Kali temple.

A few moments later, Gomati sneaked out of her home. She wasn't going for any discourse. She hoped she wouldn't be late in meeting Sivagami.

TWENTY-FOUR

Sivagami

'Where were you, Mama?' Sivagami asked angrily as Neelappa came up, panting and puffing. She was standing by the gate of her home, impatient and irritated.

Neelappa mumbled an apology without looking at Sivagami's face. Sivagami felt guilty seeing the old man standing with sagging shoulders. She didn't have the heart to scold him. Neelappa took to heart even mildly harsh words, and would retract into sullen silence.

'Let's go,' Sivagami said, patting his shoulder as a gesture of apology. Neelappa rushed to the chariot and she glimpsed that his eyes were wet. *Even a little display of kindness makes him so happy*, she shook her head with a smile.

It was past midnight when they left the main avenue. Sivagami became cautious as the chariot entered the untouchables' path. A thunderstorm threatened to break any moment, and lightning occasionally fissured the western horizon. The air had an uncomfortable heaviness, and not a leaf stirred. Sivagami saw a figure move out of the shadows from behind a banyan tree ahead. She tapped Neelappa's shoulder, and the chariot stopped.

'You are late,' Gomati complained as she got into the chariot. Sivagami nodded. She couldn't tell the woman that she'd had to make other arrangements.

On her instructions, Neelappa guided the chariot off the untouchables' path and through the lepers' cremation ground, entering the forest from there. They needed to avoid the sentry post on the way. The chariot entered a thick grove and Gomati touched Sivagami's wrist in warning.

'We need to walk from here. And we need to hide the chariot.'

Sivagami and Gomati got down while Neelappa took the chariot some distance away. He camouflaged the chariot using tree branches and hurried back to them carrying a tiny lamp.

'Vajra?' Sivagami asked in a worried voice. She didn't want the horse to make a noise at the wrong time.

'He will be calm,' Neelappa reassured her, as he walked behind the two women with his sword unsheathed.

The jungle was thick and dark, with the forest canopy obfuscating even the dull light of the moon. Neelappa shielded the lamp with the cusp of his palm, allowing it to light only the path ahead. It took some time for Sivagami's eyes to adjust to the darkness. What she saw filled her with foreboding. There were dilapidated structures all around, partially hidden by creepers and trees growing from the crevices. It looked like an abandoned temple, perhaps unused for hundreds of years.

They entered a clearing, in the middle of which was a derelict temple, its roof caving in. They walked towards it with careful steps. Something slithered away as they stepped into the pillared hall that was open on three sides. At the far end, there was an idol, almost twelve feet tall. It was hidden in the shadows, but its eyes shone an eerie blue in the darkness.

Neelappa restrained them from stepping forward and pointed to the floor. On the ground were traces of a strange rangoli design made with red powder. A sudden flash of lightning lit the hall, and Sivagami gasped at what she could now see. The huge idol of Rakta Kali stared down at her. With ten arms and ten heads, each more grotesque than the other, Kali looked fierce and intimidating. However, what horrified Sivagami wasn't the idol—it was the garland she wore. She was used to seeing garlands of skulls in temples. Usually the skulls were sculpted from wood. But this idol had the severed heads of humans. Some were in an advanced stage of decomposition and some had already turned into skulls.

Suppressing her urge to vomit, she moved to the idol. She paused a few feet away and then turned back, fighting tears. The skulls were not of adults, but of children. Gomati was crying softly.

'How long has he been doing this? And why haven't you reported this to any official so far?'

Sivagami's fear and revulsion had turned into anger.

'I only found out recently, devi. He suddenly seemed to have more money and precious gifts, and that made me suspicious. It coincided with the rumours of the ghost in the city, and I knew he was making money off it. I was sure my father-in-law had got some rich patron, and was doing occult pujas for him. There are many children who forage for food in the area behind the temple, where leftover prasadam is thrown.

I became close to one of them, and the boy complained about his missing friends. He said he was scared of a ghost that came in the night and took away children sleeping on the pavement. I assumed it was a child's imagination, and then, one day, the boy disappeared.' Tears rolled down Gomati's cheeks.

'Why didn't you rush to the authorities?'

'With what proof, Amma? The women of the agrahara don't enjoy that kind of freedom. And my father-in-law is powerful. I don't know anyone in an influential position that I can trust. I can't go to an ordinary dandakara and complain about the chief priest of Mahishmathi. The only person I could have informed …'

Gomati started crying softly. 'The only honest person I could have informed was long dead by then.'

'Skandadasa?' Sivagami asked, surprised that was the only name that sprung up in her mind when Gomati talked about honesty. 'But how did you know him? He was the mahapradhana of Mahishmathi.'

Gomati gathered herself and said, 'He was everything to me once.' Her voice was defiant, as if she expected Sivagami to challenge her. The way she said it made it clear that she still cared for the man deeply.

'But how?' That question came out inadvertently. Sivagami hadn't meant it the way it sounded.

'But how?' Gomati's lips curled in derision. 'That was the question even my father asked when I said I wanted to marry the man I loved. There is no scholar greater than my father in Mahishmathi. He can quote all the Vedas backwards. Reciting all the Upanishads is child's play to him. He has learnt all the six systems of philosophy in depth, written books on them. And he is a great man, have no doubt about it. How many Brahmins would adopt a bear dancer's son and bring him home? How many upper-caste men would allow an untouchable inside their house and teach him the Vedas? How many scholars would have the courage to face the orthodox and defeat them in debates by proving that the Vedas don't sanction caste and that the Smritis have no scriptural basis? How many would train this untouchable to become his successor and ensure he succeeds as mahapradhana of the country? My father is a great man indeed.'

'You are the daughter of Mahapradhana Parameswara?' Sivagami asked incredulously.

'Yes, but not anymore. I stopped considering him as my father the day he forced me to marry Rudra Bhatta's son. My great, learned father, who believes in the equality of all men, baulked when it came to his own daughter's marriage to an untouchable. All his progressive thinking ended there. The man who had even fought with the king to ensure Skandadasa succeeded him as mahapradhana, he thought about jaati, gotra and kula when it came to the marriage of his daughter. And he forced me to marry Kalicharan Bhatta. So what if the man is a drunkard, abuses women, is a fanatic and mentally unstable—he belongs to a great kula, gotra and jaati,' she said sarcastically.

'And Skandadasa didn't fight for you?' Sivagami asked.

'And become a thankless devil in the bargain? My Skandadasa would have committed suicide before he did anything that would hurt my father. And I would have been disappointed had he done anything like that. I would have gained a husband I loved, but then, it wouldn't have been

Skandadasa but a man who put his selfish wants before gratitude. My Skandadasa wasn't a man like that.'

Sivagami could hear the pride in Gomati's voice. Even after so many years, she was defending Skandadasa's actions. She couldn't understand the kind of gratitude that would overwhelm one's love. But who was she to talk about gratitude? Wasn't she the one who killed the man who had brought her up?

'It was my father's fault. And mine too. I should have ended my life then and there. It was he, my Skandadasa, who persuaded me to live. He loved life so much.'

And he threw it away for an unworthy empire, thought Sivagami, though she didn't voice it aloud.

They heard footsteps approaching the temple and Gomati dragged Sivagami behind the idol. They could hear each other's heartbeats. Neelappa quickly hid behind a pillar. A long shadow fell on the intricate drawing on the floor. Sivagami peeped out from behind the idol.

Rudra Bhatta was carrying a rooster and a curved sword in one hand, and a lamp in the other. He placed the skull-shaped lamp at the centre of the drawing and began a strange chant for Rakta Kali. 'Amma, Kali, Rakta Chamundi,' he cried. 'You are thirsty. You want blood. You aren't like other gods and goddesses who are satisfied with mere offerings of coconuts, garlands or a few copper coins thrown at your feet. You are real. You are the truth. You want blood, for with blood we all are made. Isn't it the duty of sons to quench their mother's thirst? Your drink is coming, your food is coming, Amma. This time, it is a girl. I hope your thirst shall be quenched tonight.'

Rudra Bhatta took out colourful powders from the bag slung over his shoulder and spread it on the floor. He sprinkled some water from a jug, chanting all the time, and started sketching a tantric design on the floor with the powders. He kept looking over his shoulder, as if expecting someone. Holding the sword with both hands, he closed his eyes. After a few moments of frantic chanting, he held the rooster and stood up. He ran thrice round the tantric drawing, and then, in a swift move, severed the head of the rooster. Blood spurted from the neck of the bird, and he directed some towards the Rakta Kali idol, and then some into his own mouth, before flinging the headless body on the floor.

He made a circle of blood around the drawing and started swaying in a trance, chanting mantras.

Sivagami leapt out from behind the idol, grabbing the trident from its hand on her way. She kicked Rudra Bhatta, and he fell on his back. She pressed him down to the floor with her foot and pressed the trident to his throat.

A scream died mid-way in Rudra Bhatta's throat. He was dazed by the sudden appearance of Sivagami. He lay stunned and immobile.

'D-don't k-k-kill me, Devi ... Amma ... Kali ...' he pleaded.

'Not so easily, not so soon, Rudra Bhatta. You have a lot to answer for before you die,' said Sivagami. It required all her self-control to prevent herself from thrusting the trident into his throat. Anger throbbed in her veins and she looked as if the Rakta Kali idol had come to life. Gomati, watching the scene from behind the idol, unconsciously pressed her palms together in obeisance.

'Why did the king kill Devaraya?' Sivagami asked. The priest blinked, uncomprehending.

'You don't remember Devaraya? Look at my face, you devil.'

Rudra Bhatta stared at her. As recognition finally came, his face contorted with rage. 'You bitch,' he screamed and grabbed Sivagami's ankle. Sivagami raised the trident high to strike him and the priest's eyes bulged in terror. Sivagami brought down the trident. Gomati screamed. The trident struck the floor, a hair's breadth away from his cheeks, throwing sparks over Rudra Bhatta's face. She pressed the trident against his neck again, drawing drops of blood.

And Rudra Bhatta started talking, but dragging the story out as much as possible. His son, whom he had instructed to receive Bijjala, would come with the prince at any moment. He needed to distract this girl Sivagami until then.

'It all started with Devaraya finding out about the deadly secret of Gauriparvat,' Rudra Bhatta began.

TWENTY-FIVE

Gundu Ramu

They had travelled up a narrow path which opened out onto a plateau. Ahead of them was a fort, and the dwarf marched them through the gate of the fort to reach the entrance of a cave. Inside, a huge fire was burning, illuminating the entire area in a golden light. The cave looked like the mouth of a giant, with its carved cobra face giving it a sinister look.

Gundu Ramu looked around. They were almost mid-way to Gauriparvat peak. The mountain peak rose above them, steep like a needle, and the cave looked as if it had been carved out at the throat of Gauriparvat. The smell of rotten eggs lingered in the air. What was an object of reverence in the city looked neither divine nor mystical up close. Gauriparvat looked as if it were a beast crouching to swallow everything in the blink of an eye. Gundu Ramu felt the earth throbbing under his feet. From the peak, purple and black smoke curled up into the sky.

'Only two hundred and thirty-two? Where are the rest?' An imposing man who towered above Gundu Ramu asked Hidumba. Gundu Ramu was dead tired with the weight he had carried and the heat from the torch that the man was holding felt unbearable to him. Hidumba, sitting on Gundu Ramu's shoulders, glared at the man.

'Only two hundred and thirty-two,' Hidumba mimicked. 'Should I have dragged the dead bodies too, Durgappa?'

The man's beefy face flushed red. 'Mind your tongue, dwarf.'

'Or else Bhoomipathi Durgappa will pluck it and give it to the crow? Amma, I am scared, I am scared.' Hidumba cackled. He slapped Gundu Ramu's head and yelled, 'Put me down, fatso.'

Durgappa started inspecting the goods the dwarf had brought. The children in chains, listless and exhausted, stood up when their masters approached.

'This one, this one, not this, this one, not this, not this ...' Hidumba droned on, prodding each of the boys as he walked past them. He was sorting them out like a vegetable vendor grades potatoes.

'Where are your bodyguards?' Durgappa asked Hidumba.

'Dead,' said the dwarf, without breaking his inspection.

'Where is the old devil Vamana?' Hidumba asked after they had sorted the boys out by size.

From the mouth of the cave, a silver-bearded dwarf slowly walked towards them, leaning on a stick that was double his size. He stumbled as he reached Gundu Ramu, and the boy reached out in time and held up the old dwarf. Fire crackled near them, the flames dancing in the bitterly cold wind that blew from the valley.

'Thank you, son,' Vamana said with a toothless smile. Then he frowned when he saw so many children.

'Why are you here, son? Who are you?' he asked in a voice that carried an edge of panic.

'No, no, no,' he cried, and ran towards the chained children. He fell down, scrambled up, and continued to run towards them. 'No, no, no.'

Hidumba and Durgappa laughed.

'We ... we just finished our job. Why has this batch come so fast?' Vamana cried. 'And they are so small.'

'We need smaller ones, old nut. You were the one who said that most of the ore yielded next to nothing. Now, find more. Find mine shafts that yield plenty of the goddamn stones. We need a shipload of them. And we need it fast,' Hidumba said.

Vamana turned to him. 'Fast? We have twelve more years.'

'No, you don't. You have a few more months—two or three.'

'Three months? Are you insane?' Vamana's lips trembled in anger. 'Making fun of me, Hidumba? The Mahamakam got over a year ago. What are you blabbering?'

Hidumba walked up to the old dwarf and poked a stubby finger into his chest. 'What a blasted moron you are, Vamana. Don't you know that the Mahamakam never concluded? That the Kali statue sunk and the Vaithalikas staged a coup that was thwarted? And now your king needs all the stones he can get and he wants them fast.'

The old dwarf's shoulders sagged. 'What ... what. How is it possible? Three months? Are you mad?'

Bhoomipathi Durgappa rushed to the old dwarf. 'Vamana, when we need advice from a lowly officer, we will ask for it. Do as you have been told.'

'Everything will get destroyed. Devaraya—'

At that moment, a low rumbling vibration shook the ground. From the dark sky rose the panicked screech of Garuda pakshi. The old dwarf's grip on Gundu Ramu's wrist tightened. Purple and black smoke billowed out of the mountain top and rocks came tumbling down. The children screamed in terror as the rocks rolled towards them, crushing a few of them.

'The end is near, the end is near, Amma Gauri ...' Vamana cried as things settled down and the mountain resumed its cold indifference. Vamana shook his staff at Durgappa and Hidumba and cried, 'Devaraya was right. We are committing a great sin, and Amma Gauri will punish us all. A country built on such a sin will not last.'

Hidumba smacked the old dwarf and sent him sprawling. Hidumba went up to kick the fallen dwarf, but Durgappa restrained him. Hidumba screamed at Vamana, 'I will flay you alive, bastard. Talking against your country? Talking against your king? You want to destroy our beloved Mahishmathi? If you don't like Mahishmathi, go to some other country.'

Durgappa carried Hidumba and put him down near the mouth of the cave. He pacified Hidumba while Vamana lay whimpering on the ground. Gundu Ramu sneaked over to the fallen dwarf and tried to lift him up. Vamana steadied himself on Gundu Ramu and stood up, holding the staff the boy handed to him.

Durgappa came back and said in a reconciliatory tone, 'Vamana, why can't you just do what you are told? One has to do one's duty. My duty is to ensure security at Gauriparvat and keep an account of each and every Gaurikanta stone that leaves this mountain. Hidumba's duty is to extract the quantities that the king needs. Your duty is to show the mother lodes where the stone can be mined. Let us do our duty and be at peace.'

'Everything will be destroyed. Amma Gauri is angry,' Vamana mumbled.

Gundu Ramu saw that the soldiers of Durgappa were carrying the bodies of the children who had been crushed by the rocks. He watched as they went to the shoulder of the mountain and flung the bodies of the children down the cliff. He was horrified. He was sure a few were alive, even if barely so.

Durgappa and Hidumba perched on a rock by the cave and opened a casket of gooseberry wine. The soldiers came back and they unchained the children. Vamana was sitting on his haunches at the cave, watching them. When the last of the children were unchained, he gestured for the children to follow him. Terrified and crying, they started walking towards the cave mouth. A soldier counted them as they passed. Gundu Ramu stood watching them amble by, some holding hands, some acting brave. Some might have been siblings, for the elder ones tried to carry their crying brothers on their hips.

When the last one had disappeared into the cave mouth, Vamana cried, 'There is one more. The large one who helped me.'

Gundu Ramu didn't wait to be prodded by a soldier. He walked with heavy steps towards the cave, fighting the rising panic and fear. The children had grown silent. When he reached the cave mouth, Vamana held his hand to support himself.

'Take me to the front, son,' he said in a kind voice.

Inside the cave, water dripped from the roof, and the walls were smooth and slimy. There were interconnected crates there, into which the children were crammed. The crates had wooden wheels that stayed in ruts dug into the rocky ground. Gundu Ramu counted twenty crates before they reached the front. Harnessed to the first crate, were four mountain rams.

The light became dimmer and dimmer as they walked farther inside the cave mouth.

'Help me get in, son,' Vamana said. They had come to a halt by the crate in the front, which was narrow and had a small bench seat. Vamana made space for Gundu Ramu and gestured for him to sit next to him. Once Gundu Ramu had squeezed in, Vamana shouted for light, and a soldier came with torches and tied one on each crate.

Vamana closed his eyes in prayer. Gundu Ramu turned back to see that the children had stopped crying and were looking around in amazement. Some were whispering excitedly and pointing at the slime oozing from the cave wall. Some looked scared and were holding on to each other.

Vamana snapped his whip, and with a jerk the train started moving. The sound of the wheels bouncing in the ruts echoed in the cave.

'We are going to the womb of Amma Gauri. We are all her sons. Only she can protect us,' Vamana said. Gundu Ramu felt a cold finger of fear tracing his spine. The way ahead was pitch dark, the dull light from the torch reflecting on the walls and lighting only a patch of circle ahead. Rodents the size of rabbits scurried away as the train rumbled and creaked through the gently sloping path. The train jerked to a halt and some children laughed and whispered.

'Hold tight, son,' Vamana said. Gundu Ramu tightened his grip on the wooden railing. He looked back at the children again; they seemed excited and afraid at the same time. They couldn't see what he was seeing ahead. The gentle slope ended a few feet away and what lay ahead was a dark abyss. He understood why the train was drawn by mountain rams instead of mules or horses. In his native village, he had seen them darting up steep cliffs as nimbly as a horse would gallop through the royal highway. They were great climbers, as agile as monkeys and as strong as mules. That also meant ...

The train started with a jerk and gathered speed, and soon the ground under them fell away. Gundu Ramu felt like he was flying in the air. He landed with a heavy thud on his seat, only to bounce up again. The cave was filled with shrieks of terror from the terrified children as the train rolled down. Sometimes the left set of wheels were in the air, sometimes the right set scraped against the cave walls.

The cave narrowed as they spiralled down the treacherous path. They went through walls of water, drenched and shivering only to encounter foul-smelling smoke that swirled around, making them cough. Sometimes they went through portions where the walls shone with a dull blue glow, which was followed by thick darkness on either side of the train.

'Don't breathe, don't breathe, toxic gas,' Vamana cried and coughed hard. A searing pain ripped through Gundu Ramu's lungs. His eyes burned and skin blistered. The train entered a roaring waterfall and emerged on the other side to flames that jumped from the wall and tried to lick them.

Gundu Ramu saw it first. Sharp stalactites from the ceiling plunged like daggers ahead.

'Duck, duck, duck,' Vamana cried, lying down on the narrow bench. Gundu Ramu tried to squeeze himself flat too. The children screamed as a torch hit one stalactite and sparks flew in the air. A child jumped to escape the falling embers and was instead hit by a protruding stalactite. Gundu Ramu saw him topple over and vanish under the train.

'Stop, stop,' Gundu Ramu cried. The train continued to speed down, taking another turn.

'A boy has fallen over. Stop, stop,' he screamed.

'Sad, my son. Too sad. But that is how your great king selects the suitable ones. Those who survive are the fittest for his job.'

Gundu Ramu grabbed the reins from Vamana and yanked hard. The rams bleated and stopped and the crates collided against one another. He jumped out and ran back.

Vamana cried, 'Son, son, what have you done? Amma Gauri, help us!'

Gundu Ramu ran down the tunnel, keeping his head low. Squeezing past the last box, he could see the boy lying limp in the distance. A low hum filled the air then, and Gundu paused. He could see the tunnel curving upwards into the darkness. The hum was getting louder, and he could hear Vamana screaming for him to return to the train. *Fast, fast,* his panicked scream echoed.

As the hum increased, Gundu Ramu heard the crack of the whip and the train started off again. He ran towards the boy, but before he could reach him, a huge rat darted out of the darkness towards him. Gundu Ramu froze. The rat sniffed at the boy, and Gundu tried to shoo it away from where he was standing. Unmindful of Gundu Ramu, the rodent started nibbling at the nose of the unconscious boy. Gundu ran towards it, hurling abuses, and the darkness above him exploded in thousands of rats. They covered the boy who was lying limp, and before Gundu Ramu could comprehend what had happened, the rats scattered. In place of the boy was only a skeleton. A few rats still sat there, nibbling at what was left of the boy.

Gundu Ramu screamed in terror and ran back towards the train. With a terrifying hum, the rats began chasing him, pouring down from all sides, like water rushing out of a breached dam.

TWENTY-SIX

Mahadeva

Bhanu Gupta regained consciousness when he heard the rumbling of an approaching chariot. He was in a half-dream, half-awake state, lying in the bushes by the side of the untouchables' street. In his dream, he had heard two chariots rushing away from the city. By the time the third chariot approached, the effect of Kattappa's strike was wearing off. He stood up on unsteady legs and slowly walked towards the road. The chariot appeared as if from nowhere, and he instinctively ducked into the bush.

The dim, low-hanging light at the bottom of the chariot swayed from side to side, throwing confusing shadows and circular patches of light on the street as it passed him. His trained eyes picked up the contour of the passengers. A man and a woman were in the chariot, and Bhanu Gupta blinked, trying to adjust his vision. *Prince Bijjala and a woman,* Bhanu Gupta whispered. By the time he was able to make out that it wasn't a woman but the eunuch Keki, the chariot had vanished.

Bhanu Gupta had lost the trail of Kattappa, and the spy was sure that what Kattappa had been transporting in the handcart was Shivappa's body. Was the rebel slave already dead? Or was Kattappa playing the same trick he had played once, as the king had revealed to Bhanu Gupta before he was sent on the mission.

Bhanu Gupta ran to find Prince Mahadeva, to whom he was to report as per the king's instructions. He knew where he could find him—Guru Dharmapala's ashram.

In the ashram, a group of disciples were talking to excited devotees, requesting them to remain seated and not rush towards the guru when he arrived for his discourse.

Mahadeva was sitting in the front row, among the many other noblemen of Mahishmathi. The fragrance of incense mixed with the stench of sweat from the milling devotees. Thousands of oil lamps had been aesthetically placed on the platform, where an elaborate stone throne with a tiger skin spread over it was standing.

When Mahadeva had first met Guru Dharmapala, his eyes brimmed with tears of ecstasy. This was the guru the prince had been seeking. Mahadeva wanted to ask the guru whether he would ever marry Sivagami, but in the magnetic presence of the guru, he became tongue-tied. Such questions appeared trivial and mundane.

The guru talked about the inevitability of death and the irrelevance of worldly attainment. 'How does it matter whether you were a king or a beggar when you die?' the guru had said. 'You are not going to take anything with you when you go.' The guru stressed this point through various stories and songs. 'The world is an illusion, and we are living in someone's dream. And the one who is dreaming about this world is living in someone else's dream, and so on and on. An infinite regress. Dream within a dream within a dream within a dream till infinity.'

'When you know the world isn't real, when it is a maya, an illusion, why bother to love only one? Why not love everyone, everything,' asked the guru. 'Why run behind possessions like a new horse, a big house, a better silk dress and such trivial things when you know you are the universe.' That moved Mahadeva to tears. 'Love for one person is selfish, love for the entire universe is noble,' the guru said. 'You know you are living a dream, don't make it a nightmare by fighting for money, power, women and such trivial things. You have a destiny. You have a quest. You have a duty to come out of the dream. Wake up, and you will find that you didn't exist in physical form. You exist as a spark, as a thought in the mind of the great god of time, Mahakala Shiva. In your sleep, you think you are a different entity. When you wake up, you know you are part of that great time, the Mahakala. You are him and he is you.'

It was all very confusing to Mahadeva. In his dark moods, he thought the guru was talking gibberish, but he was afraid to entertain such doubts. Maybe he wasn't intelligent enough to understand the guru's profundity. When he summoned up the courage to say that he didn't understand, Guru Dharmapala smiled at him compassionately and pressed his divine palm on his head. 'You are a beginner in this quest, son. Sages have toiled their entire lifetime to grasp the universal, the ultimate truth. Through the control of breath, through correct postures, through ritual practices, you can only prepare your mind to receive the eternal wisdom. But you need the grace of the guru to be enlightened. For the grace to flow, you need to have absolute belief in your guru.'

'But what happens after I get enlightened?' Mahadeva had blurted out. The moment the words were out of his mouth, he felt he had committed a great crime. He had asked an unspeakable question. But he had wondered about this before. In various books, he had read about gurus achieving enlightenment. But after enlightenment what, he had asked. He pondered over that question and never received a satisfactory reply.

Guru Dharmapala laughed aloud. 'After enlightenment, you start seeing everything clearly. You know what is what. That is all.'

Mahadeva nodded, but the answer did not satisfy him. He was afraid to say that he liked the dream he was living. He liked the misery he felt when he thought of Sivagami. The pain was sweet. The longing made him feel alive. What use was staring at one's navel and counting one's breath when the world outside exploded with the ecstasy of life? What use was clarity, when the dreamlike state he lived was so sweet. And what was it that the guru meant by clarity. Who knew. Perhaps he was lacking absolute belief in the guru.

More than his future with Sivagami, there was another question that was giving Mahadeva sleepless nights. He had heard about the children missing from the untouchables' village. Mahadeva had meticulously plotted the places from where the children had gone missing, along with the dates they had gone missing. He had found a strange pattern. The children went missing around the day of the new moon.

And he had found another thing that disturbed him. It had started with a casual remark from Hiranya when he had met him. The general warned Mahadeva not to come under the spell of gurus. 'You are a prince, and you should stay away from ashrams. A wise prince knows how to use godmen to his advantage,' Hiranya had said.

Mahadeva smiled at him, but then the general added that he felt uneasy when both the princes were under the spell of Guru Dharmapala. Initially, Mahadeva was puzzled. He had never seen Bijjala in the ashram.

'My brother would never come to the ashram,' Mahadeva corrected the general.

'Of course, of course. Not like you. Not every day. But he goes away on certain nights, especially for the new moon day discourses,' Hiranya said.

Mahadeva was troubled by this remark. Was there some relationship between his brother's disappearance and the missing children? Maybe his jealousy of his brother was making him think evil thoughts about Bijjala, Mahadeva chided himself, but the doubt kept gnawing at him.

The sudden blare of a conch alerted the audience. From a thousand throats the cry of 'Guru Dharmapala, Jaya Satyachara' rose in unison. The atmosphere turned electric. Two well-built monks started beating a huge drum in a rhythm that spiralled faster and faster. Two fire dancers somersaulted on the stage, revolving torches that burned on either ends. A horn sounded, and soon, hundreds of conches were being blown together. The drum beaters were covered in sweat as the drumming became frenzied. Cymbals clashed. People went into screams of near hysteria. From one end of the stage, Guru Dharmapala entered carrying a trident in his hand. He was wearing only a deer skin around his waist, but several beaded necklaces bounced on his chest. His eyes were blazing, reflecting the torches that spun around. He gave an animal scream.

'Raudra Bhava, Raudra Bhava,' the audience cried in ecstasy. The guru had chosen to appear tonight as the angry avatar of Lord Shiva. Guru Dharmapala started dancing, waving the trident wildly.

'Shivoham, Shivoham, Shivoham,' the guru cried. *I am Shiva, I am Shiva, I am Shiva.*

'Shiva, lord Shiva,' people cried from all sides. Adult men started weeping like babies. Women rolled on the ground, clutching their hair and crying the guru's name. Despite himself, Mahadeva stood up and started singing the Shiva Thandava stotra, the energetic song praising Lord Shiva written by Ravana.

As Mahadeva sung the Asura emperor's song, the guru's glance met his, but there was no smile on the guru's face. He was in a frenzy, spinning round and round, his matted hair moving in circles above his head, sparks flying every time the trident scratched the floor when he jumped, swirled and twisted.

'Shivoham,' the guru cried, beating his chest with his fist at every pause in the shloka being sung. The audience started beating their chests and crying 'Shivoham', keeping rhythm with Mahadeva's song. Mahadeva had never been so moved, never felt so elated that tears rolled down his cheeks as he sang. He choked with emotion, but no one noticed. The crowd was beating their chests and crying 'Shivoham, Shivoham, Shivoham', and Guru Dharmapala had gone into a trance. Mahadeva's eyes brimmed with tears as he watched the guru. He felt a sudden coldness at his feet and looked down. His blood froze. A cobra was weaving its way through the crowd and it had just gone past him. It crawled up the stage and started moving towards the guru who was now standing still, with his eyes closed, trident in one hand and the other open in the sign of benediction. An uneasy silence descended, except for the dull rhythmic beats of the drums. As everyone watched with bated breath, the cobra started crawling up the legs of Guru Dharmapala. It coiled around his body and crawled up while the guru in his Shiva form stood still like a statue. The cobra wound around his neck and opened its hood, its cold grey eyes glittering in the light of the spinning torches and its split tongue moving out and in.

The crowd went down on their knees, weeping, screaming, crying together. The chanting picked up. 'Guru Dharmapala, Jaya Satyachara, Shivananda roopa, namoham, namoham.' Mahadeva found himself on the floor, weeping for no reason. *I have seen God, I have seen God,* he repeated to himself. A hand tapped his shoulder and he looked to his side. Bhanu Gupta was in a prostrate position near him.

The spy whispered, 'Your brother and that eunuch are going towards the jungle beyond the lepers' village in a chariot.'

Mahadeva nudged his horse to gallop faster as they cut through the darkness. He had wasted precious time making his way through the crowds in the ashram. Where was his brother going with Keki? He knew Bijjala couldn't do without wine and women. But there was no need to leave the palace for that. After reaching eighteen, both princes had been getting a handsome allowance from the royal treasury, and they each had their own wings in the palace. Bijjala had built a harem and populated it with the best of women. He had even constructed a hall where musicians and dancers came to perform before him. He had a reputation of being generous with artists and musicians. Bijjala was popular among a group of soldiers who considered him brave. They saw his arrogance as a sign of a royal temperament.

In contrast, Mahadeva had built a library and was in the process of collecting manuscripts from various parts of the world. He spent most of his leisure time reading books or walking through the streets of Mahishmathi, sometimes in disguise, sometimes as himself. He knew he was a subject of ridicule among the servants. Bijjala's behaviour was becoming of a prince. Mahadeva was aware of the rumours being spread about him, including the one that he was impotent and that was why he had no interest in building a harem. He was aware of the gossip regarding his interest in Sivagami. He didn't care. As a vikramadeva, he was entitled to travel on an elephant, a privilege he shared only with the king, the queen and the mahapradhana. He was eligible to carry his own flag and a train of fifty-one male servants and twenty-one female ones, something Bijjala longed for. Mahadeva rarely used any of these privileges for he found them meaningless. He walked to his office often, ignoring the giggles and whispers of the servants. Many called him the saint prince, some called him mad and a fool. He didn't care either way.

Yet, he recognised that he was jealous of his brother Bijjala, and he struggled with it. He had seen his father taking swift decisions; he had the ability to see far ahead with clarity and implement things with a strong will, and he thought he could see the same quality in his brother. Mahadeva felt he himself lacked such resolve. He had a strong sense of justice and knew he was growing rigid on what was right and what was wrong. His father's actions often confused him: sometimes the king seemed like the most generous person in the world, and at others, he was cruel beyond Mahadeva's imagination. His brother suffered from no such confusion. He never bothered about what was right or wrong. Bijjala went by his instincts, sought pleasure when he could, became angry when he felt so, and was generous when he was in the mood. *Bijjala lives in the moment, as Guru Dharmapala often advises, while I am a fool who is always confused,* thought Mahadeva as he rode through the dark winding path.

Mahadeva skirted the outer road that went parallel to the river, with the untouchables' village on one side. He crossed the sentry point and, to his irritation, found that both the sentries were fast asleep. He woke them up and chided them. The terrified soldiers fell at his feet and pleaded that he spare them. No, they hadn't seen anyone crossing their sentry point. Annoyed, angry and at the same time, feeling pity for the poor souls whose job it was to man a sentry point in this wilderness, Mahadeva let them off with the threat of a pay cut.

He had wasted time on the sentries, but to guide them was also his duty. Mahadeva urged his horse to gallop faster to make good the lost time. Occasional lightning lit the lonely path. A leopard darted across his path and vanished into the jungle. The death cries of a wild boar rent the air. Mahadeva felt sorry for the boar, but that was the rule of the jungle.

Mahadeva would have preferred to have some soldiers with him, but he was afraid of what he would find. In the event that Bijjala was guilty as he thought, he didn't want anyone to witness his brother's guilt. At the same time, he knew his brother would try to harm him, if he got an opportunity. Before leaving the ashram, he had asked the spy to inform his personal guards to track and follow him. Since he had a head start, Mahadeva would have sufficient time to confront Bijjala and find out the truth, and if his brother tried to harm him, his personal guards would come to his rescue.

The thought that Bijjala's crimes would pave his path to the throne made Mahadeva uneasy. *No, I am not doing this to destroy my brother, I am doing it because it is the right thing to do,* he assured himself.

He took the path winding up the hill and caught a glimpse of a chariot vanishing round the corner. He urged his horse to gallop faster.

Keki was sitting in the rear seat of the chariot, allowing Bijjala to ride. Akhila was lying on the floor of the chariot, unconscious. Keki had drugged her food at Revamma's mansion, and after a fight with Rudra Bhatta when his chariot had gone missing, Keki had hurried to Bijjala's palace with an unconscious Akhila. At least today Shivappa should appear, she hoped.

'I wonder what Pattaraya is up to. The fool had promised the sky,' Bijjala said as they sped through the countryside.

'Have patience—' Keki stopped abruptly. Something had caught her attention. She stared into the pitch darkness that stretched endlessly behind their chariot, and then lightning lit the path behind. She froze and held the chariot rail for support. Had she seen someone galloping behind them?

'Prince ... prince,' she whispered, her voice edged with panic. Bijjala grunted as he guided the fast-moving chariot with admirable skill towards the lone light shining ahead. He could see Kalicharan Bhatta standing at the entrance of the path leading to the temple, holding a flaming torch.

'Someone is following us,' Keki said.

Bijjala didn't slow down. 'Whichever fool it is, he isn't going to see tomorrow's dawn.'

In the next flash of lightning, Keki saw him clearly. The rider was gaining on them.

'Prince, it is your brother!' Keki cried.

Bijjala cursed and looked behind. Now the sound of horse hooves was clearer. From the distance, Kalicharan waved his torch. Bijjala smirked. 'My brother is going to die today.'

Keki looked at Akhila, who was regaining consciousness. How would they explain Akhila's presence in their chariot?

'Prince, I think we need to abort our plan.'

'For that fool? Never. It is a God-given chance to finish him. We will blame it on Shivappa's ghost. Or some such story.' Bijjala laughed and whipped the horse to gather more speed.

A brisk wind shook the trees. A thunderstorm was advancing from distant Gauriparvat. Another flash of lightning made Keki realise that their situation was truly desperate. Mahadeva would reach them at any moment.

'Where has that priest's son vanished?' Bijjala cried. Keki saw that Kalicharan had fled. Perhaps he had seen Mahadeva and had gone to warn Rudra Bhatta. An idea started forming in Keki's mind.

Keki said, 'You think Prince Mahadeva would be foolish enough to come alone? There will be more soldiers reaching anytime. Allow me to handle this, Prince.' Without waiting for Bijjala's permission, Keki lifted Akhila and flung her to the side. The girl crashed into the bushes and disappeared.

Bijjala screamed, 'What are you doing, you fool?'

Before Keki could answer, Mahadeva's horse came near their chariot and started racing parallel to it.

'Ah, Prince Vikramadeva Mahadeva,' Keki cried, as lightning lit the entire jungle. 'Did you also come to stop that evil priest?' There was the sound of deafening thunder, almost drowning out the eunuch's words.

TWENTY-SEVEN

Sivagami

'The children are used to mine Gauriparvat?' Sivagami asked incredulously. She couldn't believe her father was responsible for such cruelty. Rudra Bhatta was seated at the foot of the Rakta Kali statue and Sivagami was standing, her trident pointed at his chest.

'Not in the beginning,' said Rudra Bhatta. 'When mining was started, it was done by slaves and workmen on wages. The Gaurikanta stones yielded huge amounts of money and Mahishmathi, which was a vassal kingdom of Kadarimandalam at the time, was able to raise an army to win its freedom. As prosperity increased, it could buy more slaves, have a bigger army and subjugate its former coloniser.'

'How could mere stones give so much prosperity?'

'They aren't mere stones. Some of them contain a lotus-shaped diamond called Gauripadmam. Traders came from all around the world to get these precious stones that shone in the night. Each Gauripadmam diamond was worth an empire, but to get even a small diamond, one needed huge quantities of Gaurikanta stones to be broken apart. Not all cores had the Gauripadmam. The maharaja announced a good price for the Gaurikanta stones brought to him. Devaraya would search for the Gauripadmam by breaking each stone. Soon, everyone was tempted to join the search for money: pirates, desperadoes, fortune-chasers, hoodlums—all went to Gauriparvat for the Gaurikanta. Gang wars broke out. Tribes attacked each other. Villages were burnt. The tribe of Vaithalikas, who considered Gauriparvat as their mother, fought a desperate war to protect the mountain. They succeeded in barring the approach to Gauriparvat. Their warriors perched on trees with poisoned arrows, taking out anyone trying to approach their divine mountain. Soon, the stones stopped coming to Mahishmathi. Somadeva, who had been secretly raising an army to free Mahishmathi from Kadarimandalam's yoke, became desperate.'

Rudra Bhatta stopped talking suddenly and tensed up. Sivagami listened. She could hear the faint sound of horse hooves hitting the jungle path from afar. It seemed as though the rider was approaching them. She gestured to Neelappa and he slipped into the jungle to investigate. Rudra Bhatta twisted his head and saw Gomati. He exploded with rage.

'You characterless woman. I was doing all these tantric pujas for you. To cure your infertility and you … you …'

Gomati came forward and stood in front of him.

'Mama, it isn't me who is responsible, but your son. He is of high kula, gotra, jaati and whatnot, but he is impotent. And you are curing my "infertility" by sacrificing children?' Gomati scoffed. 'You were doing it for money, cheating some big man.'

Rudra Bhatta struggled to get up. His eyes shone with murderous rage. Sivagami pressed the trident to his throat and he became limp. 'Speak,' Sivagami commanded.

Rudra Bhatta stared at her with all the hatred he could muster. 'You will go your mother's way, whore,' he spat out.

The blood rushed to Sivagami's head. She smashed his face with the blunt end of the trident and, in a trice, the pointed ends were back pressing at his throat. Rudra Bhatta screamed in terror. She pressed her foot on his chest and yelled, 'Speak!'

A petrified Rudra Bhatta quickly resumed. 'Parameswara found out about a split in the Vaithalika tribe and decided to exploit it. The Vaithalika chief Malayappa's sister was jilted by a young man, and the girl committed suicide. The chief ordered the execution of the young man. But the man was more popular than the chief, and he ousted the chief and his family. Desperate, the chief of the Vaithalikas took asylum in Mahishmathi. It was for vengeance that he gave away the rights of Gauriparvat to the Mahishmathi king, who promised to kill the young man who had dishonoured his sister. Parameswara wasn't satisfied with the deal, though. The minister wanted Mahishmathi's claim on Gauriparvat to be iron-clad and permanent. He made Malayappa promise his own eternal slavery and that of his descendants to the Mahishmathi throne. Revenge and honour were more important to Malayappa, and he signed away his freedom. The Mahishmathi army moved in under Thimma, butchered the usurper and his men, and destroyed the age-old Vaithalika village. The tribe scattered, some surrendering to Mahishmathi as slaves while others fleeing to the forest. Malayappa's son, Kattappa, serves as a slave of Mahishmathi even now. Once Gauriparvat was firmly under Mahishmathi's control, the mining officially started. Devaraya built a facility to break Gaurikanta stones in Mahishmathi, but the mine dried up soon. That shocked the king.'

After a moment's hesitation, Rudra Bhatta continued. 'Gauriparvat stopped yielding Gaurikanta stones and the king felt that his ambition to lead his country to freedom was being thwarted. Whatever could be mined got lost in inter-tribal rivalry and hardly any stones reached Mahishmathi. It was then that a dwarf called Vamana met Parameswara and offered his services. He was an expert in ferreting out mother lodes of Gaurikanta from the belly of the mountain. For some time, he was able to offer some respite. But greed and demand kept growing. Devaraya had found out that the sledge from the Gaurikanta process was a good fertiliser, and soon barren lands turned fertile if ashes from the process were spread over them. It was given as prasad from the Gauri temple every year during an annual ceremony, and people believed the land turned fertile thanks to Amma Gauri. Stone production hit a wall again. There was only so much a dwarf could do by himself.

'Pattaraya, who was a young merchant then, came up with a brilliant idea. He negotiated with the king for the contract to provide the stones. He stitched together an alliance of various tribal and caste lords, by giving them an equal share in the profit. He and men chosen by him eliminated any opposition. The remaining Vaithalika villages were torched, and those Vaithalikas who refused to leave were executed. The bhoomipathi guild came up with the idea of using small children to ferret out the stones from the narrow tunnels.'

'The king and the others agreed to this?' Sivagami couldn't believe her father had supported this idea.

'The king turned a blind eye, because he was in the middle of a war for freedom. Already the army under General Thimma had defeated and repelled the Kadarimandalam army in the first battle of Patalaganga. Maharaja Somadeva knew Kadarimandalam wouldn't keep quiet—a much mightier army would be formed to repress the rebellion. So he needed a bigger army. The slave fighters and mercenaries cost a lot of money. Slave traders were bringing more and more slaves to the Mahishmathi port, and they needed to be paid. Many of them were willing to wait for payment and gave the slave warriors on credit to the king with the hope of getting at least one Gauripadmam.'

'To win freedom, the great King Somadeva was willing to buy slaves?' Sivagami asked, the disgust in her voice obvious.

'It was a life or death situation for all of us,' Rudra Bhatta said. 'The king offered bhoomipathi posts to everyone he thought needed to be appeased or rewarded. A treaty was signed with the war- and caste-lords for the transport of Gaurikanta stones. Bhoomipathi Durgappa, the tribal lord and a renegade Vaithalika, became the lord protector of Gauriparvat, manning the forest and the fort around the peak. Bhoomipathi Akkundaraya, the head of the river people, became the transporter of the stones till it reached Bhoomipathi Guha's land, where the stones were filled into a Kali statue and brought in to Mahishmathi.'

'Why the deceit? Why can't the stones be brought in openly,' Sivagami asked. Rudra Bhatta stopped talking. He was listening to something and a smile flashed across his lips.

Sivagami stared at Rudra Bhatta. Was he trying to spin a yarn to distract her and attempt something desperate? She gripped the trident tight, alert for any sudden move from the priest.

'Speak,' she commanded. 'I asked, why the deceit? Why can't the stones be brought in openly?'

'There was a small pox epidemic, and half the population of Mahishmathi was dead in a matter of months. A rumour spread that Amma Gauri was angry and she was taking revenge on Mahishmathi for mining the stones. When the stones were next brought into the city, a riot broke out in the streets. That attracted the attention of Kadarimandalam. Somadeva knew that, if he was to succeed, he could not force his way on the people. The maharaja decided to bring in the stones clandestinely. Publically, he vowed on Amma Gauri that there would be no more mining in the holy mountain. Then he went a step further and declared that they should worship Gauriparvat, and Amma Gauri became the country's presiding deity. The Kali Nimmanjan festival was started supposedly to appease the goddess, and the stones were hidden and brought inside the city in the Kali statue.'

'Did Devaraya support this deceit?' Sivagami asked, knowing full well what the answer would be.

'Yes, he did. In fact, he constructed a workshop where the stones could be broken down. I don't know where it is, but we know it is somewhere inside Mahishmathi city.'

Something was not adding up. Sivagami knew the priest was withholding something—or worse, perhaps he didn't know everything. As if reading her thoughts, he said, 'Everything about the Gaurikanta is secretive. No one knows everything, except perhaps the king and the mahapradhana.'

'Did Devaraya know children were being used to mine the stones?' Sivagami asked.

'No, he didn't. He only knew that mining was happening and he was happy to serve the king. His visit to Gauriparvat changed everything. He came back as a traitor. He wanted the mining to stop. He threatened to tell the public that children were being used to mine the holy Gauriparvat. Already there were rumours floating around about it. Every day, some poor mother from a tribal village travelled from afar to complain to the emperor of Mahishmathi about her missing child. She would never get an audience with the king. The city-dwellers didn't bother too much about it. Those who were kidnapping children ensured that they were not taken from villages belonging to Mahishmathi, but from remote tribal villages in the forests between Kadarimandalam and Mahishmathi, so it didn't really affect the city-dwellers. But Devaraya threatening to expose the secret of the kingdom was another matter. He was the second-most important man in the kingdom. He was the king's bosom friend, a celebrated inventor, a man to whom the country owed its prosperity. If he revealed that the holy Gauriparvat was being mined despite the promises of the king, and that children were being used for it, it would have resulted in riots in the street. Devaraya threatened to tell the public everything unless the mining was stopped. That was something Maharaja Somadeva couldn't afford to do. He pleaded with his friend, he threatened him, coaxed him, tempted him. Nothing worked. Devaraya was adamant. Finally, Maharaja Somadeva called the rest of the bhoomipathis for an emergency meeting.'

Just then, Neelappa came running into the hall and said, between gasps for air, 'Someone is coming. He has parked his chariot and is walking through the jungle.'

'Ha,' Rudra Bhatta cried triumphantly, 'it's my son. You are dead, whore. You are dead.' He started laughing.

Gomati looked terrified. Sivagami paused for a moment, calculating whether it would be worth fighting it out with the priest's son. She might have to kill him too, and she didn't know for sure how Gomati would react.

'Neelappa, tie him up.'

Neelappa approached Rudra Bhatta and tied up his hands and legs. When the priest tried to scream, he thrust his turban inside his mouth and wrapped it around the priest's head. He lifted the priest on his shoulders and waited for Sivagami's instructions. Rudra Bhatta was making choking noises and struggling to get off the slave's shoulders.

'Rush to our chariot. Gomati, follow Neelappa. Give me a moment.'

Sivagami rushed out of the hall, towards the jungle. Neelappa, carrying Rudra Bhatta and Gomati, ran in the opposite direction towards their chariot.

Sivagami watched as Kalicharan stumbled through the bushes towards the temple. She slipped past him and reached where he had parked his chariot. Sivagami unharnessed Kalicharan's horse. Neelappa came up in her chariot and halted near her. She jumped into it, without letting go of the reins of Kalicharan's horse. Neelappa snapped his whip and Vajra took off. Kalicharan's horse was terrified and it neighed in fright. It started running parallel to their chariot.

Sivagami saw Kalicharan running out of the temple. He stood in shock for a moment, and then began to chase them.

Hearing its master's voice, his horse started struggling to free itself from Sivagami's grip. Sivagami held on, gripping the side of the speeding chariot with one hand, and the struggling horse's reins with the other. Low-lying branches hit her face as the chariot sped forward through the jungle, rattling and bouncing over the uneven path. Kalicharan had no intention of giving up, neither had Sivagami. Without his horse, he wouldn't be able to follow her.

Then she realised she had made a mistake. Ahead on the path, a few hundred feet away, another chariot was parked. The sounds of men arguing came to her. She grabbed the reins from Neelappa and swerved the chariot at the last moment, crashing into the jungle. She let go of the reins of Kalicharan's horse, and in one swift move, took the whip from Neelappa's hand and struck it on its hump. The panicked horse ran in the opposite direction and Kalicharan ran behind it, leaving Sivagami's chariot to chart its own course. When she looked back, the men were staring at Kalicharan running behind the horse. Hopefully, they hadn't seen her. She cut through the thick undergrowth and emerged out on the forest path. They rushed towards Mahishmathi city.

'We need a place to hide this devil, Neelappa. I haven't finished with him,' Sivagami said to Neelappa.

'I know a place,' Neelappa said, thinking about the storehouse that had held Shivappa hostage.

'You are taking an insane risk, Sivagami,' Brihannala said, as Neelappa locked the storehouse by the wharf. 'Why don't you do it here. The river is nearby. We have enough weights to ensure the deed will go undetected.'

'Revenge has a recipe, Brihannala. Unless you follow it, it will taste bland,' Sivagami said. Brihannala roared with laughter. Sivagami didn't like the ring of that laugh. It sounded like she was indulging an adamant child. In the dim light of the torch, Brihannala's face had an impish look.

'I shall wait for you to come with him. I shall make necessary arrangements in the place you want at the time of your choice. Your captive shall be safe here till then. But let me warn you, it is risky.'

Sivagami nodded gravely, turned on her heels and hurried to the waiting chariot.

By the time she reached home, she was drained by the events of the day. But more than anything, she was worried for Gundu Ramu. Was he still alive? She had to reach Gauriparvat at the earliest. She hoped it wouldn't be too late for Gundu Ramu by then.

TWENTY-EIGHT

Gundu Ramu

Gundu Ramu ran for his life. Rats were crawling in from everywhere and the tunnel was filled with their squeals and shrieks. Some rats jumped on his legs as he ran, and he could feel their sharp incisors puncture his skin. Screaming in terror, Gundu Ramu shook off the rats hanging from his calves, clinging to his back, running up his dhoti. As he ran, he plucked a torch from the wall and he started using it as a shield. The fire kept the rats at bay, but the torch wasn't going to last forever. When he swung the torch, the rats would stop in their tracks, some backtracking, some sitting on their hind legs and barring their rodent teeth, some squealing and darting here and there, toppling over each other. The moment he turned, they would rush towards him like a turbulent river.

He could see the train turning a curve far ahead. With a sinking heart, he saw it vanishing. He desperately looked around for an escape route. The tunnel branched into many smaller tunnels, but most of them were too narrow for him to consider taking. Some had rats pouring out of them as well. He spotted a wooden door with coiled serpents carved on it and tried to open it, but it didn't yield.

He continued to run, stumbling on the uneven floor and scrambling up before the pack of rats could devour him, sometimes skidding, sometimes stopping to catch his breath while keeping an eye on the pack. He thought he could hear a faint roar. His heart skipped a beat. He started chanting 'Amma Gauri, Amma Gauri' repeatedly when he remembered that he was in the womb of the Goddess. And it was hell.

The roar became louder as he fled. The air felt damper, and the floor was even more slippery. As he turned a curve, the roar became deafening. At the end of the tunnel, thick curly fog rose. The smell of rotten eggs was overwhelming. He stopped at the end of the passage and peeped out. A sheet of water plunged down into a tunnel-like cave. Far below, he could see another river—it was molten lava, and it flowed into the pool made by the falling water. He knew he was at Mahishimukha, the origin of the Mahishi river.

He was looking at the heart of Amma Gauri, made of molten rocks that sizzled and hissed in anger. The songs that his father had taught him came to his mind. *Amma Gauri's heart is as hard as rock and as soft as water. From her heart that bleeds flows the river of compassion—the Mahishi river. The river feeds the belly of countless millions. She is the grace of Amma Gauri. Trust in her and she shall hold you like a mother holds her baby.* A plunge down the waterfall would be a return to the womb of the only mother he had known—Amma Gauri.

Gundu Ramu pushed himself through the hole and, digging his nails into the wall, he carefully started climbing down the sheer rock. There was a gap of a few feet between the sheet of water and the slimy wall. A rat jumped on his face, slipped and vanished into the abyss. Water pounded down on him as he looked up and saw he hadn't climbed down more than fifteen or twenty feet. To his right, he saw a rotten creeper dangling out of a cavern in the rocky wall. There was some space there. A cave, a refuge—his mind was a blur. He pulled himself there bit by bit, struggling against the water that wanted him inside Amma Gauri's bleeding heart.

He dragged himself in and lay on his chest, his legs hanging down into the cascading water. Bit by bit, he crawled forward till he was inside the small cave. On one side was the wall of water, and on the other, uneven rock. He could barely move his limbs in his cramped refuge. He sat on his haunches, hugging himself and shivering, a bit from cold but more in fear.

His hand felt something smooth and round on the floor. He picked it with trepidation. He stared at it. He was holding a skull. He shut his eyes tight and put it back. He could feel a rib cage near him. The skull was small. The cave must have held someone like him many years ago. That poor one hadn't made it out of this cave alive.

Amma Gauri, Amma Gauri, he chanted, to keep his fear at bay. *Die, die, die,* roared the river. The boy clung to life, clutching the promise he had given to a young woman who had fed him. *Amma Gauri, Amma, Amma,* he chanted. *Let me not die till I meet my akka.* The heart of Amma Gauri, deep and dark, molten and bleeding, hissed from the bottom of the hell.

'Don't move, don't move,' a voice said, and the boy lay frozen with fear. He didn't want to open his eyes. His legs were tied tight and he was being lifted from the ground. He dared not open his eyes. He was moving. Someone was carrying him on their shoulders. 'My father has come back, nothing to worry,' Gundu Ramu whispered to himself. 'Amma Gauri, you have sent my father.' Tears of joy came to his eyes, and he smiled. Then he remembered that his father had been dead for a long time. Was he also dead?

'Hold on tight,' the voice said, and in the next moment, Gundu Ramu gasped as water pounded his face. He screamed and thrashed about. 'Hold on, hold on, son, hold on, hold on, hold on.'

Water cascaded down, drowning out Gundu's scream. He felt himself swing out and into the water, each time a few feet higher. Someone was hoisting him up. Gundu Ramu held on for dear life.

'Easy, boy, easy,' the kind voice said. Gundu screamed in terror and fainted.

When he opened his eyes, he was inside a cave. Around him sat several children, staring at him. He scrambled up, frantically searching for the book in the folds of his dhoti. It was missing. He let out a howl of agony and the children scattered.

'My book, my book,' Gundu Ramu screamed, standing up. He bumped his head on the low roof and sat down, dazed.

Vamana held out a steaming pot of gruel and said, 'Drink this. You're drenched.'

Gundu blinked at the dwarf and turned his face away. He had lost the book. He had lost the only reason to live.

'This is not how you thank an old dwarf who descended to hell to save you, my son. Gratitude is the most important virtue. Be thankful.'

'I want to die,' Gundu said before he buried his face between his knees and wept.

'Die you shall, like everyone else,' the old dwarf said, running his fingers affectionately through Gundu's hair. 'But not so soon, son.'

He put something in Gundu's hands and Gundu sprang up. Sivagami akka's book. He hit his head on the roof again, and quickly sat down. He didn't mind the pain. He clutched the book close to his heart and sobbed quietly.

'How did you get that?' the dwarf asked, handing over the gruel to Gundu Ramu. The boy didn't know how to take the bowl without putting the book down. He blinked like a fool. The dwarf extended his hand. 'Don't worry, son. I can't read,' he said with a chuckle as he took the book from the boy's hand. 'But beware of this accursed thing. Whoever has held it has only met with misfortune.'

Gundu Ramu started slurping the gruel, but his eyes never left his precious book. The dwarf ran his fingers over the manuscript and said, 'I never expected it to come back here again.'

'That is Sivagami akka's,' Gundu Ramu said between gulps of the gruel.

'Who is that?' the dwarf asked, and Gundu started telling him his story. The children sat in a circle as he recounted his life as a bard's son, how his father was killed, how he had reached the orphanage in Dasapattana, how he had met Sivagami, and how he was caught by Hidumba.

When he finished, the dwarf said, 'She might be Devaraya's daughter. I didn't know someone from the family had survived. Had I known this book was so accursed, I would have never given it to him. It brought death and misfortune to him and his family. You should throw this thing away.'

Gundu Ramu grabbed the manuscript from Vimana and held on to it tightly.

'Do you want to know how I got this book in the first place?' Vimana asked. When Gundu Ramu nodded, he said, 'Long ago, when I was a young man, I led an exciting life. Poor, I was, and I was never as tall as most men, but I was blessed with a lot of cunning. I was a thief's apprentice. My short stature meant I could crawl through tunnels that my master dug into rich men's homes, and then stealthier valuables. We heard that the barbarian tribe of the Kalakeyas was holding something precious inside their Varahi temple. It was rumoured that it was the most precious of all diamonds—some said it was Nagamanikya, the diamond made by a king cobra by solidifying its poison. It was believed that it could give the owner mystical powers: the power to fly, the power to vanish at will ... I never believed in all that nonsense, but there were fools willing to pay any price for it. My master decided to steal it. Foolish decision, for who but a mad man would enter the den of cannibals and try to steal something they hold precious. To cut a long story short, my master got caught and was promptly eaten up by Kalakeyas, but I managed to escape with the treasure box. To my disappointment, I found that it contained nothing but this book, written in some strange language. Not that it mattered which language it was, for I know nothing about reading or writing. I carried it with me in memory of my master, and tried to find someone to decipher it. What if it contained some hints about where the treasure was buried? I learned about the legend of the Kalakeyas, who were mighty kings many thousands of years ago. It was said that they had done something to displease Amma Gauri, and she had cursed them to become cannibals. Most of such old women's tales are stupid, but I knew they contained a kernel of truth. Why were they worshipping a book written by some old sage when the Kalakeyas were civilised and ruled half the earth? I had found out who had written it, and that it was in the old tongue of Paisachi—but no one knew how to actually read it. Without my master, I was as good as lost, for no one would employ a dwarf. I found out that the king of Mahishmathi was looking for dwarfs to work in mines and I came here to feed my little body. I carried this book with me, just like you did.'

After a pause, he continued, 'Since I thought the book contained the location of treasures and the pictures in it resembled the landscape of Gauriparvat, I kept the book hidden and started searching for the treasure inside the mountain caves. It had maps of many secret paths, and I studied them intently. I kept it hidden in the same place from where I retrieved you sometime back.'

'But tell me ... why have they brought all of us children here?' Gundu Ramu asked.

'Oh, I thought you would've guessed. For the same reason that all the guards and supervisors are dwarfs. As time passed, the main tunnels stopped yielding Gaurikanta stones, and we had to dig deeper and deeper. The tunnels are very narrow and only dwarfs can enter, but there aren't so many dwarfs in the world. Hence, children are forced to come here and do slave labour.'

'And when they grow up?' Gundu Ramu asked.

'Most never survive long enough to grow up,' Vamana said. He touched Gundu Ramu's wrist and smiled. 'Don't worry, son. Some do grow up, and they become the slaves who transport the mined stones. Akkundaraya takes them to Guha's land and they build the Kali statue as a mark of gratitude to Amma Kali for sparing their lives. No one sees them after that.'

'But ... but why does Amma Gauri allow such cruelty ... using small children for such work?'

'Who can fathom the minds of gods?'

'Why does the maharaja allow it?'

'Ah, that is easy. Greed,' Vamana said.

'Greed?'

'Essentially, the difference between me, a petty thief, and the maharaja, is only in the scale of our greed. The man who steals from one is a thief, the man who steals from everyone is the ruler.'

'I don't know what you are talking about. So much cruelty, so many children killed and tortured for greed. It is terrible. Neither the god cares, nor the king.'

'We mould the gods like we are ourselves, and we get the rulers we deserve, son. You are too young to understand. I hope you never grow old, though that is a terrible blessing to give here. But if you have the misfortune of living long enough, understand this: No one cares.'

The dwarf stood up. Gundu Ramu caught his hand and said, 'But what happened to the book? How did it reach Sivagami akka?'

'Ah, sometimes I am wrong. There are some fools in the world who care. Unfortunately, they never survive,' Vamana said. After a moment's silence, he said in a low voice, 'I have his blood on my hands.'

Gundu Ramu saw a tear track its way down the old dwarf's lined cheeks. It was embarrassing to see a grown man cry and he averted his gaze.

'Devaraya was the only official who bothered to check how the mining was being done,' Vamana said in a voice trembling with emotion. 'He crawled through the impossible tunnels on his hands and knees. He was shocked to find that children were being used to mine the stones. He ordered the mining to be stopped, but Durgappa and Hidumba laughed at him. They ignored his orders. They said the maharaja had sanctioned it. Devaraya didn't believe it. When I saw him, I thought, here is a man I can trust. I had been feeling strange things for the last many years when I moved through the belly of Gauriparvat. The smell was strange, the vibrations I felt and still feel are evil. Something sinister was about to strike. I went to fish out the book from the cavern by the falls, and it was then that I saw the skeleton of some poor boy who might have tried to escape like you did. That is why I thought I should come and check, and found you alive there.'

'What happened to the book?' Gundu Ramu asked impatiently.

'Ah, the book. I fished out the book and gave it to him. From the way his hands trembled as he flipped through the pages, I knew he was terrified. He thanked me profusely and said that he was confident that his friend, Somadeva, would stop the mining once he met him. If nothing convinces my friend Somadeva, this will, Devaraya said, clutching the book. I felt pity for the man. For all his wisdom and brilliance, he was naive. He was doomed. I wanted to warn him, but I convinced myself that I was wrong. Once in a while, very rarely, good wins over evil. Perhaps, this was one such rare occasion, I told myself. I should have known better. Devaraya rushed to Mahishmathi with the book, and the next thing I heard was that he and his family had been executed. The world had survived another rare infection of the good. The world had become normal again. A real world driven by Hidumbas and Durgappas and other bhoomipathis. A world where men like Somadeva ruled. A world that has no place for Devarayas.'

'But what is there in the book that caused him to rush off like that?' Gundu Ramu asked.

'Honestly, I don't know, son. Devaraya knew Paisachi language and was clearly terrified of what he saw in these pages. But this old dwarf can tell you one thing: book or no book, the end is nearer than we think.'

'I must reach this ancient manuscript to Sivagami akka.'

'You are never going to leave this place, son,' Vamana said, shaking his head sadly.

'Sivagami akka will come, and this evil will end,' Gundu Ramu said.

'Ah, the hope of the very young! How do you know she will come?'

'Because she is my Amma Gauri.'

TWENTY-NINE

Mahadeva

'How will I bear this horror? Amma Gauri, such a shame. Such cruelty,' Keki cried, beating her chest with clenched fists.

The gory sight of the garland of putrefying heads on the Kali statue made Mahadeva sick. How cruel was the priest, to have sacrificed all those innocent children, he thought, sitting on the cold steps of the temple. Bijjala shouted orders at the soldiers who had arrived. 'Quick, search everywhere. I can't believe the rajaguru would do something like this. Catch him. Bring him to me.'

The dilapidated Kali temple was teeming with soldiers who had followed Mahadeva. The chariot of Rudra Bhatta was found hidden in the bushes. His son Kalicharan and the horse were missing. So was the rajaguru.

Bijjala came and sat beside Mahadeva. 'You shouldn't have come, brother. Such sights will upset you.'

Mahadeva knew Bijjala was right. He felt guilty that he

had suspected his brother. He said in a hoarse voice, 'I am sorry, Anna. I ...'

'Suspected I was involved in this gory affair?' Bijjala laughed. 'How naive you are, my brother. You shouldn't be worrying about such things when your elder brother is there to take care. Now, go to the palace and take rest. Leave this to me. I shall find that priest and strangle him to death,' Bijjala said, clenching his teeth. Mahadeva shared the sentiment, but that wasn't how the law worked.

'No, Anna. We need to catch him alive. We need to hold a trial and give him a chance to prove his innocence.'

Mahadeva saw Bijjala's face grow dark. 'Such monsters deserve no trial. They should be summarily executed.'

'Even the worst criminal deserves to be heard before we pass judgement,' Mahadeva said and stood up.

Bijjala exploded in rage. 'Hear this nonsense,' he shouted, and the soldiers who were carefully taking out the remains of the slain children stopped their work. They walked towards the two brothers. Keki too came towards them.

'Hear this, my comrades,' Bijjala addressed the soldiers. 'My brother wants to pardon Rudra Bhatta, the devil who killed all these children.'

The soldiers gasped. There were angry murmurs. 'I never said that,' Mahadeva said, his face flushing red with anger.

'Then what did you say?' Bijjala asked scornfully.

'I said we can't kill him without a trial.'

'Same thing.'

Mahadeva shook his head in exasperation.

'Oh, now it is my fault?' Bijjala said. 'I am a fool, right, great Vikramadeva?' Bijjala snapped his fingers before Mahadeva's face. 'Look here, Vikramadeva Mahadeva. I can't understand what you are saying, great scholar. I am a soldier. Just like my comrades here. Did you understand what my beloved brother said now. Did you? You? How about you, the tall one in the back? Did you get it?'

The soldiers stood quiet, not wanting to take sides in the spat between the princes.

'Everyone knows how gutless you are. For Bijjala, there is only one law. If someone has done such a heinous crime, he deserves the most horrible death, as early as possible.' Bijjala turned to the soldiers. 'Enough of wasting time here. These are my orders. If you find Rudra Bhatta, behead him. The one who brings his severed head will receive ten thousand gold coins.'

Mahadeva sensed the palpable excitement of the soldiers. Ten thousand gold coins would tempt anyone. He knew he was fighting a losing battle, but if he didn't act now, he wouldn't be able to look at himself in the mirror.

'I, Vikramadeva, who is senior in rank, though junior in age to Prince Bijjala, hereby order this. Anyone who harms Rudra Bhatta before he is proclaimed guilty by the sabha of the maharaja shall be arrested and punished as per Mahishmathi law.'

Bijjala scoffed. 'This is my word. I shall protect the one who kills Rudra Bhatta with my life. We are soldiers, comrades. Let the pundits debate about law. We will do what is right. This is the word of Bijjala. Now I want a couple of you to go to the untouchables' village. Inform them about the tragedy. Tell them Prince Bijjala is seeking their apology. Tell them Bijjala understands their pain. Though nothing can compensate their grave loss, tell them that Prince Bijjala would be giving the parents of every child who was killed one thousand gold coins and farmland that can yield a thousand measures of rice every year.'

Mahadeva helplessly watched the effect of Bijjala's words on the soldiers he had just bought. He couldn't understand why Bijjala was insisting on beheading the rajaguru before finding out the whole truth. Surely Rudra Bhatta couldn't have committed such cruelty without the help of other people? A trial would expose them ... That same doubt arose in Mahadeva's mind. What if that was the reason Bijjala was adamant about killing Rudra Bhatta without a trial? Bijjala didn't want the truth to come out. The more he tried to shake off the disturbing thought, the more it clung on.

With a heavy heart, he walked inside the temple. It was tough to keep his eyes away from the gory sight of the children's skulls. He pulled his gaze away and walked around the hall, drinking in the details. The daylight that was seeping in didn't reduce the horror a bit.

The stink of putrefying flesh hit him hard as he walked towards the idol. A few soldiers who were cleaning the premises made way for the prince. He saw the ritual drawing on the floor. The blood on it was still fresh. There were some signs of struggle on the floor—a jug of water lay upturned, the ritual drawing was smudged in a corner, and most telling, the trident of Rakta Kali was missing.

It seemed to him that someone had surprised Rudra Bhatta here.

He noted that there was a large patch of oil on the floor. He tried to recollect the relevant verses from the Thaskara

Veda, the ancient manual for thieves and robbers. As a prince, it was one of the sixty-four specialised subjects he'd had to learn. He remembered a verse that said the thief had to rub off the oil that dripped from the lamp or torch, for a good officer of the king would be able to calculate how much time he had spent at the crime scene by looking at the size of the patch. The bigger the patch, the more time the person holding the lamp had stood still at the place.

Evidently, they had been here for some time.

Mahadeva decided to investigate the premises around the temple. Immersed in thought, he walked through the jungle, and the disturbing thought returned. How did Bijjala reach the exact spot where Rudra Bhatta was doing his sacrifice? Why did he choose to come with Keki, and not with a band of soldiers? The bushes lay crushed around him. Rain had turned the ground slushy, and there were footprints, chariot-wheel tracks and horse-hoof marks in the mud. They had concluded that Rudra Bhatta was the culprit as they had found the rajaguru's chariot. But the bushes on the other side of the forest path were lying in a particular fashion, as if something was hidden inside them. Mahadeva went near the bush and studied the ground carefully. There was a depression in the soil, indicating a chariot had stood there for some time, most likely hidden. Whose chariot was that? With his training, Mahadeva was aware that every chariot's wheels left a distinct mark on the soil. He knew it was neither his chariot nor that of Bijjala, as they had been standing a little farther. He walked back to the chariot of Rudra Bhatta, and with his fingers, measured the width of the wheels and the depth of the rut it made on the ground. He checked it against the markings in the bush. They didn't match. It meant someone else other than Rudra Bhatta had been here. And by the indentation the chariot had made and the quantity of horse dung, Mahadeva was sure whoever had come had arrived before Rudra Bhatta and was waiting for him.

There was a chance it had been the priest's accomplice. Someone who was hiding the priest now. Maybe Bijjala should be given the benefit of doubt. His brother might have come to investigate, as he claimed. So who was Rudra Bhatta's accomplice? Who had skilfully helped the priest escape their net by creating a diversion?

But that line of thought didn't go with what he had seen inside the temple. Someone had kept Rudra Bhatta forcefully pinned to the ground. Or was it the other way round? Did Rudra Bhatta force someone on the ground—perhaps a child for the sacrifice? But the mark on the ritual drawing had been almost head-shaped, and big enough to belong to a grown up. If it was an enemy that had attacked Rudra Bhatta in the temple, what had prevented him from killing the rajaguru here itself? That would have been the safest path. Perhaps his arrival had surprised whoever was inside the temple, and they had bolted.

Mahadeva decided to trace the path they had taken in the night. Something was nagging him. There was some odd familiarity in the marks which his mind had registered, but which his brain couldn't process. Mahadeva paused under the shade of a tree to think. Suddenly, he heard something. *Was that a groan?* Crows were cawing above him. From somewhere the harsh cry of a peacock pierced the air. Monkeys swayed from branch to branch, screeching and scolding each other.

Then he heard a muffled cry—'Bhutanna', which made no sense to him, and then he heard a child sobbing.

Mahadeva pushed his way through the bushes and saw a girl of about twelve, sitting on the ground. She appeared dazed and had bruises all over her body. Mahadeva knelt before her, but her eyes were glazed. Her lips trembled, and when Mahadeva touched her shoulder, she shrank from him.

'Daughter,' Mahadeva said, but she kept whispering, 'Bhutanna, you didn't come. You didn't come.'

It was as if she wasn't aware of his presence. 'Who are you, daughter? How did you reach here?' Mahadeva asked, dreading the answer he would get. He was almost sure that this was the girl Rudra Bhatta had brought for the sacrifice.

'Ah, here she is,' a voice came from the bushes, and a moment later, Keki and Bijjala stood before Mahadeva. The girl snapped her head towards Keki and her face contorted with fear. She screamed and gripped Mahadeva's wrist. Her nails dug into his skin as she watched Keki coming towards them.

'The poor child may be in shock, Prince. She would have been the next victim of that rakshasa Rudra Bhatta. The timely arrival of Prince Bijjala ... and, of course, you, saved her.'

Keki knelt before Akhila. 'Darling,' she said.

A shudder passed through the girl and she started having fits. She thrashed her limbs about, and there was froth at the corners of her mouth.

Keki took out a dagger, and Mahadeva grabbed her wrist.

'You have to make them hold iron, Prince. That is the way to prevent fits,' Keki gave her best smile, but it made

Mahadeva's blood run cold. He pushed her away and took Akhila in his arms. Without a word, he started walking towards his horse.

'Where are you going, brother?' Bijjala asked. 'Leave the girl with us. She can't travel on a horse. We have a chariot. We will take her to her home.'

Mahadeva hesitated. He did want to spend more time on the premises to see if he could find out anything more about the person or people who had surprised Rudra Bhatta.

'Yes, Prince. We will leave her back at the orphanage,' Keki said, and bit her tongue.

Mahadeva turned sharply. 'How do you know she is from the orphanage?'

'I don't know where she is from. But we need to keep her somewhere until we find her parents, right?' Keki said, proud about how she had recovered after that slip of the tongue. 'What better place than the orphanage?'

Mahadeva looked at his brother and Keki. Something wasn't adding up. He wanted to talk to the girl when she recovered. He had a feeling that it would help him get closer to the truth. Mahadeva left the clearing, with Bijjala and Keki behind him. He whistled and his horse came trotting. He put the unconscious girl on the saddle and tied her to it with his turban. He jumped up on to the saddle and galloped towards the city.

Bijjala turned to Keki. 'If that girl talks, we are doomed, eunuch.'

Keki smiled and said, 'She won't.'

THIRTY

Sivagami

The sabha that day was unusually calm. Sivagami had expected a flurry of activity surrounding the rajaguru's absence, but it seemed as if there was a deliberate silence about it. She knew the soldiers and dandakaras were sweeping the streets for the missing priest and both the princes were directly involved in finding him. Sivagami wasn't sure how long the storehouse where she had kept Rudra Bhatta would remain safe. She was dependent on Brihannala, and that didn't give her much comfort. She was impatient to finish what she had planned and then reach Gauriparvat somehow.

The king was cheerful and witty as usual. The more she saw him, the more hatred she felt for him. She was sure Somadeva was aware of the cruel ritual that had taken place in the Rakta Kali temple. Yet, he was acting as if nothing had happened. The man was diabolical.

The moment the sabha was over for the day, she rushed to the waiting chariot and had Neelappa take her outside the city. She had to wait until it was dark for what she wanted to do, and the detour was necessary to confuse any spy who may be following her.

When it was midnight, Neelappa took her to the deserted Mahamakam arena. As the chariot approached the arena, she could see a pile of wood arranged at the bottom of the pyramid. The eunuch bowed to her as he would to a reigning monarch. As she walked up the steps of the Gauristhalam, the Rakta Kali trident in her hand, memories rushed to her mind. Memories she had fought to suppress for more than fourteen years. But there wasn't a day the nightmare had spared her. And the memories that she had grappled with, for so many years, burst forth. She was five years old again, helpless, angry, scared.

'You are taking an insane risk, devi. And I bow before your courage,' the eunuch said, looking around the empty ground. It was pitch dark, the night after the new moon. The sky was pregnant with rain.

Sivagami walked to the stone throne and sat on it. It felt cold and hard. It was time to deliver justice. Sivagami would bring the empire built of greed, avarice and immorality down. For a moment, her thoughts went to Gundu Ramu, and her only prayer was that she wouldn't be too late. But after hearing Rudra Bhatta, she knew she had to do this now—for her father, for her mother.

Sivagami stared out into the darkness that enveloped the Mahamakam grounds. She could see the dim outline of Gauriparvat etched in the dark night sky. There would be a hundred Gundu Ramus trapped in the dark underbelly of that monster. After hearing about what was happening in

Gauriparvat, it was difficult for her to look at it with the same reverence she'd had since childhood. Gauriparvat represented everything that was wrong with Mahishmathi. Clouds swirled above the peak. A brisk wind was blowing.

Brihannala threw Rudra Bhatta at Sivagami's feet. In the dull light of the lamp that Brihannala held, she could see Rudra Bhatta's face contorted with fear. She could hear Neelappa adjusting some of the logs at the bottom of the Gauristhalam pyramid.

The Brahmin started cursing her, 'You will have the sin of Brahmahatya. The greatest sin is to kill a Brahmin. You will never be happy in life. Your own son will betray you. Your husband will betray you. Everyone—'

'Shut up,' Sivagami snapped. 'You, a Brahmin? You are nothing but a conniving devil, and you shall rot in hell.'

'Daughter,' Neelappa shouted, alarming Sivagami. He was staring into the darkness. A light was moving towards them, fast. It swayed rhythmically as it approached.

Sivagami's decision was quick. 'Neelappa, light the pyre. Now.'

Brihannala stood up with a smile. She toppled the pots of oil she had kept in a row at the edge of the pyramid. The oil pots burst as they hit the timber pile, spreading the smell of groundnut oil in the air.

Rudra Bhatta was staring at Brihannala and Sivagami. He looked confused, not understanding what they were talking about. The chariot was approaching them at great speed. Brihannala dangled the lamp over the pile of timber and asked, 'Sivagami, now there is no going back. Are you sure?'

Sivagami, sitting like a queen on the stone throne of Maharaja Somadeva, gestured impatiently, and Brihannala dropped the lamp on the pile of timber. With a whoosh, the pyre caught fire, lighting up the entire arena.

'Rudra Bhatta. You have misused your holy office and lied, cheated and murdered all throughout your life. Your king Somadeva turned a blind eye to the misdeeds committed by you and many others. But that doesn't mean dharma will not be served. When the king fails in his dharma, every subject must become the protector of dharma. For the crime of many child sacrifices, for the crime of accusing an innocent woman of immorality and murdering her in cold blood, and for countless other unspeakable crimes, I, Sivagami devi, give you the death penalty. You shall die as that innocent woman died many years ago. This is the word of Sivagami.'

Rudra Bhatta let out a scream of terror. He tried to run but Sivagami rushed to him. She caught him by the scruff of his neck and his eyes bulged in fear.

'Rot in hell,' Sivagami hissed and pushed him down. For a brief moment, he tottered at the edge of the platform, and then he toppled headfirst into the raging fire. Sivagami shifted the trident from her left hand to the right, and sat on the throne to watch him burn.

With the killing of Rudra Bhatta, Sivagami had declared war on Maharaja Somadeva's evil empire. Unmindful of the approaching danger, she continued to sit on the king's stone throne. A heady feeling of power rushed through her veins as the screams of Rudra Bhatta died down. The smell of charred flesh hung thick in the air.

I have delivered justice. I will save the people of Mahishmathi, she promised herself. For a fleeting moment, a vision of herself sitting on the throne, this time dressed in regal clothes, came to her mind. She could hear the roar from lakhs of throats: Jai Sivagami devi! She could see the soldiers standing in columns, with their lances and spears, and the cavalry marching past. She could hear the roll of drums and the blare of horns, she could smell the fragrance of sandal water sprinkled on her. Above her was the pearl-studded umbrella. A massive golden flag of Mahishmathi flapped in a brisk breeze. A golden sun showered his benevolence from the heavens on her and her happy people.

The light from the burning pyre washed over the Gauristhalam like waves, and she felt powerful and divine. Power felt good. The power to punish, the power to kill, the power to do good.

'Sivagami!'

Mahadeva's scream woke her from her reverie. She looked at the prince standing with his sword unsheathed. Behind him stood hundreds of Mahishmathi, soldiers. And in the crowd, she saw Keki and Prince Bijjala. She turned back to Brihannala and found that the eunuch had vanished.

'Arrest her for killing Rudra Bhatta,' Mahadeva ordered his soldiers.

To be continued ...

Acknowledgements

This book series is a tribute to the vision of a great director, artist, and human being, Sri S.S. Rajamouli. *Bāhubali* is a landmark film in the history of Indian cinema, and the sheer scale of it is mindboggling. One can only wonder at how much effort would have gone into making such a classic. Taking the responsibility of working on a prequel of such a story was a daunting task. Had it not been for the absolute freedom, encouragement, and kindness shown by S.S. Rajamouli, this book would never have been possible. I am indebted to him for life, for the trust he has shown in me.

Sri K.V. Vijayendra Prasad is one of the greatest living screenplay writers in the Indian film industry. Sri Prasad, who is S.S. Rajamouli's father, has penned many classics, among which *Bāhubali* happens to be one. My first meeting with him is still etched in my mind. It was his story I was going to rework and expand, and I was apprehensive about how he was going to take it. He was grace personified and the tips and advice he gave me on writing are more precious to me than anything I have ever achieved. I consider him my mentor and this book is my humble tribute to his art.

Prasad Devineni and Shobu Yerlaggada, the producers of *Bāhubali*, the film, and promoters of Arka Media, deserve special mention for their unstinting belief and trust in my skills as an author. *Bāhubali* has gone much beyond being a great film. It has become a global brand. I hope I have lived up to their expectations and hopefully added some more sheen to the brand. Having worked with many producers in the past, I can vouch for the fact that people who give complete freedom to the writer are rare to come by. Thank you, gentlemen, for being there to support and encourage me whenever I was assailed with self-doubt.

I had almost finished my fourth book, *Devayani,* and was about to submit it to Westland when this amazing project came up. Gautam Padmanabhan, CEO of Westland, is more a friend than my publisher, and it was he who advised me to shelve the book I had been working on for the last two years and take up the Bāhubali trilogy. His enthusiasm gave me confidence.

I should thank my editor Deepthi Talwar for the mammoth effort she put in to edit the book at a blistering pace. She deserves special thanks for putting up with a writer who was assailed with insecurities and who kept harassing her every hour with a new rewrite. The map was designed by Vishwanath Sundaram, the graphic designer and VFX artist of Arka Media. He was assailed by two perfectionists, S.S. Rajamouli and yours truly for even minute detail, and he has done amazing work. Thank you for the great piece of art.

Krishna Kumar, Neha and Shweta of Westland deserve special mention for all the public relationship work they have done for me. Arunima arranged for some fascinating interviews. I am grateful to the press and TV journalists too for the extensive coverage of the book.

Preetam of Arka Media who handled the social media campaigns along with Hemal Majithia and his team in Oktobuzz Media deserve special thanks.

My friends often say that my better half Aparna deserves a Nobel prize for tolerating me. Thank you for being there, my dear. It may be a great trial to live through my mood swings, but after more than fifteen years, I am sure you are used to it. My children Ananya and Abhinav have been my greatest critics and inspiration. They bring me down to earth often from my flights of fantasy. And my pet dog Jackie deserves a special mention, as he was the one who often heard my stories during our long walks together.

My extended family has always stood by me, even when I wrote books that challenged their beliefs and convictions. They have been my source of inspiration from childhood. My siblings Lokanathan, Rajendran and Chandrika, my in-laws, Parameswaran, Meenakshi and Radhika, and my niece and nephews, Divya, Dileep and Rakhi have always made our family get-togethers lively with many debates about the Ramayana and Mahabharata.

My friends for more than three decades, Rajesh Rajan, Santosh Prabhu and Sujith Krishnan; other friends like Sidharth Bharatan Jayan CA and Venkatesh Satish Lolla, and Anubhooti Panda who was my beta reader of various drafts, all deserve special thanks for keeping me inspired. My batchmates of EEE 1996, from The Government Engineering college, Trichur, especially Cina, Gayatri, Ganesh, Malathi and Maya, who have read some of my works, and Mathew, Gopu Keshav, Anjali, Brinda and Habibulla Khan, who have never read and are never going to read any of my works, but still encourage me to write, all deserve my heartfelt gratitude.

My special thanks to all the readers of my books. Your words of criticism, praise and suggestions have been my inspiration and the reason I continue to write.